TOMORROW'S MEMORIES

Tomorrow's Memories

JOSEPH D. AYD

jAy18t

1952

DODD, MEAD & COMPANY · NEW YORK

Printed in the United States of America
by the Vail-Ballou Press, Inc., Binghamton, N. Y.

FOREWORD

$\mathcal{T}$OMORROW'S MEMORIES is the story of Ruth Sterner, an average Catholic girl. She experiences all the thrills and heartaches of high school life. She dreams of being color girl at the Naval Academy and loves life, her friends and dancing —yet, to her comes the grace of a religious vocation. This she embraces as wholeheartedly as the other events of her life. But Ruth would find it difficult to explain why God called her rather than some friend who is just as generous as she is, but more exceptional in ability. All Ruth knows is that God wants her to do a work for Him that only she can do, the way He wanted Peter, or the girl down the street, or the boy who used to hurry past the house each day on his way to school. For the ways of God are mysterious; and it is His to choose and ours to accept.

A girl may enter the convent for any number of reasons: to save her soul, to sing, to help save other souls, to nurse, to sew—to do any of the thousand and one things different nuns do. But she won't stay very long unless she is doing it out of love of God, which doesn't express itself in a lot of high-flown notions about being a bride of Christ. It is expressed in a deep conviction—no matter how entangled in pleasant or unpleasant emotions—that this is what God wants her to do.

Before she becomes a nun, a girl may know little about the religious life, for it is doubtful whether anyone can explain the joys of such a life. One could talk about the friends it gives, the prayer, the games, the studies, the work. They are joys, but anyone can experience them. The essential differences are grace and the love of God, which are difficult to explain.

Practically no one understands the joys of the religious life until they are experienced. And this is so, precisely because practically no one can explain them to anyone else. The grace of vocation came to many, but not all, religious through the example of teachers they had in school. There they actually saw concrete examples of joyous peaceful happiness and love of God. These people can no more explain just what there was about the teachers than the teachers can explain the happiness that is there. *Love of God* is not easily understood, but, difficult or not to understand, it is a great and moving force.

"RUTH!" the echoes of an exasperated but doggedly persistent soprano voice shook Ruth like a rude rousing hand. Two sleepy eyelids moved slowly, mechanically, revealing two uncomprehending blue eyes.

"Come on, Ruth, wake up!"

Recognizing the voice as that of her younger sister, Ruth Sterner disregarded it and rolled over on her side as she saw the bright sunlight of a November morning dancing noiselessly through her bedroom window. She wished her sister were as quiet!

But Marge, who was sixteen and only a year younger than Ruth, was not to be ignored as though she were a baby sister. Besides, her voice rang with a sure authority which must have come from their mother, so Ruth muttered, "Okay, okay, I'm awake."

With a satisfied smile on her face, Marge had turned to leave the room when her eyes lighted on something on Ruth's dresser.

With a triumphant "Well!" she picked up the picture which had caught her eye.

To see what it was that so interested her sister, Ruth once more rolled luxuriantly in her bed. When she discovered that Marge had her prized picture, all sleep was dashed from her eyes as she bolted upright, demanding possessively, "Leave that alone, Marge Sterner!"

"Don't get excited; I'm not going to take it," Marge replied nonchalantly. "Where'd you get it?"

"I cut it out of yesterday's *Sun*."

After one more careless glance at it, Marge let the newspaper clipping slip from her fingers and glide to a stop on the cluttered top of Ruth's dressing table among the various trinkets and souvenirs that had been deposited there on her return from football games, dances, and other social events. The picture was so surrounded by fancy buttons and bows, programs, and colorful school banners, scattered over the basic array of dainty rose-colored jars and bottles, that only an eye accustomed to the ordinary litter would have noticed it in the first place.

Marge looked teasingly at Ruth. "Not a very good picture of Jim, is it?"

To admit to herself that the picture had defects was one thing, but to own up to the fact in front of Marge was quite another. That would be the fatal error of giving her sister something to tease her about, like giving her a pin and saying, "Stick me."

"Of course," Marge went on when Ruth said nothing, "when a girl gets in the state you're in, she can't tell a good picture of her boy friend from a bad one."

"And whatever gave you the idea that Jim Stevens is my boy friend?" Ruth asked with a roguish sparkle in her eyes.

"To enumerate all the signs, step by step, would take too

long, and you have to get out of that bed some time. But when a girl, who met a boy just before the beginning of school, goes to see him play every football game, goes out on dates with him, and cuts his picture out of the paper, in my books it means that the boy has become her boy friend." And Marge added hastily, when she saw Ruth about to reply, "Now don't try to tell me you go to all the Loyola High School games just because you like Loyola. I'm not that naive."

Ruth bit her lower lip, then said disarmingly, "Well, you have to admit Loyola has a good team, and even the *Sun* says Jim is good."

"I suppose you'll be telling me next that one Jim Stevens is the best football player in Baltimore," Marge protested. "All I can say is you've certainly made progress with Jim since you met him. If he spends much more time around here, he might as well move in."

"I guess we were just meant for each other," Ruth smiled with mock coyness as she slid under the covers again, pulling them up to her chin. "Close the window before I get up, will you please, Marge?"

"Okay, but don't go back to sleep—dreaming of your hero." Marge pushed the window down and walked out of the room on a note of superiority—the superiority of one who is free from the snares entangling others. But Ruth, feeling completely unhampered by the bonds that Marge supposed were binding her so tightly, laughed quietly and lay back to think about Jim Stevens.

Slim and broad-shouldered, Jim was thoroughly American, though his uncontrollable sandy hair, blue eyes, and ruddy complexion gave him something of the appearance of a Swede. While Ruth had been tempted to laugh at the unruly lock of hair which kept brushing Jim's forehead at their first meeting and afterward, she felt a warm joy in the way his eyes said hello and invited conversation. For Ruth, Jim's hair and eyes had become the symbols of his whole character, which was independent, tempered by a warm friendliness.

When Ruth had gone to see Loyola play its first football game of the season, Jim hadn't known she was there until after the game, when she waved to him as he was leaving the field. His face was streaked with perspiration and dust and a lock of his hair was sticking out from under his helmet, but he called hello and waved back. After the St. Paul game, the second of the season, he looked for Ruth, and she had been so proud when he walked over to her and in front of a crowd of girls from school and asked, "Hi, Ruth, got anybody to take you home?" And when Ruth shook her head negatively, he said, "Wait for me, and I'll give you a ride."

She had waited. And from that time on Jim had been seeing her regularly, though not as often as Marge and the rest of Ruth's family liked to make out when teasing her.

Suddenly Ruth kicked off the covers, bounded out of bed, and went to her dressing table to look at Jim's picture again. Proudly she said, "And the *Sun* does think he's a pretty good football player. Fact of the matter is, he's darn good!"

After replacing the picture in a more prominent spot, Ruth stretched her arms in a yawn that meant everything was right with the world as far as she was concerned that morning. Running her fingers through her hair, she shook her locks vigorously and made a face at herself in the mirror before drawing herself up to her full five feet six inches, hands extended above her head preparatory to touching her toes—to prove to herself that she could still do it.

Despite the grunts which escaped from her during the bending and stretching processes, Ruth was satisfied, deciding, much to her own delight, that she had not too large a waistline, with all her hundred and twenty-one pounds. The fact that she had seen some rolypoly girls at school touch their toes with ease was readily put aside as irrelevant as she fluffed her hair once more, then knelt beside her bed for a few minutes of morning prayers.

"Good morning, good morning, good morning! It's a beautiful day in Baltimore." Walking spryly into the kitchen, Ruth caught her mother from behind and kissed her half on the ear and half on the cheek. "Good morning, Mrs. Sterner, you're looking fine this lovely morning. How do you manage to keep so young?" Freeing her mother, she looked hopefully at the stove. "Now, after all that," she said, "how about some breakfast? Or have the rest of the ravening Sterner horde eaten everything up?"

Mrs. Sterner, a small, matter-of-fact woman with attractive gray hair and youthful skin, paid little attention to Ruth's bantering chatter; such goings-on were quite characteristic of all of her children. "Did you make your bed, Ruth?" she asked quietly as her daughter was foraging in the refrigerator for oranges and cream.

That was a question to be avoided, so Ruth didn't answer it. "Okay," she said instead, "I don't need any breakfast. I don't need anything. I feel like a million. Just look at me!" She spun around on her toes and threw herself into the arms of her mother, who turned quickly from the lunch she was preparing to brace herself and catch her daughter—and give her an admonishing shake. Then they both laughed, and Ruth loved her mother for laughing with her.

When Ruth had finished washing her breakfast dishes, Mrs. Sterner instructed her to fix her hair properly before lunch. But Ruth merely twined a loose strand of her mother's hair around her finger and pulled. It was beautiful hair and it had been gray ever since Ruth could remember.

"Now, Ruth, stop your nonsense and do as you're told."

"I'll fix it superbly after lunch," Ruth promised, tweaking the perky bow of the bright blue ribbon she had tied around her hair after a few hurried passes with her comb.

"Do it now."

"All right, Mom, soon as I read the paper."

"Now!"

"All right," Ruth replied as she strolled into the living room where she picked up the morning paper and settled into a chair. When she turned to the sports section, she called to her mother in the kitchen, "Wish I was going to the Notre Dame–Navy game today."

That brought Mrs. Sterner from the kitchen. "Now, you listen to me, young lady. I told you to fix your hair."

Standing up to her mother impishly, Ruth called her "Mrs. Sterner" because she liked to appear very formal at such times. "You shouldn't let yourself get so excited, Mrs. Sterner," she advised severely as she thrust the paper into her mother's hands and ran for the stairs, calling back over her shoulder, "You're a dear, Mrs. Sterner." She heard her mother's chuckle above the clatter of her feet.

After helping to clear away the lunch dishes, Ruth had curled up in a comfortable chair in her room and was deep in a book when Marge called and said someone wanted to see her. Ruth went right on reading, supposing her sister was looking for help with something or other she was working on in the cellar. She wasn't in the least interested in getting involved in any of her sister's projects, which were just one step closer to sanity than the harebrained things her brother Paul was always plotting; only there was some excuse for Paul, since he was but a fifth-grader, while Marge was in her third year at high school. Also, aside from the fact that she was not expecting anyone, Ruth considered it poor manners to announce company by shouting up the stairs!

After calling several times and receiving no answer, Marge came storming up the steps and said, "Come on, slowpoke, your one-and-only is downstairs."

"Piffle," replied Ruth as she turned the next page. It was an interesting story, and none of Marge's undertakings was going to lure her away from it.

Marge firmly took the book from her sister and insisted that Jim Stevens was downstairs to see her.

"Do you really mean it?" Ruth was still incredulous but there was dawning excitement in her blue eyes.

Marge groaned, "What on earth do you think I've been trying to tell you?"

"Why didn't you say it was Jim?" Ruth demanded, rushing past Marge and down the stairs. Marge threw up her hands in a hopeless gesture. "I suppose I said it was Santa Claus!" She put the book on the desk and started down the stairs. But before she had reached the bottom she collided with Ruth, who was returning even more rapidly than she had gone.

" 'Scuse me, Marge, hon," she said breathlessly, without stopping her movement. "Talk to Jim a few minutes while I change my dress, will you?" Marge didn't catch all of the rest of what Ruth said, but she did make out the delighted announcement, "He's taking me to see the Midshipmen march through the park on their way back from the game."

"Okay." And Marge continued on her way down the stairs, amazed at how easily her sister could bustle from one thing to the next—when it had something to do with boys and dates.

Because the police had already stopped traffic from passing through Clifton Park when they arrived, Jim had to park his car on Washington Street. They jumped out, and Jim seized Ruth by the hand.

"Come on, we'll have to hurry!" he urged. "They don't stop traffic until it's almost time for the Midshipmen to arrive, and we want to see them before they break ranks at the railroad bridge."

Until they heard the booming of the bass drum and the distant *umpha-umpha* of the Sousaphones, which, Jim explained to Ruth, are "those tremendous horns that twist around the player's neck and pop up above his head," they walked rapidly along the sidewalk of the park. But at that warning sound Jim decided they'd have to go faster if they were going to see the returning Middies swing through the Harford Road entrance to the park. "Here," he said, "we'll cut across the grass." And he began to run down a slope behind the bandstand where the park band gave concerts in the summertime.

Ruth, who was being pulled along behind Jim like the tail of a comet, tried to stop him. "What will people think?" she protested.

Independence stood out all over Jim's face when he answered with a laugh, "Who cares?" And he continued to tug on Ruth's hand, helping her up an incline toward the street where policemen on motorcycles were scurrying by. All around

Ruth and Jim, children were running in the same direction as they were; some of them tackling one another and rolling gleefully in the grass; others strutting like drum majors, lifting their knees and twirling tree-branch batons; but all of them drawn by the call of march music.

"I bet I look a sight," Ruth panted as she and Jim took places along the curb, just inside the entrance of the park, where the Navy band, as if in response to a plea from the crowd, struck up *Anchors Aweigh*.

"You look swell," Jim answered. He said something else, too, but Ruth didn't hear him—she was lost in the music. It pulled and pulled at her until in spirit she marched right out of herself and fell into step with the band. She even felt the urge to seize a horn and start blowing—not that she could have gotten a sound out of it, but that's just the way martial music affected her whenever she heard it. Her whole body moved with the magic of its beat. Only after the band had passed was she able to contain herself again and begin to notice the men marching before her.

As the music died away all that could be heard was the steady *scrutch-scrutch* of the Midshipmen's heels on the pavement, and that was almost as rhythmical as the music. White caps moved up and down together; white-gloved hands swung in perfect synchronization . . . *scrutch-scrutch* . . . one company singing, "Army, Army, call the doctor, 'cause you're going to need him soon" . . . *scrutch-scrutch* . . . Ruth caught the eye of a company officer moving before his command; a smile spread over his face and his hand shot up and down in a signal to his men. "Hotcha, hotcha, hi ya, babe!" the call came as hands went to caps and caps came off in unison.

In spite of the fact that she didn't want to, Ruth blushed,

wondering all the while whether the people around noticed it. She even thought that maybe the salute hadn't been intended for her. But, she told herself, he *did* smile at me before giving the signal. Pride at being thus honored brought a new aliveness to her, for that salute was given only to girls whom company commanders considered attractive.

Ruth didn't notice the other Middies as they passed by or hear the other calls that came; they weren't for her. She was enveloped in a dream of Annapolis and June and graduation week at the Naval Academy. On the day of the presentation of the colors she pictured Ruth Sterner, color girl, marching at the side of an admiral, between them the flag to be presented to the commander of the leading company of the graduating class. It was just as she had always dreamed it would be, ever since the first time her father had taken her to witness the ceremony when she was in the sixth grade. The flag fluttered in the breeze and her white dress tossed at her ankles. She had on a blue sash and a tremendous white wide-brimmed hat. Everything looked so beautiful, with all the fresh color of spring and flags and uniforms; and it was enchanting when she, Ruth Sterner, presented the flag and kissed the commander of the crack company of the Naval Academy.

A tug at her arm by Jim brought her back to reality. "Parade's over, little girl."

"Oh," Ruth gave a startled cry. "Yes . . . the parade is over." But she didn't move, even though she and Jim were the last two left standing at the curb.

"Well, are you going to stay there making moon eyes at the Middies until they reach Annapolis?" Jim asked, only half jokingly.

Ruth laughed at him and said he was jealous because the

Midshipmen had saluted her.

"They could have picked out some girl who was alone. They didn't have to pick on somebody who had a date, did they?"

"Of course they did, silly, if they were going to pick out the best-looking girl around," Ruth said as she pushed Jim into a pile of leaves that crackled joyously under his feet, as if they were laughing with Ruth. Between giggles she warned Jim not to touch her in front of the people in the park. "You know it's true, what I said about the best-looking," she continued with glorious delight in her voice and in her eyes, "or you wouldn't have invited me to your Thanksgiving dance with you."

"I suppose it is," Jim agreed, cautiously unconvincing, "but you're going to look funny with these leaves in your hair." He crushed a handful of leaves over Ruth's head. Their laughter carried over the November air—clear, cold air, full of autumn's tang, burning brown leaves, and carefree laughter.

2

$\mathcal{T}$HE following Friday evening there was one empty place at the Sterner dinner table. Young Paul was late again. And Ruth was perturbed because it would make her late with the dishes, and it was the night of the Loyola-Southern football game. "Mom," she demanded, "why don't you make that boy get here on time for meals?"

"Yes, Mother," Marge mimicked Ruth, with a twinkle in her eyes, "why do you not place him under the stringent disciplinary injunctions of his older sister?"

"Why don't you stop telling everybody you've been studying the dictionary again?" Ruth came back at her.

"What's the matter, Ruth? Do you find my conversation incomprehensible?"

Mrs. Sterner said nothing, letting the girls go on with their repartee. She knew one or the other would grow tired of it soon and the conversation would return to normal, or one might become angry, in which case she would, of course, have to put a stop to it. Such spirited exchanges were usual occurrences at the Sterner house, and there was no denying that she enjoyed listening to them. Ruth and Marge were still going at it when Mrs. Sterner called out, "Paul?" She thought she had heard the front door open quietly, and for her that was a signal of foreboding, because Paul always came in the back way, and never quietly, except when there was something wrong. "Paul," she repeated, "is that you?"

A barely audible "Yes'm" came back, for it sounded simultaneously with the squeak of the bottom stair.

"Where have you been?" asked his mother. "Come here."

"In a minute."

"Right away," commanded his father. And the fifth-grade boy came slowly into the room with his head bowed low. When his mother again demanded to know where he had been, Paul, without raising his head, mumbled something that no one understood.

"Look at me," Mrs. Sterner ordered, catching Paul under the chin and lifting his head. "Where have you . . ." The words died on her lips when she saw her son's face.

Marge cried, "Mom, did you ever see an eye like that one? Isn't that the most beautiful black eye you've ever seen in your life?"

"Shut up!" Paul retorted bitterly, knotting his fists. But Marge continued to gaze at him, trying to suppress a smile, until her brother shouted, "I hope you're satisfied. I've got a black eye. So what?"

"So what?" interjected his mother. "So you'll stop shouting, young man, and tell me what happened."

"Nothing." A resolute silence locked Paul's lips until Mr. Sterner spoke up. Then Paul, knowing it was safer and less painful to tell just what had happened, admitted he had been fighting.

"That's quite obvious, Paul." His mother was tired of this sort of thing. That was clear to Paul by the tone of her voice and it boded ill for him. "With whom this time?"

"Lou Weber."

"John," Mrs. Sterner said to her husband, "I've told him a dozen times not to fight with that boy, but he won't listen to me. You've got to do something with him."

"But he called Ruth a dope," Paul protested.

"Oh, he did!" Ruth spoke up. She threw her arm around Paul, who for once didn't shake it off. "I hope you socked him good and hard."

In this case, however, Ruth's honor meant little to her mother, and Paul was sent to his room without anything to eat. But after she had helped Marge with the dishes, Ruth sneaked a sandwich to him. While he was eating, her brother told her of how he had fought and won.

After that Ruth had to rush to get out to Baltimore Stadium in time for the football game.

Jim had given her a ticket and asked her to wait for him afterwards so they could go out for something to eat. And that thought predominated everything as she watched him score two of Loyola's three touchdowns to win for his team.

" 'Lo, honey," a limpid voice cooed behind Ruth as she stood outside the Loyola dressing room after the game. "Waiting for your heartbeat?"

Recognizing the voice as belonging to only one person, Ruth groaned inwardly and turned to greet June Thompson.

June, petite, saucy, dewy-eyed, was a junior at the Institute of Notre Dame, and felt not the slightest bit inferior to Ruth or any other senior at the school. Now, smiling a baby-faced smile, she looked at Ruth with patronizing green eyes, which the latter found more than ordinarily repellent tonight. Yet Ruth had to admit there was a certain prettiness about June, the prettiness of blonde hair meticulously cared for, of perfect teeth, of soft skin. And with all these she had the attractiveness of stylish clothes, pressed to the last pleat.

"Hello, June," Ruth said rather stiffly. "I'm waiting for Jim Stevens, if that answers your question."

"It does that, dearie," June replied with a fetching shake of her blonde locks and a knowing glance over her small nose. "And in case you're interested, sweetheart, I'm waiting for that great, big, strong fullback, Gene Cole. A li'l girl like me needs protection."

Ruth did not want to have to say anything else to June at this point, for that might have been unpleasant for both of them, so she found Jim a particularly welcome sight as he emerged from the dressing room. With a brief "Excuse me" she left June and started toward Jim, only to hear June's "Hi, there, handsome" reach him before she did.

"Come on, Jim," Ruth urged. "Let's get away quickly." She put a hand on his arm. "You were terrific tonight."

"Best man on the field," Jim added jokingly, only his eyes weren't smiling, and she knew something was wrong.

"Ruth," he said, "I'm awfully sorry, but I can't take you home tonight. I have to leave you at the gate."

"That's all right, Jim." But it really wasn't. "Is there something the matter?"

"Ruth, I can't go into all the details because Mother's waiting for me, but it seems she made a date for me with a young friend of the family who has just moved to Baltimore without telling me anything about it until I was ready to leave for the game tonight. Honest, I didn't know a thing about it, Ruth. I would have called you, but by the time I got through arguing with Mother I was late already. I did call you from the stadium to try to explain, but you were on your way then. This is the first time I've had a chance to tell you."

A sad softness crept into her voice when she asked, "Didn't your mother know you had a date with me before she asked this other girl?"

"I'm afraid not, Ruth." Jim leaned against the wooden railing dejectedly.

"But what did she say when you told her you had a date with me?"

"She only said she made her date before we made ours and that we have to drop ours." Jim was miserable, and his already ruddy complexion had turned full red. "She tried to make it a case of family loyalty, too, and said the least I could do was to take my own mother home when she comes to see me play football. Of course the fact that Dad's with her doesn't make any difference. Usually she wouldn't come to see me play because she doesn't approve of it, but she came tonight just to insist that I take Barbara out. Golly, Ruth, I'm sorry. But I can't stand here talking about it. Mother's probably tearing her hair out now. I'll make it up to you."

"Never mind," Ruth said bitterly. She thought of June Thompson who, if she saw Jim walk off, would tell the whole school that Ruth Sterner had been stood up. "If you don't take me home tonight, you needn't take me any place any more."

"But, Ruth," Jim pleaded, "be reasonable."

"I think I'm being perfectly reasonable. Your mother is the one who is being unreasonable. Even if she wants you to take this other girl out, she should at least allow you to take me home first. That's a very simple rule of good manners."

"I agree with you, Ruth, but she's still my mother."

"All right, you had better have her invite Barbara to go to the Thanksgiving dance with you."

"But I don't want to take Barbara. I want to take you."

"Well, if you don't like this Barbara, I'm sure your mother can find somebody else. Maybe she has already; you'd better ask her." Ruth's eyes flashed anger and she breathed quickly.

"I'm sorry," Jim said very quietly. "I'll phone you later; this won't happen again."

"Oh, don't let it bother you." Ruth tried to laugh over a lump in her throat, but she made a poor job of it. "It doesn't matter, really."

"Good night, Ruth." Jim turned abruptly and walked away, and Ruth knew her irony had hurt him. She watched him go and was sorry. Too late she heard June Thompson's giggle behind her. June was snuggled up against the side of the Loyola fullback; she was talking to him and laughing. When they reached Ruth she asked, " 'Smatter, gorgeous? Where's Jim?"

"Oh, he's over there," Ruth replied, pointing in the general direction of the parked cars remaining on the stadium lot. She was so embarrassed she couldn't tell whether or not she sounded convincing. June gave her a strange look and moved on.

After waiting a few minutes for June and her friend to disappear from her sight, Ruth started out in the opposite direction, hoping she wouldn't meet anyone who knew she was supposed to have a date with Jim Stevens. And although she was glad most of the people had gone from the stadium by that time, she felt alone, cold, and friendless, like the trees she passed on the sidewalk.

The ride home that night by bus and streetcar seemed endless and only served to put Ruth into a deeper depression. Other young people on these conveyances seemed so happy, and here she was alone, jilted!

Well, she finally admitted to herself, it's better to find out now than later if Jim's a mamma's boy. Yet she couldn't convince herself that he was; there was something too manly about him for that, something independent like that mop of sandy hair of his. But then why hadn't he taken her home?

After a while, Ruth tried to talk herself into forgetting the whole affair. There were plenty of other boys around, some of them every bit as nice as Jim Stevens. In her own neighborhood there were Tod Edwards and Pete Decker, both of whom dated her fairly regularly. In fact, Tod always considered Ruth as his girl friend. He was taking her to the movies the following night and to the Calvert Hall—Mt. St. Joe football game, where he had every intention of showing Ruth he was a better player than that guy Stevens. Now Ruth hoped he would.

"Phooey on Jim Stevens," she said aloud to herself as she walked home from the car stop. But it was all so much make-believe, because she knew all the while that Jim couldn't help it; that it was his mother's fault, not his.

"What's the matter, Ruth? Loyola lose?" asked Mrs. Sterner, who noted how silently Ruth was hanging up her coat.

"No, they won."

"Is there something wrong, dear?"

"No, Mom."

Mrs. Sterner watched with an experienced eye as her daughter dejectedly climbed the stairs to bed. That there was something wrong was as certain as the fact that Ruth had forgotten to kiss her. She'd love to know what the difficulty was, to comfort Ruth, to help her; but it was her daughter's problem, and if Ruth thought it important enough in the morning, she'd probably hear about it. It doesn't do a girl any harm to wrestle with her own problems for a while. Mrs. Sterner smiled and quietly went on with her sewing.

3

SEVENTEEN and smiling, Ruth Sterner put one last dab of powder on her nose, pursed up her full lips, pinched some extra color into her cheeks, and went to meet Tod Edwards, who was waiting for her in the parlor.

"Hi!" she called to him. "Be with you in a second, soon as I get my hat and coat."

Looking into the mirror as she put her hat on, Ruth told herself that her black hair had a sheen equal to June Thompson's today. And as if to let June know she realized it, she arched her brows and hummed, "Tra-la." She wished June could see her now.

It was a grand, blue, sunshiny day to begin the struggle for the Catholic football championship. And while Ruth sat in the stands of Mt. St. Joe's stadium she hardly realized how long before game time she had arrived, for she was enjoying the cool breezes blowing playfully across the field. She watched the people file into the stadium, at first in thin trickles, then in a steady flow that split into rivulets coursing through the various aisles and rows of seats. It was all so colorful. The day being a very moderate one, enveloping coats and blankets were not necessary.

At first Ruth paid more attention to the people than to the teams warming up on the field. But once the game got under way she kept her eyes fixed on Tod Edwards, not only because he had brought her to the game, but because that's where the eyes of practically all the fans rested. Tod did everything right this afternoon; the loose-limbed, one-hundred-and-forty-eight-pounder skirted ends, brushed off tackle, wriggled through the center of the line to keep his team in a game that would have ended in hopeless defeat for Calvert Hall without him. Almost singlehandedly Tod pushed across two touchdowns for the Cardinal and Gold to equal the twelve points St. Joe had garnered.

To be waiting for the star at the end of the game was a thrill for Ruth, more so when she saw a crowd of Loyola football players leaving the stands with their coach. One boy left the group, and Ruth recognized Jim Stevens coming toward her. She looked the other way.

"Hello, Ruth," Jim said as casually as he could, as if they were still on the best of terms. "Do you have anyone to take you home?"

"Of course," she answered coldly. She wasn't in the habit of going places without having some boy to take her home.

"I'm sorry."

"Well, I'm not."

"Ruth, will you forget about what happened after the game the other night? I couldn't help it."

Unmoved, Ruth replied bitingly, "Maybe not, but there may

be other times when you won't be able to help it either. And I'm not interested in being stood up or pushed around."

"It won't happen again."

"How do I know it won't?"

"Because I say it won't."

"And what kind of assurance is that?"

Jim looked at her very seriously; he had a surprised look on his face. He hadn't expected this coldness, this unwillingness to accept his word. "It's the best assurance I can give," he said quietly.

"And what about your mother?"

"I've already told her I'm taking you to the Thanksgiving dance, and no one else; otherwise I'm not going."

"But I told you I'm not going with you."

"Before that," Jim protested, "you said you would go."

"Well, I'm not going."

"I'll call for you around eight-thirty the night of the dance," he declared with sudden assurance.

"I won't be ready."

"I'll wait then." Jim walked away as if he had no doubt whatever but that Ruth would be ready when he called to take her to the big dance. And she wondered if he were as sure as he seemed to be.

When Tod Edwards came hurrying out of the locker room with his duffle bag thrown over his shoulder, he didn't look much like a football player. Ruth thought he looked more like a kid who had offered to carry some player's bag for him. And when his hair was plastered down with water the way it was now, he looked especially young and skinny, for his hundred and forty-eight pounds just about covered the bones of his stooped frame.

"Hi, Ruth! Like the game?"

"Swell, Tod. You were terrific."

Tod smiled and took her by the arm. "Come on, we'll stop and get a Coke and sandwich some place."

Nodding toward the bandage on Tod's sharp nose, Ruth asked, "Did you hurt your nose badly?"

"No, just skinned it on somebody's pants or jersey. It'll be all right in a couple of days."

Ruth looked at the injured nose, the tired eyes, the face from which all color had been drained so that Tod's lips stood out as if they had been painted, and wondered whether it was worth while to give so much to play a game. But she knew Tod would say that it was. And if a game was worth playing at all, in Tod's view it was worth giving every effort, even if it hurt. That's the way he was, for although he was the youngest-looking of all Ruth's friends, he was the most serious-minded, at times carrying his self-conscious maturity to vexing degrees.

Never very talkative, Tod told Ruth he thought his team could now beat Loyola, then he let her do most of the chattering. And Ruth knew he was happy and proud to walk along with her at his side without shouting that he had almost won the game, or bragging, or boasting. At times like this, when his sense of maturity was balanced, Ruth liked him, liked him the way she had liked him in grammar school when he had first shown himself less rambunctious than the other boys and more interested in her.

When Tod invited her to go to the Loyola–Calvert Hall game with him, Ruth refused because her family usually went to that game together. Both her father and her brother Dan, married now and a dentist, had graduated from Loyola and the

Sterners had made it an annual custom to see the school's big game of the year. But Tod stopped by every afternoon after practice to tell Ruth how things were going, and he took her on a date Saturday night. He was around the Sterners' so often those days that the family was beginning to think it was like summer time, when Tod and many of the young people in the neighborhood spent part of every day there.

Thanksgiving turned out to be a dismal day. Chill, cloudless, and colorless, it was disheartening as well as discomforting, and it seeped through one's clothing like ice water. It was too much even for Mr. Sterner and he reluctantly decided that the family would not attend the Loyola–Calvert Hall game. When he made the announcement on the way home from church, Ruth objected strenuously, and Paul cast his vote to go along with her. They went, but only in the face of their mother's firm conviction that it was nonsensical for anyone to stay out in the open all that time on a wretched day like that.

And by half-time Ruth found herself sitting alone, for the chilling net of rain that clung to everything heightened the effect of the cold until even sturdy Paul was blue-lipped and his teeth rattled uncontrollably. He had asked for his carfare and left, saying it was a lousy game anyhow.

It was Thanksgiving . . . Thanksgiving when everything should be bright and snappy, with a brilliant sun riding a clear blue sky; when there should be friends about and laughter. And here was Ruth, sitting alone in the Stadium, shivering in the dank, dreary air that swallowed up the clang of the bells. Doubling up her fingers into fists, Ruth slipped them into her coat pockets to try to thaw out the painful cold at their tips. Then she fixed her attention on the second half of the game, which was as dull and fumble-riddled as the first, except for

Tod's beautiful play on the opening kickoff when he had run, reversed, changed pace, side-stepped, swerved, and slid to the thirty-yard line in Loyola territory. After that nothing had happened; two lines faced one another like so many snorting dragons, breath vaporizing like smoke before their faces. And so it was all through the second half until Calvert Hall fumbled a Loyola quick-kick by Ken Carpenter, and a Loyola end recovered on Calvert Hall's twelve-yard line.

In spite of herself, Ruth was excited when she saw the ball handed to Jim on the next play. He swung wide around the end, Ken Carpenter trailing him all the way. Perfect blocking removed everyone from Jim's path except the opposing end, who had diagnosed the play correctly and was closing in on Jim. As the two drew closer together, Ruth jumped up on the seat in front of her and screamed with the thousands of others in the stadium. Her voice shrilled wildly when she saw Jim toss a lateral to Carpenter and throw a vicious block at the Calvert Hall end. Her cheers were drowned in the pandemonium that broke loose around her when Loyola scored. Then she suddenly realized that she had been cheering for Jim and promptly sat down. He's lucky, that's all, she told herself.

"Hello, Ruth," called Gil Stevens. Jim's younger brother broke from a crowd of Loyola rooters and came over to ask Ruth how she liked the game.

"Swell." Ruth tried to smile, but loneliness played tricks with her lips. "Tell Jim he was very good."

When Ruth started to walk away, Gil stopped her. "Why don't you wait to see Jim? He'll be out soon."

Unable to see any reason why she should tell Gil she and Jim were on the outs, if he didn't know it, Ruth said, "Sorry, Gil, I have to hurry home to Thanksgiving dinner. Your mother here to see Jim play today?"

Gil walked toward the gate with Ruth, who was remarking to herself how very much like his brother he looked. "No," he answered, "Mother doesn't approve of Jim's playing at all. She's funny that way, always afraid we'll get hurt. I couldn't understand it when she went to the Southern game."

Since she really didn't know Mrs. Stevens, Ruth was reluctant to pass judgment on her. The one time she had been introduced to Jim's mother, she had said, "How do you do, dear" and had gone on talking to a friend. Ruth thought she might be snobbish and finicky; she'd never let her sons get their hands dirty if she could help it.

"Well," Ruth said when they reached the gate, "you don't want to wander too far, Gil, or you won't find Jim. So long."

"Yes, that's true," Gil agreed. "Good-bye, Ruth."

Ruth went home—cold and alone. She told herself she could have waited for Tod, but since she had told him the day before that she would go right home, he wouldn't be looking for her. And she didn't want to chance meeting Jim Stevens, especially after she had told Gil she had to hurry home to dinner. She did have to hurry home because she wanted to help her mother with the preparations—but most of all because she didn't want to see Jim. Dinner wouldn't start until Tod got there, for Ruth had invited him to have dinner with her family.

Thanksgiving dinner with Tod and her family, the penetrating warmth of home, and the way Tod tried so hard to be natural, even though it made him most unnatural, made Ruth forget the dank day outside. She talked a lot and laughed at the way her father kept telling tales (most of them highly embellished, she was sure) of the days when he was a young man in high school. Tod was not noticeably quiet, and everyone except Paul included him in the conversation. Between Paul and Tod there was not a great deal of cordiality, and Ruth supposed her young brother didn't like the way Tod was trying to act the part of a man, or something like that.

After dinner Ruth didn't think of asking Tod to help with the dishes, as she would have asked Pete Decker or some of the other boys who would have considered it fun to be able to show off. But while Tod wouldn't have refused, he wouldn't have enjoyed it either. So she got her hat and coat and they took a bus for downtown. She had wanted to watch the Santa Claus parade, but Tod considered that foolish. And while they were waiting in line for the movies, she told herself it wasn't a good day for a parade anyhow.

The show they saw was a farce, which was distasteful to Tod, so much so that he wanted to leave before it was over; but Ruth, who was enjoying the nonsense, talked him into staying. That, however, did not alter Tod's judgment that the makers of the picture were a bunch of fly-brained nincompoops who were taking good American cash for a lot of childish absurdities.

"But, Tod, a farce is supposed to be foolishness."

"I guess it was okay if you liked it, but I still think it was awful."

"Old Mr. Serious." Ruth laughed and she would have mussed his hair if she had been sure Tod wouldn't think it childish and get angry.

"It's good to be serious," Tod protested.

"Most of the time, yes." Ruth couldn't resist nudging him with her elbow. "But it's good to let your hair down and have some fun occasionally."

"Other people can do silly things if they want to," he frowned, "but I don't think they're grown-up. That's what's wrong with the world, not enough grown-ups."

"Okay, I don't laugh for the rest of the day," Ruth said winsomely. Good, old, serious Tod, she thought, and laughed to herself.

If Calvert Hall had won the game that morning, it would have made a good topic for conversation. But Ruth thought it best merely to congratulate Tod on the game he had played before letting it become a memory; she had forgotten to do this at the dinner table. Tod smiled at her and said, "Thanks." But he wasn't in one of his talking moods. To Ruth that didn't matter, because she could tell when he was satisfied and when he wasn't; and today Ruth knew he was content to walk along and say nothing, the way he was satisfied to come and sit on the front steps for hours on a summer night without saying a dozen words the whole time he was there. She knew he enjoyed that just as he was enjoying their walk now. She liked him for it; it was good to walk with someone you liked and say nothing, knowing that you liked and were liked.

When Ruth reached home, Marge told her, "Hey, the phone's been ringing all night for you."

Arching her eyebrows demurely, Ruth asked, "Who was it?"

"Jim Stevens."

"Oh." And the period meant that the calls didn't matter.

Nonplused at her sister's indifference, Marge added, "Aren't you going to ask what he wanted?"

"No." Ruth hung up her coat and started for the stairs. "I could guess, but I really don't care."

"Well, he said to tell you he'd call for you tomorrow night around eight-thirty."

"He did?" With a sophistication new to Marge, Ruth added, "Boys are strange, unbelieving creatures. Most difficult to understand. Oh, well, I can't worry over it. I'm going to bed."

Marge threw up her hands in despair. "I give up. One day you're nuts about him, and the next you don't give a darn."

"Don't trouble your pretty little head about it."

"Oh, go drown yourself in a Coke."

In her room Ruth smiled coquettishly at herself in the mirror. She'd have to decide soon whether or not she was going to stand by her refusal to go to the dance with Jim. She had to admit he was persistent, and she liked that. She wanted to go to that dance, too. But it was fun holding him off this way. She knew now that he had been serious when he had said he wasn't going to the dance if she didn't go with him; he couldn't possibly ask anyone else at this late date. Inside herself she knew she was going to the dance, but she wouldn't admit it yet.

As she lay in bed that night she could hear the familiar sounds she had learned to love at night: an express truck rumbling down the street, trains in the distance, boat whistles still farther off, automobiles, and streetcars, and human voices. She loved them all and found them more than usually bewitching tonight, muted as they were by the moisture-ladened air. Her lips gradually separated in a smile as she thought of all she had to be thankful for; it had been a successful day, after all. And she wasn't really sorry for tantalizing Jim—he deserved it. But she'd go to the dance with him if he wanted to take her, because from the very day she had met him she had wanted to go to a Loyola dance with him. She thought it was a mighty good thing for her that Jim didn't take himself as seriously as Tod. Otherwise there might be trouble!

4

"JIM'S downstairs." Paul scampered into Ruth's room and started out again.

"Paul, tell him to wait." Ruth smiled impishly. "And don't tell him I'm almost ready."

"Okay." And Paul bounded down the stairs two or three at a time, making more than the usual racket.

When Ruth decided she had kept Jim waiting long enough, she went to the living room and was horrified to see Paul tossing his dirty, old football to Jim.

"Paul," she demanded, "get that ball out of here!"

"Aw, Jim was only going to show me how to throw a pass."

Before Ruth could give further vent to her ire, Jim broke in, "I'll show you some other time, Paul. We have to hurry now." He held Ruth's wrap for her. "Thanks for coming."

At the car Ruth's heart fell lower than her toes, and she could have walked on it, for there in the back seat were Mr. and Mrs. Stevens, who were to act as chaperones at the dance. Jim introduced Ruth to his father. She apologized for keeping them waiting, and they started for Loyola at Blakefield.

Rolling along the street, the tires made a heavy, liquid sound like the noise pancake batter makes when it is poured on a hot griddle. It had rained all day, but now a cold wind was driving the rain away, leaving behind little puddles that stood alone and shivered or spurted out from under the wheels of passing cars. An occasional spray of raindrops, shaken from the trees, splattered against the windshield, dampening Ruth's spirits, which were chilled and fervid by turns, since she knew the eyes of Mrs. Stevens were piercing right through the back of her. All the things she wanted to say to Jim were forgotten, and she didn't know what to say to his parents. Mr. Stevens seemed nice enough, but Jim's mother didn't invite conversation. The headlights jaggedly searched the road ahead in much the same way that Ruth felt Mrs. Stevens' eyes going over her. Usually Ruth had little difficulty beginning a conversation but, sitting next to Jim as they drove along tonight, ideas just wouldn't come. Unfair as she felt it to be, she nevertheless thought Jim's mother was passing judgment on her. She was late; she couldn't carry on a conversation; she was . . . she was being treated unfairly. Ruth looked disconsolately at Jim's strong hands gripping the steering wheel. Here she was realizing that dream she had dreamed ever since the day she had met and liked him; but in all those dreams Jim's mother had had no place; nor had she been considered in all the brilliant remarks Ruth had imagined herself making. And now even those remarks were forgotten—most of them at any rate; and any Ruth remembered seemed dull and senseless under the circumstances. Mrs. Stevens wouldn't be impressed by them. Mentally Ruth shook herself for being so stupid. When they arrived at Blakefield, it seemed to her she hadn't uttered a two-syllable word the whole way. It was a relief for her when Mr. and Mrs. Stevens got out at the main entrance of the school, and she and Jim went together to park the car.

From the outside the gray stone building at Blakefield looked warm, and its lights spilled an inviting gold mat on the road beside it. After hastily checking her make-up, Ruth pinned on her corsage and returned to where Jim was waiting for her. Together they hurried up the stairs to the library where the orchestra had already begun to play.

"Oh, Jim," Ruth exclaimed as they entered the hall, "it's beautiful!" And her eyes happily scanned the scene before her: book-lined walls lending atmosphere, though the volumes of potential knowledge were stored in a series of alcoves which left the whole center space open; in other parts walls of paneled oak; oak overhead reaching from side to side of the building; oak on the stage; oak blending with the brown linoleum of the polished floor and the rich coloring of autumn leaves—it was a soothing sight, mellow as candlelight.

"A gang of us spent all day decorating it," Jim said proudly. Then taking Ruth by the arm, he added, "Don't stand there all night gazing; let's dance. We can fill in with other partners now and then so it won't be monotonous! I especially want you to have a whirl with Ken Carpenter. He's my best friend at school. But right now I'd rather we danced together than anything."

"So would I," Ruth agreed after they had already started to move across the floor to the rhythm of the music, working their way in among the other dancers. She was glad he hadn't said anything about the ride out. Probably he hadn't enjoyed it any more than she had.

If there was anything Ruth preferred to dancing, she couldn't think of it tonight as she glided about the floor with Jim and, later, with some of his special friends. But it wasn't only the dancing that had her treading on air tonight; Jim had something to do with that. So smooth and sure was his step that Ruth was certain he must have been dancing ever since the time he was two.

"You're almost right," he told her when she finally mentioned it to him. "Mother started me off to dancing school before I could write my name. It seems she holds that dancing is one of those things a gentleman simply must be able to do well. Poor Dad never was much of a dancer according to Mother's standards. But Gil and I will be good dancers or Mother will know the reason why."

"Your father seems to be very nice."

"Dad's tops!" There was sincere admiration in Jim's eyes when he said it. "He's lots of fun, too; you'll like him. And don't worry about Mother—she's mighty nice, too, once you get to understand her ways."

The thought of Mrs. Stevens brought a host of conflicting emotions to Ruth. Unreasonable as it might be when she hardly knew Jim's mother, she couldn't help feeling a certain animosity toward her. If she happened to be a bit standoffish, Ruth supposed she had a right to be, because Mr. Stevens was one of the big lawyers of Baltimore. But she didn't have to be so terribly cold and distant. Ruth gave her head a little shake. Why waste a second of such a super evening on thoughts like that?

"What're you thinking about?" Jim asked.

"I'm just afraid the night will end too soon. I'm having such a good time."

"You know you're making quite a hit with my friends, I suppose."

"They're making quite a hit with me."

"That guy Carpenter's already looking for a date."

"That'll be just fine."

"Says who?" Jim wanted to know.

"I like Ken," Ruth admitted frankly. She pictured to herself the young fellow with the square jaw already giving promise of a heavy beard. She was pleased with the tiny wrinkles at the corners of his eyes and mouth when he laughed.

"But now that I've told you how popular you are, I'll tell you you're going to sit out the next dance because I've promised it to the best girl I know."

"And doesn't this *best* girl have a companion?" Ruth wasn't angry, but she had a few mean thoughts about Jim, wondering whether he had told her she was popular only to have her sit in the corner and think about it while he danced with someone else. Her resentment, slight as it was, was evident in her question.

Seeming to enjoy Ruth's discomfort, Jim said slightingly, "She does, but I'm afraid he wouldn't be interested in dancing with you."

Ruth's eyes burned with anger. "Oh, he wouldn't!"

Still unaffected by her reactions, Jim remarked nonchalantly, "You look fierce when you're mad."

Knowing that Jim had the upper hand, Ruth vowed that he'd be sorry about this! She was of the opinion that she could still put him in his place, if she could only think of the proper biting remark. But she found it was useless to try. Whenever she was angry, smart replies just wouldn't come to her. It had been that way ever since she was small. Her brother Dan always got the better of her if he could make her angry when he was teasing her. In place of anything better, she said, "Angry's the word." And fighting to control herself for fear others would notice her, she added, "And I'm not angry."

"Oh, but you are. If you could see your eyes flash." Jim squeezed her hand and said seriously, "They're pretty that way, full of blue fire."

Pretty or not, compliments or no, Ruth wasn't to be easily pacified, and she told Jim so. And when in an effort to control herself she missed Jim's lead and stepped on his foot, her "Excuse me" was more a matter of form than regret. After that Jim decided he'd spoil Ruth's night if he carried things any further. He told her casually that the next dance was his mother's.

"Oh!" Ruth's mouth didn't close as it should have after the exclamation—it hung open in astonishment. "Why didn't you say so in the first place?"

"It was more fun this way." Jim laughed.

"Jim, don't say anything to your mother about this; she might misunderstand. If she thought I didn't want you to dance with her, she'd be angry."

Jim laughed again at Ruth's breathless desire not to offend his mother.

Not knowing at just what he was laughing, Ruth retorted, "All right, Mr. Smarty, we'll see whether or not I sit out the next dance." Poise returned with determination. "While you dance with your mother, I'm going to ask your father to dance with me."

Like the boy who called wolf too often, Jim found his joke out of hand, for Ruth paid no heed to the note of seriousness in his voice when he told her, "Mother's heart will probably do flip-flops of jealousy if he does."

"Nonsense!" Ruth couldn't imagine Mrs. Stevens getting excited because a high-school girl asked her husband for a dance. Anyway, she was determined she was not going to sit out the dance and have Jim tease her. So when the orchestra completed the number it had been playing during their discussion, she accompanied Jim to his parents, who were seated with the rest of the chaperones. After several introductions, Ruth turned to Mr. Stevens. "Jim says you wouldn't be interested, Mr. Stevens, but would you care to dance with me while he is dancing with Mrs. Stevens?" With a warm smile she faced Jim's mother and asked, "You don't mind, do you, Mrs. Stevens?"

"Go ahead, dear, that will be nice." Mrs. Stevens' cool reply drove all the enthusiasm from Ruth, but her husband's quiet acquiescence kindled a fresh warmth. At Mr. Stevens' agreement, Ruth grimaced playfully, intending it for Jim's eyes, but it was his mother who saw it and gazed sternly at her. Feeling the full burden of her blunder, Ruth watched miserably as Jim began to dance with his mother, whose eyes still pinned her in place. Her lips were moving, and Ruth knew she must be talking about her son's "impossible" friend. The words would be sharp, Ruth feared, as sharp as Mrs. Stevens' chin and other features. Everything about Jim's mother was precise, much more exact even than June Thompson. There wasn't a hair out of place, and every fold in her dress struck Ruth as being intended by her. Her every movement was measured, exact, impersonal.

"Well, Ruth, are we going to dance?" Mr. Stevens asked in a voice that swept her up in its cordial realness.

Hesitantly she replied, "I—I don't think Mrs. Stevens liked the idea."

"Of course she did," Mr. Stevens said with embarrassed bluster. He wasn't at all like his wife, in whose presence Ruth was uncomfortable. He was real, a man like her father or Mr. Mason who ran the confectionery near the parish hall.

"All right," she agreed, adding as they began to dance, "this certainly is an honor for me."

Mr. Stevens told her she wouldn't think so by the end of the dance, for he had never been a good dancer and his exercise of recent years had consisted of nothing more vigorous than walking. "I'm afraid you don't know what you've led me into, young lady," he continued. "After this, my wife will want to drag me out on the floor for every dance."

"Really, I'm sorry, Mr. Stevens, if I've caused you any trouble."

"Oh, I wouldn't exactly put it that way, Ruth." The corpulent man, who was such a good sport, was already gasping for breath, while beads of perspiration broke out on his forehead at the effort he was expending. "Oops!" he exclaimed as he landed rather solidly on Ruth's toes. "Mrs. Stevens would give up after one or two of those." He laughed again. "I must say, I haven't had so much fun in quite a while." Ruth liked him for his gameness, though she couldn't help hoping Jim would never become so heavy and bald. Jim without his sandy hair. No, that just couldn't be!

Looking at her husband, who stood puffing and mopping his brow at the end of the dance, Mrs. Stevens gave a slight sigh of exasperation, as if it were a fault to become overheated. Nodding to Ruth, she said, "You must dance with Mr. Stevens again some time, dear." Then very impersonally, somewhat like a mother taking her small son from play to his nap, she grasped her husband by the arm and walked away, leaving

Ruth staring after her.

The realization that she had actually made this a wretched evening for Mrs. Stevens hurt Ruth deeply. "Jim," she said, "I'm afraid I've spoiled the night for your mother."

He could have said I told you so, but he didn't. He tried to disregard the whole thing. "Don't be silly."

"I'm sorry I asked your father to dance with me. I could tell she didn't like that." They started toward the downstairs recreation room where refreshments were being served. "Did your mother say anything to you about my asking your father to dance, Jim?"

"Forget about it, Ruth. It wasn't important." But Ruth felt it was important, more important than Jim was willing to admit. He stopped her on the way down the stairs and asked, "Say, did I tell you how terrific those yellow roses look on your dress? I think they make about the nicest corsage I've ever given a girl."

Ken Carpenter and his date passed them, and Ken called over his shoulder, "Don't let the old politician give you a lot of hot air, Ruth. He's always practicing his voice."

"I won't, Ken; I'm on to him." Seriously Ruth asked Jim, "Do you really want to be a politician—or should I say statesman?"

"I want to be one, all right, and I'll tell you all about it some day, if you're interested. But right now let's get some of those refreshments."

At the far end of the recreation room there was a fireplace where a gold-blazing fire cast grotesque shadows against the walls. Two lighted candles shed a yellow luster on the tablecloth of each of the tables spread throughout the room, while overhead lights gave off a pale orange color that fused with the red of the leaves and the yellow of the corn shocks decorating the room. There was no mistaking the autumnal spirit.

When Jim, after placing some punch and fancy cookies before Ruth, launched into a panegyric on what a great bunch of people the mothers were for providing the refreshments, she leaned over and whispered in his ear, "Politician."

The orchestra had just begun a medley of waltzes when Ruth and Jim returned to the dance floor. Still flushed from the heat of the fire, Ruth's face took on a deeper hue as she and Jim whirled and whirled, caught up in the rhythm that has set hearts and feet dancing since the day the first waltz was played. For Ruth waltzes meant Strauss, and Strauss meant Vienna and the spectacle of varicolored uniforms, the Danube, and people dancing, dancing, dancing. Only when she was actually dancing a waltz did she realize how much she preferred it to any other step. That rhythm—she couldn't stand still when she heard it; she had to move with its magic, because it seemed to lift her right out of herself. And the lightness that came when her head cleared after a series of whirls was indescribable.

When Jim congratulated her at the end of the number, Ruth was radiant, for if there was anything she was proud of, it was her ability to waltz. The warmth she felt within herself was not the result of mere physical activity. "I wish they were all waltzes," she said.

The time passed rapidly and almost before Ruth realized what had happened, the dance was over and she stood in self-conscious silence, the silence that came over her when she felt the nearness of Jim's mother. Hastily, she volunteered to walk to the car with Jim.

As they hurried along Jim pointed to the moon which was struggling to stay out of a sea of wind-driven clouds. " 'The moon,' " he quoted, " 'is a ghostly galleon, tossed upon cloudy seas.' " His finger moved toward the road which reflected the moon in its wetness, "And the road is a ribbon of moonlight. And in just a few seconds the highwayman will come riding, riding, riding." Ruth smiled happily at the thought of Jim and herself walking up a ribbon of moonlight.

The Stevens' car went a different way from the one taken by most of the others, for Mrs. Stevens insisted that Jim return home with her and Mr. Stevens rather than stop at Murray's, the Hot Shoppe, Drumcastle Farm or any of the other popular places where friends were taking their dates.

It seemed a long ride to Ruth because again she didn't know what to say. Jim's mother said nothing, and his father was tired. She had a feeling that Jim said nothing either because he was annoyed with his mother. As they drove along Loch Raven Boulevard, Ruth watched a few stars trying to pin down some of those clouds in the sky, but they soon gave way to the street lamps; and the quiet of the country was drowned in the sounds that linger with a city even when it is asleep.

While Ruth was opening the front door to her house, she was hoping she'd never have another date with Mrs. Stevens! Jim, who was standing beside her, was talking quietly and she liked it, but she was conscious that Mrs. Stevens was waiting for him. "Well, Jim," she said when she had the door open, "it's been a perfectly wonderful evening. Thank you very much."

"No thanks to me, Ruth." His eyes were clear and earnest. "I enjoyed it as much as you did." She watched his fingers circle the brim of his hat a few times before he continued, "I guess it's good night."

"I suppose it has to be," Ruth said, no more anxious than he to end such a perfect night.

Jim mumbled something about all good things having to come to an end before he changed to his best oratorical style to add, " 'Parting is such sweet sorrow that I shall say good night till it be morrow.' "

"How nice! Jim where'd you get that?"

"From Shakespeare. Juliet says it to Romeo, I think. I'll tell you all about it if you'll come to the first hockey game with me next Friday night."

"I'd love to, Jim."

"Then it's a date. But good night now; Mother and Dad will get tired of waiting in the car." As he went down the steps he called back, "Pleasant dreams."

Pleasant dreams, the words kept ringing in Ruth's ears. How could dreams be anything but pleasant after such a night? Thinking back over it, she skipped the disagreeableness of Mrs. Stevens, satisfied that she would not come along to a hockey game with Jim. Ruth wasn't sleepy; she could still hear the music and see the gay couples gliding buoyantly across the floor. When she recalled the waltzes with Jim, she was tempted to dance around the room; but a whirl or two before hanging her dress in the closet had to satisfy her, for there was danger of waking Marge, who slept in the twin bed next to hers.

"Mother Mary, it was wonderful! Thank you, thank you." Ruth knelt for her night prayers. "Mother Mary, here I am saying my night prayers early in the morning. Don't let me be grouchy when I get up. Good night—but how I wish the night were just beginning!"

5

WHEN Ruth went to Mass the following Sunday, she walked with the self-assurance of a girl who knows she has friends and happiness. There was a vibrant confidence in that walk, in the tilt of her head, the swing of her arms. She could have hugged little old Sister Leo when she saw her after Mass, gathering her third-graders for the children's Mass, just the way she had been doing it since Ruth was in her class *ages* ago. Sister Leo was the unwrinkled kind of nun who put new warmth into the hearts of her former pupils by bowing to them and smiling wherever she met them, even in church. Old she was, but no one could guess how old. To Ruth she looked the same as she did the day she first came to teach her in class. She walked with all her years, slightly stooped under the burden, but smiling the smile of peace. Ruth remembered how she had wanted to be a nun when she was in the third grade, just because she wanted to be like Sister Leo, who must be so very holy. She smiled at the Sister who, she knew now, was even holier than she had thought. Heaven does walk around on earth sometimes.

"What's the matter, don't you speak to your friends any more?"

Ruth recognized Pete Decker's voice. "Hi, Pete," she answered, and waited for him to catch up with her. "Sorry, I didn't see you."

"What's the matter? In some kind of trance?"

"Maybe."

"You sure must have been. I don't see how you could have missed me. I was trying to get your eye all the way out of church." Pete looked off into space and said, "And I do so stand out from the rest of men."

"Tell me more," Ruth said jokingly, as they started up the street together.

"Oh, shucks!" Pete turned up his coat collar. "You girls are bad for my humility, always agreeing with me."

"How's Betty?"

Owl-eyed, Pete replied, "Divine as ever." He patted his flaming pompadour of red hair that rose in two or three decks above his forehead. "I'm really making time with the goddess. You other girls are nice, but Betty. . . . Ah!"

"Pete, you're crazy!" Ruth loved to watch his animated gestures—those arms were never still. For that matter, not many of his features were either; he had one of the most expressive faces she had ever seen.

"I know, but it's fun. Who wants to be sane and ordinary? Nearly everybody's that way, but very few people are red-headed, red-hot, and robust. And let me hasten to inform you that I'm proudest of the red-hot because that's my own talent. The red hair runs in the family, the robustness comes from eating as much as I sell in Dad's store, but the red-hotness comes from myself alone."

"And whatever does that mean?"

"What does it mean?" Pete repeated the question with outstretched, incredulous arms. "Why, it means all those little marks of genius I've developed; all those things you and Betty and the other girls are so fond of. The French might call it *savoir-faire*. Of course I don't know what that means, but it sounds red-hot to me."

"I don't know how Betty stands you, Pete."

"No trouble at all. She never disagrees with me and lets me do all the talking."

"I want to be around the day that happens."

A meaningful laugh from Pete, and then, "So do I. But I can dream, can't I? What's life without dreams?"

"I think you see too many movies."

"So do I, but I'm happy."

When they reached her house, Ruth asked, "Won't you come in for a while?"

"No, thank you," Pete said ceremoniously. "I have to run along. Give my regards to that lovely young sister of yours, a most charming person, and what an exquisite vocabulary she is developing."

"She's probably been around you too much lately."

Pete smiled. "That could only prove a great boon to her." And he was off in a flutter of excitement.

Ruth was in school the next day, and Monday at the Institute of Notre Dame is as difficult as Monday in any other school. The Institute is a large establishment. It is a motherhouse of the School Sisters of Notre Dame, a grammar school and a high school for girls. The brick building has stood serenely in its place on Aisquith Street many a year, and like a lady quietly growing old, has watched everything around change. At one time the neighborhood surrounding the Institute was a residential district, but it wore out and became a slum area. Transformed anew, it now stands as a Federal housing project. But during all the years of aging and rejuvenating around the Institute, Catholic girls were growing into young women within her walls and passing on to take their places in the world. For over three years now Ruth Sterner had been one of those girls growing into young women.

Although Sister Philothea was lecturing brilliantly—or at least Ruth supposed she was, since Sister always did, of course, whether any of the girls understood her or not—Ruth sat musing about the things the old building must have seen and heard during its years of standing: First-graders crying for their mothers . . . seniors supposing themselves to be mature women . . . sophomores trying to act like seniors . . . hundreds of first Holy Communions . . . the fervent first vows of young Sisters . . . the beautiful holiness of those who had grown old in the service of God.

"Funny," Ruth murmured to herself, "inside it's always the same; outside it's always changing. Soon we'll move on and other girls just like us will come to take our places. I wonder if the building will notice it?"

"Miss Sterner, you might profit by paying attention to what is being said!" The voice from the front of the room was stern. Until now Ruth had almost forgotten that Sister Philothea was still talking—it was so much more enjoyable to dream, and so much easier during the last period on Monday afternoon. She excused herself and made an effort to pay attention to what

Sister was saying, although she couldn't help feeling that Sister might have let her dream away the last ten minutes.

As soon as class was over, Ruth gathered up her books and hurried after Jane Arnold, who sat nearer the door than she did and was already in the corridor. "Jane," she called as she left the room, "wait a second, will you?"

"Miss Sterner!" It was Sister Philothea again, Ruth knew. Her blood ran cold as she turned and answered meekly, "Yes, Sister?"

"Young ladies at the Institute do not run and shout in the halls. Don't let me hear you do it again."

Lucky thing she's too tired to keep me in, Ruth thought to herself while replying, "Yes, Sister—I mean, no, Sister. It won't happen again, Sister."

When Ruth caught up with Jane, she whispered, "A friend of mine. What does she think I am, a freshman?"

Jane's eyes twinkled unsympathetically. "Well, why must you sleep in class? That was the start of everything."

A quickly-suppressed snort told Jane what Ruth thought of her remark. Then the latter smiled and said she had been pondering an idea for a feature article for *Windows*. The mention of anything for the school paper always brought an interested look to the face of its editor, and Jane was excited immediately. An editor can find ordinary articles without any trouble, but feature stuff is different. And Ruth insisted her feature on the building would be different. "Not the ordinary sort of thing; every school paper has that. *Windows* wants something special." She paused dramatically.

"Well?" said Jane, quite evidently not interested in theatricals, but her curiosity whetted nonetheless.

"Look, couldn't we do this? Couldn't we make the building

a person and have her tell her own life's story, the people she's seen, the Sisters she's known the longest. You know, all that sort of thing. What do you think?"

Jane didn't know, but with dispatch becoming an editor, she appointed Ruth to undertake the task, and with a quick movement of a slender index finger she checked off the matter on an imaginary pad. Walking with a grace Ruth always admired but was unable to imitate, the willowy senior led the way toward the editorial office. "Tell me, Ruth, do you do all your thinking in Sister Philothea's class?"

"Let's not go into that." Ruth had her own opinions of Sister Philothea and her class, and since they weren't very complimentary, she preferred to keep them to herself. Once at home she had mentioned her, and Dan, who had studied Greek at Loyola, had told her Philothea meant friend of God or something like that. There were times when Ruth thought God was the only one with whom Sister Philothea could be friends. Even when she admitted honestly to herself that she was prejudiced because of the number of times Sister had been obliged to call her down for not paying attention, Ruth still couldn't work up any great spark of enthusiasm in her heart for this teacher. She thought part of the trouble lay in the fact that Sister was so thin and stern-looking; she would have preferred to have her look like Sister Bernard, who bounced when she walked but always had a smile on her face.

Once in the editorial office, Jane put Pat Boyle to work typing good copy, while she told Ruth to start on her feature. The sharp clickety-click of the typewriters beat a spellbinding rhythm as the girls went to work on their paper.

" 'Lo, everybody!" June Thompson sang out with her sugary voice. She was late as usual. "How's this sound for my social column? At Loyola's Thanksgiving dance, what I.N.D.ians were escorted by Don halfbacks?"

"I'll bite," said one of the girls.

"Peggy Lambert and Ruth Sterner," June primped her blonde hair.

"Jealous?" Ruth asked.

"No, honey," June half-sneered, half-smiled. "I was invited by another star, but I was already engaged for the evening. However, my sweet, Gene Cole told me all about it yesterday, tra-la."

"Oh!"

"Made quite a hit with Jim Stevens, they tell me. He's a nice kid, Ruth." June, who had gracefully arranged her petite form on one of the chairs, got up and walked over to Ruth. "I think I could like him myself, but I can't be dating *everybody.*" She turned to Jane without seeming to notice the glint in Ruth's eyes. "Jane, when are you going to talk these old-fashioned nuns into letting me smoke while we're working on the paper?"

"Why don't *you* try talking them into it?"

"I did, but we don't talk the same language. Oh, well," she sighed, "it doesn't make any diff today; I can't stay. I came to tell you, Jane, I'll be two days late with my copy. I was so busy over the week end I didn't get any time to work on it. That'll be all right, won't it, hon?" June could be so sweet when she was pleading or making an excuse, her green eyes evidencing a regret most people took to be sincere.

"Sure, sure," Jane groaned, knowing there was nothing she could do about June's tardiness.

"You're so sweet, Jane. I knew you'd understand. I'd stay and do the work now, but I have to meet Mother downtown. I simply must have a new evening dress. Good-bye, girls."

"Good-bye, girls," Marie Kenny imitated June as only she could. "I simply *must* have a new evening dress."

Everyone laughed except Pat Boyle, who said June meant well.

"She could prove that," Marie contended, "by coming here to do some work once in a while instead of offering excuses."

When it was time to stop for the afternoon, Ruth hadn't made much progress with her feature, and she was glad to comply with Jane's suggestion that she take it along with her and finish it at home. While Ruth was putting her things in order, Pat Boyle waited for her, as she had done almost every afternoon since they became friends. Quite accidentally they had sat next to one another on their way home from school one afternoon when they were freshmen. They fell into conversation, and Ruth found that she enjoyed talking with the plump little girl with the serious mind. She liked Pat especially because she was easygoing and could always be nice to everyone—even June Thompson at her sugar-coated worst. Pat was the one to whom Ruth went when she had difficulties with her studies, or when she just wanted to talk seriously. Pat was also Ruth's Delphic oracle in the world of classical music and the other arts.

To Ruth's mind it was a shame some of the boys didn't recognize what a gem Pat was. What if she were plump? She had lovely, clear skin, a pleasant, intelligent face, and a wonderful personality. Although she had never been thought of as being popular, Pat had in her quiet way become one of the best liked girls in the school. She didn't have enough sparkle to be the most popular, and because she worked so much in the background, it wasn't likely that she would be chosen the girl most likely to succeed. Very few girls at the Institute realized that it was Pat's efficiency that accounted in large measure for the school paper's regular appearance, or that it was frequently the music she selected for dramatic presentations which covered up spotty acting.

"Pat, maybe you can help me with something."

"Maybe. What is it, Ruth?"

"When Jim left me at the front door after the Thanksgiving dance at Loyola, he quoted some lines from Shakespeare about 'parting is such sweet sorrow that I shall say good night till it be morrow.' Now I want to have something to say to him after our next date. You've read Shakespeare more than I have. Do you know any lines I could quote?"

Pat thought a minute. "These lines were spoken after Hamlet's death, but they ought to do: 'Good night, sweet prince, and flights of angels sing thee to thy rest!' They seem to be pretty good for wishing anyone good night."

"'Good night, sweet prince, and—and flights of angels sing . . . thee to thy rest!'" Ruth repeated the words haltingly. "Oh, Pat, that's perfect, just what I wanted!"

When Pat asked her why she didn't read Shakespeare more herself, Ruth replied, "I'll have to now, I suppose, if Jim's going to quote the stuff at me. Isn't it funny, the way boys think you're queer if you can't talk about everything they want to talk about?"

"Maybe that's why so few boys ask me out," Pat remarked. "I can't discuss sports with them and I don't know much about swing, but most of them can't talk about classical music, the theater, or books."

"Do you hold that against them, Pat?"

"Yes and no. When I can't discuss sports with boys I know

I'm to blame. However, I do think I could learn to like football after hearing you talk about it so much. The thing that makes me cross is the way boys—and girls too—get the idea that good music and the theater are high-brow. Most of them go around talking down things they've never experienced."

Leaving Pat on the car, Ruth got off and started walking toward home. When she reached the lot where Paul and his friends were playing their afternoon football, she called to him to come along with her.

"Aw, wait for just one more touchdown."

"No."

"Nuts!"

"All right for you, Paul," Ruth threatened. But she stopped to watch just the same. The shouts of the boys reminded her of the times she used to watch Dan and his crowd playing on the same lot. In those days she had always wanted to play with the boys, and when they chased her away, she would go home crying. Then her mother would say, "Girls are little ladies and don't play rough games with boys."

The play advanced to where Ruth stood, and when she saw one of the boys about to throw a pass, she set her books down, took a few steps, and jumped in front of the player for whom the pass was intended. She came down with the ball firmly in her hands and, laughing, gave it to the boy who should have caught it.

To the boys, Ruth's action wasn't funny; nor were they happy when she insisted that Paul come home after one more play, which play would be a pass, with Ruth doing the passing. When they finally agreed, Ruth selected her blockers and receiver. Her pass was a wobbly one, thrown from that strange side-arm position characteristic of girls. It reached the receiver just as Pete Decker rode by on his bike. The boy dropped the ball, but Pete yelled, "Nice pass, Ruth."

Chagrined that Pete should have seen her, Ruth quickly got off the field, picked up her books, and called to Paul, who was already involved in another play. When he didn't answer, she started home alone.

Paul soon caught up with her, declaring, "See, I knew it wouldn't take long; I got plenty of time before dinner."

Coldly Ruth replied, "You should have come when you were called."

"You're not my mother. Mom said to be home in time for dinner. I'm here, aren't I?"

Seeing she would lose that argument, Ruth changed the subject. "If you weren't so dirty, I'd let you carry my books for me."

Paul, who was studying the cracks in the sidewalk and studiously avoiding them, answered, "Yeah, well, who says I'd carry them?"

"Any boy with manners would."

"Who, for instance?"

It would have been foolish to mention Tod Edwards to Paul, who disliked him as much as he disliked singing cowboys "who don't know how to fight." And to say that Pete Decker would carry her books would have been presumptuous; of course, he would if he thought of it. But would he think of it? So Ruth said, "Jim Stevens would."

" 'Course, he's your boy friend."

Ruth blushed. "He is *not!*"

"He is too." Then Paul chanted, "Ruth loves Jim Stevens. Ruth loves Jim Stevens."

"Paul, don't say that!"

But Paul only sang out the louder. Ruth could see Pete and some of the boys gathered in front of the Deckers' place. "Oh, hush up!" she cried to Paul, who only replied, "Nuts!" and began to run, his chant trailing after him. Ruth chased him, but when all the boys turned to watch her, she stopped, embarrassed.

Unabashed, Pete called to her, "Don't stop because of us, Ruth; he'll get away."

She could have cried right then and there, but she wouldn't. Not for all the world would she cry in front of those laughing boys. With hurt pride and lost decorum, Ruth made her way home and into the kitchen, where she found her young brother standing behind his mother for protection. What was the use of a scene? Ruth stalked up to her room.

While she was there, Jim phoned and wanted to break their date for the coming Friday night.

"Of course, Jim, it'll be all right," she heard herself say.

"Golly, Ruth, I hate to disappoint you like this."

"I know, Jim. I'm not disappointed, really." But all the time she was wondering who was saying these things. It was her voice, all right, but she couldn't mean she wasn't put out about the date.

"Yes, but I feel like a heel after I asked you."

"Don't be silly, Jim. If you can't make it, then there's no reason for feeling like a heel."

"But that's just the trouble. . . ."

"What is it, Jim?" Immediately Ruth saw Mrs. Stevens' face before her, and she felt sure Jim's mother had something to do with this.

"Nothing. I'm sorry about the date, Ruth. I'll see you some time and explain in person. Good-bye."

Some time is very indefinite, Ruth thought, as she hung up after hearing the click of the receiver on Jim's end of the line. She sat at the phone wondering why Jim had called off the date. Could she have done something to make him angry? Why hadn't he told her what was wrong? She was beginning to think Jim Stevens wasn't the independent character she had thought he was; he was more like a puppet on a string controlled by his mother. But, then, she could be wrong.

Sometimes Ruth thought she didn't understand any boy except her brother Paul, whose whole life, devoid of complexities, revolved around sports, each game in season consuming his time and interest. Now Paul wouldn't have hesitated to tell her what the trouble was; in fact, the problem there might have been keeping him from telling everyone else! But when boys get older they are hard to understand. Look at Tod: he was probably the youngest looking of all the boys with whom she went out, yet he thought he had to act like the oldest; he had to be grown-up and serious all the time. Or take Pete Decker, who could talk more than any girl Ruth knew; he seldom had a serious thought. Of course, boys aren't the only queer ones. Ruth couldn't understand a lot of the girls at school, and she admitted they probably couldn't understand her either. In fact, she didn't always understand herself. Suddenly life seemed a very complicated thing.

6

SKATE! Skate! Frenzied shouts accompanied the frantic efforts of the players of two ice hockey teams in the last desperate minutes of a wide open game. A blue-jerseyed player broke away from the others with the puck, and the cheers rang louder, echoing and re-echoing off the roof of Sports Centre. Let it fly! Shoot, Don, shoot!

Strangely non-conductive of the electricity of the crowd, Tod Edwards stood beside Ruth, who was cheering for Ken Carpenter and Loyola. Obviously Tod didn't care for her excitement over Loyola, but Ruth didn't mind; she had cheered for Calvert Hall in the first game.

"Watch this!" someone behind Ruth shouted, and she forgot all about Tod as she saw Ken shoot a pass to Don Wright, who circled the Poly cage, picking up speed with every push of his skates. As his wingmen moved in to intercept the Poly defense, Don cut in front of the net and lifted a beautiful shot past the goalie, high into the left-hand corner. The cheers were almost hysterical. With two minutes left to play and the score at 3–2 in favor of Poly, this was still anybody's game.

Taking the puck on the face-off, Poly tried to freeze it. Ken Carpenter cut off a pass and started toward the Poly goal, only to lose the puck when the Poly defense men checked him and sent him sprawling over the ice. But the whole Loyola team dashed for the puck, and there was a tie-up, a whistle, and another face-off. Wright gained possession of the hard rubber disc. Ken moved in toward the crease where he was wide open. But the expected pass didn't come from Wright. Instead, Wright feinted the Poly center out of position and shot. Poly's net tender pushed the puck aside to a waiting wingman, who sped down the ice and lofted one last desperation shot at the Loyola net before the bell sounded, ending the game.

While she and Tod were skating around after the games, Ruth happened to see Jim Stevens talking to a group of the Loyola players. They seemed disgruntled about something and Ruth guessed that it was Don Wright's shot. She had heard that he was too confident of his own ability and almost entirely distrustful of his mates' ability. Even she understood that he should have passed to Carpenter on that last play, because Ken was wide open in front of the cage. But Ruth wasn't interested in that. The nerve of him, coming here tonight! she thought to herself. It wasn't so easy to put him out of her mind. Jim still occupied the center stage when he came sliding up and asked if he might skate with her for a few minutes.

"Well, what are *you* doing here?" Ruth asked as soon as they were away from Tod, and there was no mistaking the coldness of her manner and the penetrating sharpness of her gaze.

"Ruth, I'm sorry about tonight," Jim had hardly begun to explain when he was interrupted.

"Hi, Jim, introduce me." It was Don Wright, who as soon as he was presented put his arm around Ruth and began to skate with her. "From the Institute, eh? Know June Thompson? Nice kid, Junie, plenty fast."

Jim caught up with them and clamped an angry grip on Don's arm. "All right, Don, this is where I come in. Ruth's not my date and. . . ."

"Okay, Jim, don't get sore. See you some time, Ruth." With an elaborate bow to Jim, he skated off.

"Not if I can help it," Ruth said, half-audibly. Then she turned to Jim. "Well?"

"Ruth, I really wanted to bring you tonight."

"But your mother objected?" Ruth was tired of this whole thing. She could very well do without Jim Stevens and his kind.

"Yes."

"What did I do now?"

"She didn't like your asking Dad to dance with you at Blake-field that night. She thought you were too forward."

"Oh, for heaven's sake!" Ruth began to skate off but Jim caught her arm and held her back.

"You don't understand, Ruth. Mother likes to run things for us, even picking our dates."

"Well," Ruth's eyes flared, "next time let her pick those dates before you ask me."

"You're not sore, are you, Ruth?"

"No, I'm just being subtle. Really, I'm thrilled to death to have your mother care so much for me, and I just love the way you toss me off any time you please."

"It won't happen again."

Ruth laughed bitterly. "Where have I heard that before?"

"I mean it, Ruth," Jim said seriously, and something in his

manner told Ruth that he did mean it.

"I know you do. But what you seem to think is that it won't happen again because *you* won't let it. Really, though, it won't happen again because I'm not dating you any more. Now take me back to Tod, please."

"Okay, if that's the way you want it."

"That's the way I want it," Ruth said, but she thought it had to be that way whether or not she wanted it that way. She couldn't buck Jim's mother and expect to win, no matter what she thought of Jim.

Ruth didn't have much to say to Tod during the remainder of the skating session. It wasn't much fun to break off a friendship with anyone. But she took on some life once they were outside. The wind on North Avenue came in cold blasts; a lusty gust of it would trail off into nothingness, only to be followed by another big blow. Caught up in the draft, a sheet of newspaper blew past them—news rushing on to nowhere, to be read by no one in particular, though the words were tumbling head over heels to get there. Responding to the sharp command of the air, Ruth and Tod walked with the briskness of West Point cadets. Ruth wanted to wave her arms, jump about, embrace the breeze, run. "*Hmmmmm*, isn't it wonderful? We'll be skating in the park soon, if the wind dies down a little." The wind tried to blow the words back into her mouth, so they sounded like laughter when they came out. "That'll certainly be better than skating around in circles all night."

Just then Ruth sighted their car in the distance and wanted to sprint to Greenmount Avenue for it, but Tod caught her by the hand and said, "Let's walk—we're in no hurry."

Something in Tod's voice made Ruth hesitate, and if someone had come upon them suddenly, he wouldn't have been able to tell whether the tears in her eyes were there out of sorrow or because of the wind and the laughter. She looked at Tod; he wasn't angry, he was smiling. Not even Tod would have considered it childish to run tonight, when all nature seemed to be galloping merrily. No, he wasn't angry, but there was something strange about the way he held onto her hand and slipped her arm under his. Suddenly Ruth felt hot all over; it was like molten white stars bursting inside her. She didn't know what to say, and Tod didn't want to speak. They were silent.

Not until they reached her home did Tod say anything. "Ruth. . . ."

"What, Tod?"

"Ruth, I—I want to ask you something."

"Yes, Tod?"

His eyes were pleading something eloquently, but his voice was faltering. Ruth guessed what he wanted to say, and happiness and fear wrestled in her mind. "Ruth," he said, "will you go steady with me?"

Images fluttered by with the racing unclarity of a film which has jumped the track. She tried to stop it; she tried to think. She saw Tod's burning brown eyes, heard herself breathing quickly. "Wait a minute," she managed to whisper. Her own feelings amazed her. She had known and liked Tod a long time, but she had never felt like this before. There was a lump in her throat that she couldn't swallow. Only after Tod urged her to say something was she able to speak.

"I'm sorry, Tod. I didn't mean to act like this; only I don't know what to say." Her mind cleared gradually as she began to explain that she didn't want to go steady with anyone yet; that meant being somebody's special girl.

"But I want you to be my special girl, Ruth."

"We're too young, Tod." Ruth recalled what she had heard in retreats about not going steady until you were almost ready to get married. She remembered all she had read about its limiting your social life just at the time when you should be meeting all sorts of new friends and going places in groups. She liked Tod, liked him far more than most of the boys she knew, but going steady . . .

Tod sulked. His eyes became cold. "Maybe you don't love me." Ruth wasn't exactly sure what love was, though she did know it meant liking a person more than anyone else. And despite the lump in her throat, despite the fact that she wanted to cry, despite the strange feeling she had never before experienced, she was sure she wasn't in love. Love was something bigger than this, something you were sure about. But realizing her inability to explain things to Tod, she said very simply, "No, Tod, I don't want to go steady."

At first Tod's lips showed hurt, sagging corners, but they soon set in grim tightness. "Okay." It was bitter and final, like a judgment; and his eyes accused her of she knew not what, though they did somehow manage to make her feel mean and low and contemptible.

When Ruth began to realize that Tod would stand there all night looking at her with his reproving eyes unless she changed her mind, she stammered, "Tod, I—I think I had better go in."

"Okay, go ahead, but don't expect me to come around again. Turn me down now and we're through."

Thinking this melodramatic and overly serious even for a young fellow with Tod's aspirations to being grown-up, Ruth replied without considering, "Don't be silly, Tod."

"I'm not being silly. You're just not being serious," he insisted. "You don't think I know what I'm talking about. You think I don't know what love is, that I haven't thought this thing over plenty before asking you. Well, you're wrong. But if that's the way you feel about it, fine. . . ."

Melodramatic or not, Tod meant every word he said, and Ruth berated herself for having given any sign of taking him lightly; as if she could judge how deeply he felt, or as if her own thoughts were clear, when she was certain of only one thing—that she did not love Tod, however much she liked him. "Tod," she pleaded, "please don't think I'm joking. I like you very much and I appreciate your liking me enough to ask me to go steady, but I don't feel that I'm ready for anything like that. I want to meet lots of other boys and go out with them. I don't want to be tied down. Anyway, even if I liked you much more than I do, I don't think it would be wise for us to go steady. Don't you think it's rather foolish for people to go steady unless they expect to get married?"

"But I want to marry you in a couple of years."

The sureness with which Tod said it took Ruth's breath away, for she had thought of marriage only in those romantic dreams most teen-agers delight in; she had never thought of it seriously. When she thought of it now, she felt like a mere child. "Tod," she asked, "can't we go on the way we are for a while?"

"No!"

"Well, then," she whispered, biting of her quivering lower lip to hold it steady, "I'm sorry."

"Okay, good-bye." Tod turned with a finality that matched his words. "For good!"

Ruth tried to call him back to explain and thank him for her fun earlier that night, but he walked on, unheeding, straight off without looking back, shoulders that usually slouched held stiffly straight. His heels clicked sharply on the pavement, and a street light threw his shadow back toward her, but it grew shorter and shorter until he passed the light and took even his shadow away with him.

Suddenly the night was dark and oppressive to Ruth. It had lost all its charm, and had grown lonely and cold. As if trying to keep it from entering the house with her, she rushed inside and slammed the door after her. But she couldn't shut out her thoughts of Tod and Jim. Both of them were gone now.

Once in bed, Ruth tossed and turned and tried to think of nothing, but she couldn't. She heard the deep-booming *bong* of a tower clock every fifteen minutes; streetcars rumbled along outside; occasionally an auto horn sounded. Noise, noise . . . all those wonderful sounds were nothing but noise tonight, noise that made her angry when it should have been music. . . . A deep-throated whistle said farewell for a big boat as it slipped away from the lights of Baltimore harbor into the darkness of the bay. Sounds that had fascinated her before were just noise for Ruth tonight, until she lost herself in the labored *chug-chug* of a B & O freight train, tugging a load of something or other in or out of the city. Like the *scrutch-scrutch* of the Midshipmen's heels the afternoon of the Notre Dame game, it set her dreaming. Only this time it brought real sleep—and no Jim to say, "Parade's over."

7

LIKE a mountain stream jubilant with new life, the ballet music from "Faust" ran rapidly in its course. At times it was so soft and gentle that Ruth forgot its swiftness, then like that same mountain stream running wild with too much feeding, its notes spilled over one another and raced on and on, louder and louder, until they burst in a tremendous crescendo.

Experiencing her first dateless week end since she was a sophomore, Ruth was sitting by the radio, listening to the Met's presentation of "Faust" in an effort to forget her loneliness. But it wasn't having the desired effect, for Ruth was conscious, as she had been conscious for a week, of the emptiness that had come into her life. And her family hadn't made it any easier by their questioning concern, while Paul had been positively irritating with his insistence that she was in love.

"Ruth, come on down to the cellar and dance a while," called Marge who had just come in the front door with Joe Milo and Pete Decker. "Pete's got a couple of new records, and he doesn't have to be back to work for an hour."

"I'm not in the mood for dancing," Ruth objected. "Why don't you call Betty Cranwell? It would only take her a minute to come over."

"She's not home today." This information came from Pete as he snapped off the radio and took Ruth by the arm. "Come on, beautiful, you can put up with me for a short time, can't you?"

"Oh, all right," she replied without enthusiasm. Pete was pulling her after him, telling her how terrific the new records were.

With the third dance, Ruth began to feel more like herself. After all, what was more natural to her than dancing in her own cellar? The neighborhood crowd danced there frequently during the winter; almost every night during the summer. When Ruth's older brother Dan was in high school, Mr. Sterner had had the place fixed into a club cellar for him and his friends. Later Ruth and Marge inherited it. Though its "pine wood" walls were really paper and the floor was covered with waxed linoleum, it looked very much like the genuine article, and Ruth loved dancing there. For the first time that week she found herself laughing in response to Pete's clowning.

It was a phenomenon and a cause of wonder to the rest of the family that Paul Sterner inevitably turned up from his play whenever cake and Cokes were served. Hardly had Marge brought them to the cellar when he arrived panting.

"Hi, Pete, Joe!" he saluted the boys. "Can I have a Coke?"

"After you've had a bath," Ruth announced firmly.

"Aw, can't I have it now?"

"Beat it, Paul," Marge backed Ruth up. "You ought to know better than to come in here looking like that."

Paul gave a surprised but satisfied glance at his clothes. "Yeah, well you don't look so hot yourself," he called to his sister. And he shot for the stairs, with Marge in pursuit.

"Smart kid." Pete laughed. "He's going to go places. Sure knows how to put you girls in your place."

Within a few minutes Paul was back; his speed shattered his own record time for taking a bath. "Now give me my Coke," he demanded. He found himself a chair and sat watching his sisters dance with their friends.

After Joe and Pete had gone, Marge went upstairs, leaving Paul and Ruth alone in the cellar. "You mad at Tod?" he asked.

"When did you become interested in Tod Edwards?"

"I wouldn't care if you was mad at him. I don't like him, but I was just wondering whether you was mad at him, because he wasn't around here today."

"No, I'm not angry with Tod. He just hasn't been around." Then taking the initiative lest Paul ask her more pertinent questions, she inquired why he didn't like Tod.

"He thinks he's the best football player in the world. When we asked him to show us a few things in the beginning of the season, he told us to beat it. Said he didn't have any time to play with kids."

Ruth thought how like Tod that was. He really didn't think he was the best football player in the world; he only thought he was grown-up, too old to play with little boys or show them how to play the game. Paul wouldn't understand, but that was no reason for not being nice to Tod and she told him so. "You see, Paul, Our Lord told us to be nice to everybody, even people we don't like. Besides, you're happier when you try to be nice to everyone."

Talk at table that night centered around Christmas presents, each member of the family stating what was desired. When

Ruth mentioned that it would be nice if the family owned some operatic recordings, Paul was disgusted. "What do you want to listen to all that screaming for? All they do is yell like this," and he let out a few loud mi's and la's in rapid succession.

"Paul, not so loud!" His mother laughed. "Do you want the neighbors to think you're getting a beating?"

More burdensome than ten extra pounds, the days weighed on Ruth. Not that she didn't have anything to do. That wasn't it, for she had school, and shopping downtown in the gift hungry crowds, and addressing Christmas cards. But things weren't right; it just didn't feel like Christmas time. It was herself, she knew, for other things were as they had always been. Paul and his gang were hanging around the trees for sale outside Mr. Decker's store, feeling big when he let them show off a tree to a prospective customer. And when Paul came home he smelled the same way he did other years—of smoke from the fire can around which the kids stood to keep warm, and of pine from the trees. He made the same mess in the back part of the cellar as he had other years, when he tried to make moss; and he was as reluctant as ever to go to altar boy rehearsals for Midnight Mass. Marge was happily helping Mom wrap presents and plan cookies for the holidays. Dad contentedly smoked his pipe as usual. The trouble was with her.

Friday evening after dinner Ruth went to her room to dress; she couldn't stay home another night. So even though she had no one to take her, she was going to the parish C.Y.O. meeting. Betty Cranwell would be going with Pete, and they wouldn't mind her tagging along with them.

During the business part of the meeting, Tod Edwards walked in and took a seat a few rows in front of Ruth, but on the opposite side of the hall. He didn't see her, she was sure; but while she sat there not listening to what was being said, Ruth couldn't take her eyes off the slouchy form, and she wondered what he would say when he did see her. Uneasiness sat, an unseen companion, beside her.

While the crowd was putting the chairs aside before beginning to dance, Tod came over, took a chair next to Ruth, and began pushing it to the side without saying anything. Ruth watched him, and her breath came in short gasps. Why didn't he say something? Why was he staying close to her without saying anything? What had she done to him?

"Hello, Tod," she said.

His "Hi, Ruth" was followed by silence. But when Ruth, feeling she had done what good breeding required of her, turned to join some of the people about to start dancing, Tod asked sheepishly, "You with anybody tonight?"

"Yes, Pete and Betty."

"Not with any boy?"

"No." She wasn't making it any easier for Tod.

Tod's eyes looked out intently over his prominent cheekbones. "Let's make it a date for the rest of the night then?"

"All right." Ruth smiled, just a little disappointed that Tod hadn't apologized about the way he had acted when she had refused to go steady with him. But after all, she told herself, maybe he wanted to but didn't know how; maybe he was afraid it wouldn't be grown-up. Tod had some mighty queer ideas about being grown-up.

Although Tod was self-conscious at first, he and Ruth had a good time. He laughed a great deal and didn't seem to mind the way he usually did when other fellows cut in on a dance. Maybe he had been lonely during the past two weeks, too, Ruth thought, her eyes roving over the hall as she danced with Tod. They fell on Mike Hafey, standing in the doorway, talking, and not doing much of that. "Look, Tod," she said, "Mike Hafey's standing over there pretty much alone. Would you mind if I asked him to dance with me?"

Tod's reply was gruff. "If he wants to dance, let him ask like anybody else would."

"You know Mike's too shy to do that. Be a sport, Tod. You can dance the next few numbers with Betty Cranwell. I hate to see poor Mike standing around like that."

Forgetting how he liked others to ask him to dance when Ruth wasn't around, Tod grumbled, "I don't see why you should baby him."

"I don't think that's babying anybody."

"Well, it is."

"Then maybe I like to baby him." Ruth could feel herself getting angry. Of all people to talk about babying others, Tod who had to be handled like Mom's best china! And to top it all, he thinks he's grown-up!

"Maybe you do, but not when you're my date."

"Listen here, Tod Edwards," the words burned on Ruth's tongue. "I came here by myself tonight, and I only said I'd be your date because you couldn't find a girl." Something inside her told her the last remark was cruel, but she didn't stop. "I can take myself home without any help from you. I'm going to dance with Mike whether you like it or not."

She hadn't taken more than two steps when Tod replied cynically, "Okay, babe."

Babe! How she hated the word! But much as she was angered, she wouldn't, she just wouldn't turn and make a scene in front of everybody. She clenched her fists so hard her nails hurt her when they dug into her palms. But she refused to even look at Tod. She walked over and said hello to Mike. And when the next number started, she asked him simply if he cared to dance.

Mike's Adam's-apple worked up and down several times before he could manage a weak yes.

"Pete Decker was telling me you're having your prom in January, Mike. Going?" She had to keep talking until she calmed down and forgot Tod.

"No. They—they always have a big crowd; lots of students at Poly, and I don't know many of them. Besides, who'd want to go with me?"

Poor fellow, he was so bashful you just had to like him. Ruth smiled and said pointedly, "Why, Mike, almost any girl in this hall would be glad to go with you."

"I wouldn't want any girl to have a dull time because of me," he said.

"Did any girl ever tell you she didn't have a good time when you took her out?"

"You and Betty are the only girls I've been out with, and neither of you would tell me if you didn't have a good time."

"Look, Mike, you like to dance, don't you? I mean with the other girls here at the club?"

"Sure, when I can get up enough nerve to ask them." He wasn't looking at her when he added, "But that isn't often."

"That's silly, Mike. Not one of them is going to bite you or scratch your eyes out if you ask her to dance," Ruth insisted. "I think you ought to go to your prom, but I don't think you ought to ask Betty or myself, because you'd think we were only going to be nice to you. Besides, I imagine Pete has already asked Betty to go with him. That means you'll know at least two people at the dance. Maybe you could even double date with them."

Sounding almost miserable, Mike mumbled, "But who should I ask?"

"Decide for yourself, Mike. You know most of the girls here. Pick one out and ask her. Don't worry, she won't refuse." Ruth shooed Mike off after the dance and looked for Tod, expecting to have to soothe his ruffled feelings. But Tod was nowhere in evidence.

"Lady in distress?" asked Pete Decker with a flourish that would have done Cyrano de Bergerac proud. "Well, child, while we dance together, you can unburden your cares on my manly shoulders—they're padded, you know."

"Pete, you're absolutely the screwiest . . ."

"Thanks for the compliment, dear," Pete cut in. "People are getting into the habit of speaking of me in the superlative. But don't let that distract you," Pete went on without pausing. "I suppose you were looking for someone when I came up— what a pity it wasn't myself! But then you wouldn't have had the good fortune of getting me instead of some poor lad who can't hold a candle up to me, though I might let him light a cigarette for me. Well, tell me, were you, or weren't you looking for somebody?" He gave her an extra whirl.

"I've only been waiting for you to stop talking."

"Oh, my, you should know better than that, Ruth. Never hold your breath while little Peter is talking—that is, if you ever want to draw another. You were saying . . ."

"I was going to say I was looking for Tod. Have you seen him?"

"So glad I can be of service. Mr. Edwards was seen leaving the hall about twenty minutes ago."

If Tod wanted to act that way, Ruth couldn't be bothered. She wasn't going to spoil her night, not when there were plenty of other boys around to dance with.

"Say, now, would you look at that?" Pete blurted out after an unusual period of silence for him. "Now, if that isn't something! Mr. Shy Guy himself dancing with the exquisite Miss Kemper, for whom I'd gladly lay down my life, if I didn't have darling Betty. What a shame for such beauty to be wasted on one who hath not words to praise it." Pete spun around so that Ruth faced the couple he was talking about. "You look," he said, "I can't bear it."

When she saw Mike Hafey dancing with Judy Kemper, Ruth, pleased with herself, laughed quietly but said nothing.

"I see the ugly sight has stunned you, too," Pete began again. "Oh, what a task for the human mind, to understand human beings!"

"I don't see any problem, Pete. It so happens that Judy probably likes a quiet boy."

"Precisely, Ruth dear. Your insight amazes me. But the problem remains, why she should like anybody as quiet as Mike. That is the task that even I, mighty intellect that I am, face with no inkling of a solution. It's like trying to decide what Betty will want to do on our next date. And speaking of Betty, I suppose I had better return to her, or the fair damsel's heart will suffer at my long absence. For the dance, much thanks."

Ruth danced with many different boys that night before she left with Pete, Betty, and a whole crowd. They stopped at Mason's for refreshments, then scattered in different directions. Pete walked proudly with Betty on one arm and Ruth on the other. But when they reached Betty's house, Ruth told Pete she could make it home alone, it was only a block away.

Standing next to the front steps, leaning against her house, was Tod. When she saw him, Ruth pulled her coat more tightly about her and walked with determined steps toward the door.

"Ruth," he said.

"Yes?" Trying to be as unconcerned as possible, she opened her purse, took out the key, and inserted it in the lock—all the ordinary motions, just as if he weren't there. But he wasn't even looking at her.

"I'm sorry I got sore." Then Tod began walking away.

She turned and called, "Tod."

"Yes?"

"Why do you act like that?" She wasn't blaming him; she was sympathizing, really saying, "I wish you wouldn't act that way." It was something she never could understand. Ever since they were in grade school together and Tod first began to take notice of her, they had run into incidents like this which made her sad. And she knew Tod didn't want things to be that way either.

"I don't know—can't help it. Something inside me boils."

"It's okay, Tod," she said, responding to his obvious embarrassment. "Only it seems so silly to have a good time—and I've always had good times with you—and then end it by getting angry."

"I don't like it any more than you do, Ruth. You think I like to go away sore?"

"No, I don't, Tod, honestly. But why do you?"

"I don't know—maybe it's the way I'm made. Ruth, I'm sorry. If you'll forget it, I'll try to." Tod forced a smile.

Ruth snapped her fingers. "Forgotten." Then they both smiled. "Don't forget to come around during the holidays. We'll be holding open house, you know."

Tod said good night, and Ruth went in, hoping the crisis was over. On her dressing table she found a number of Christmas cards. She had forgotten to ask whether any had come for her when she had returned from school that afternoon. Marge, who had beaten her home tonight, had brought them upstairs and spread them on the dresser. A note read: "It must be scintillating (look it up, hon) to have so many admirers. Don't sit up all night, dreaming about them. And DON'T WAKE ME UP!"

Ruth opened each card and replaced it carefully on the dressing table, except the last one. It was a plain card, a lovely Nativity scene, no message; inside was written, *Jim*. She didn't know how to react or what to think. Was it supposed to make her happy, or what? She didn't know. She knew she wasn't going to send one in return, but she didn't understand what significance Jim's card might have. She stacked the cards and went to bed. Jim's was on top.

8

*T*HE choir was singing *Silent Night* when Ruth realized that
the world-changing miracle of the God-Man was about to take
place again. For soon the white wafer which the gold-vested
priest was holding so delicately over the shining paten would
be Jesus Christ born again—the sublimity and simplicity of it
all, God born again all over the world, not just in Bethlehem.
It was time to make her offering to God, and it seemed so
skimpy a birthday present, nothing like what she had planned
at the beginning of Advent. For a moment she was sad and
ashamed, but the sound of the Sanctus bell brought a calm joy,
an expectant awe. Just think, Ruth told herself, I'm older than
Our Lady was when she bore Jesus. She must have been proud
to hold Him close to her and keep Him warm, proud to be
the mother of God, happy to give Him to the world. The bell
shattered the silence, and Ruth looked up and saw the priest
holding the new-born Christ Child above his head.

When she followed the rest of her family up to the Communion rail, Ruth did not feel holy. But she knew God was with her just as truly as He was with His mother that first Christmas night, and she was proud and very happy. In her pew again, she spoke to the Divine Guest, "Happy Birthday, Dear Lord, and thank You for coming to me. Do congratulate Your mother for me. And bless my family and friends, and the Pope, the Church, our wonderful country, and the whole world. Let us all have joy, peace, and holiness. For myself I ask that You help me to decide what You want me to be in life. I've been wondering whether You want me to be a nun —but then, I don't know. Maybe You don't want me to be one. Help me, because You mean more to me than anybody else."

But a vocation was something to be pondered at other times, and Ruth was soon wrapped in the happiness of Christmas again, as the Mass continued. She was proud of Paul—who was kneeling in the sanctuary, having difficulty with a bobbing head—because he looked like a little angel to her as he tried to keep sleepy eyelids apart. His hands, cleaner than they had been for weeks, were folded before him. They never moved, though Ruth thought how much he probably wanted to use those fingers to rub the sleep from his eyes. It must have been this way the first Christmas, she told herself happily; there certainly must have been some young angels present then who weren't used to staying awake so late in the night. Maybe some of them went even farther than Paul and fell asleep.

After the blessing, during the last Gospel, Ruth could see excitement waking her brother up. She smiled and felt a desire within herself to wish each and every person in the church, friends and strangers alike, for all were Christians, a blessed Christmas.

The Mass completed, groups of people formed in front of the

church to pass the pleasantries of the season. Paul came dashing out shouting, "Merry Christmas, everybody!" No signs of sleep now!

"Paul, not so loud," cautioned Mr. Sterner, who did it more as a matter of course than as a reprimand, because he understood the exuberance of a young boy so early on Christmas morning, when all the world is alive with peace and carols tumble from the tongue at the very sight of a star or a smiling face.

Last of the altar boys to come out was Mike Hafey, the master of ceremonies. Shyly he wished the people a Merry Christmas. He was as red as a holly berry when he asked Ruth if he might walk her home. She said of course and excused herself from the crowd.

"You had the little altarboys in perfect order tonight, Mike," she said above the sharp crackle her heels sent through the cold night air.

"Yes," Mike laughed self-consciously, "but Sister did all the training." His next words came with the suddenness of something released from a spring. "Ruth, I've got a date for my prom."

Ruth felt a joyful warmness inside herself. She couldn't help feeling it at the simple sincerity of this boy who had faced a crisis and won. Mike's obvious sense of accomplishment showed through his timid voice, and he had come to share his triumph with Ruth because it was at her suggestion that he had been able to move himself to ask a girl for a date.

"Swell," said Ruth. "Who's the lucky girl?"

"Judy Kemper."

"Judy Kemper!" Ruth made her eyes widen in mock amazement. "Well, I must say, Mike, you don't start at the bottom and work up. You take the best from the beginning."

The girl whom Mike had asked to his prom was a comely senior at Catholic high. Strong-featured and agile, she captained their basketball team with a popularity that ranged from the senior class down to the freshmen. Judy was another name for school spirit to them. It meant a girl who was at every school activity, a girl with a smile that had boys from all over Baltimore wanting to date her. A vigorous character, Judy was one to bring out the best in Mike, and make him stand on his own. Vibrant was the word for her every action.

Mike launched into an account of how he had asked Judy to go with him. It turned out that they had hit it off right from the start. To Mike, Judy's poise and confidence were things of wonder, while his meekness and simplicity attracted Judy. Since the night at the parish C.Y.O., when Mike had first asked Judy to dance, he had been seeing her regularly two or three times a week, and would have thought nothing of spending more time with her, if she had not had other things to attend to. And on Judy's part the other matters lost much of their appeal; she didn't mind having Mike around—she liked it.

"Mike, why don't you and Judy come over and spend the afternoon with us? Marge and I are having some of our friends in for a get-together. It would be nice to have you."

"Thanks, Ruth, but I still don't get along well in crowds. Anyway, Judy's family is having Christmas dinner in the middle of the afternoon."

Mike talked with Ruth until the rest of the Sterners came along, then he went on his way. When Ruth and her family entered the house Paul immediately began hunting around for Christmas presents. "What'd I get for Christmas?"

"You'll find out when you come down later in the morning," said Mr. Sterner, "but now say your prayers before the manger and go to bed." To Ruth and Marge, who took his order as applying only to Paul and kept discussing plans for the afternoon, Mr. Sterner added, "The same holds for you, young ladies. Up with you."

When Ruth awoke, it was about eight o'clock Christmas morning. For a few minutes she lay in bed, wishing God, herself, and the whole world a Merry Christmas. It was a glorious morning, although the snow she had hoped for was nowhere in evidence. A stir in the twin bed next to hers caught Ruth's attention.

"You awake, Marge?" For reply, a figure rolled over in the bed. "Awake?" Ruth repeated.

"Uh-huh."

"Merry Christmas."

Marge sat up in her bed and stretched her arms. "It's cold." Then she remembered her manners. "Merry Christmas, Ruth."

"Bet I beat you downstairs," Ruth said as she banged Marge with a pillow and tossed her quilt over her younger sister. She bounded out of bed, with Marge calling from the maze of bedclothes, "We'll see about that." Disentangling herself from the quilt, Marge continued, "I could give you five minutes start and still beat you."

And Marge was right, too, for she beat Ruth downstairs by fully two minutes. Then the two girls, after wishing their mother a Merry Christmas, admonished her for not calling them to help her start the preparations for Christmas dinner, although it was quite evident that they weren't disappointed with the extra sleep. Mrs. Sterner absentmindedly thanked them for their good intentions, but she was thinking more about getting the dinner in order, so that it would be ready to put in the oven before people began to drop in on their way home from church. If it were ready, she would only have to put it on the stove at the proper time; but if it weren't, there would be interminable delay and a hungrily dissatisfied family.

"What a woman you are, Mrs. Sterner!" Ruth threw her arms around her mother and began to push her from the kitchen. "You're certainly coming in with us to see what the living room looks like. Come along, in with you!"

"All right, Ruth." Mrs. Sterner laughingly resisted her daughter's pushing and pulling. "But you let me walk like a lady, or I won't come at all. Gracious, I thought you were getting over your tomboy ways since your brother Dan left the house."

"I'll let you in on a secret, Mrs. Sterner, if you're interested."

"What is it?"

"I don't ever intend to get over my tomboy ways, as you call them, because if I did, you'd be the first person to wonder what in the world was wrong with me."

Mrs. Sterner admitted Ruth was probably right about that. The girls raved so about the decorations in the living room that their mother told them she would have known it was their work, even if she were a stranger. They wanted to distribute their presents immediately, but Mrs. Sterner said they'd have to wait for their father and Paul.

"Where's Dad, anyway?" asked Marge.

"Where is he every Christmas morning? At the children's Mass at St. James'. You know he never misses the children singing German Christmas Carols. But we'll have the grand opening when he gets back. Wake Paul and get yourselves some breakfast. Now let me go back to my kitchen."

Until the distribution of presents, Paul was sleepy and touchy. Ruth's efforts to cheer him up only aggravated him.

But once he had his football outfit he was lost in ecstasy. Now he was a football player complete, down to the ball, which Ruth gave him. "Oh, boy! Oh, boy!"

Shortly after eleven-thirty, Dan and his wife Rose arrived to bring all the Sterners together for their Christmas dinner, as they planned it should be always. Ruth, who had been watching for them, opened the door and kissed them and wished them the season's greetings.

"See how nice she can be when she expects something, Rose?" Dan couldn't wait two minutes before teasing his "kid sister."

Ruth ignored him. "Where have you people been keeping yourselves?"

"Why, Ruth, it's only eleven-thirty," Rose replied.

"Don't make any excuses to the child, Rose." Dan loved to call Ruth a child because he knew it piqued her. "Now, Ruth, you run along and play with your dolls while we greet Mom in the kitchen. Here's a nickel for you."

Much as she wanted to, Ruth couldn't think of a smart remark to make. It was always that way; Dan was just too fast for her. Anyway, she refused to pout and act like the child he called her.

"Dan, look at the football Ruth gave me for Christmas!" cried Paul when his older brother and his wife came back into the living room.

"Is she going to show you how to kick it, too?" Dan asked. "You know, she used to be pretty good at it a few years ago."

"No, she doesn't play football any more."

"Rose, what do you think of that? My little roughneck sister has given up playing football. Doesn't she play any games with you now, Paul?"

"No. Besides we don't want girls playing with us. They're liable to get hurt."

"That's strange. She always wanted to play football and baseball with us." Dan turned to Ruth. "Gosh, if you've really given up these things, maybe you won't like the present I have for you."

Without comment, but with deliberately studied actions, Ruth took the package from Dan. After removing the wrappings, she lifted the lid of the box, shut it again immediately, and declared huffily, "You think you're smart, don't you, little boy?"

Dan laughed heartily, and Paul attempted to get the box from his sister to see what was inside, but she wouldn't let him have it. With difficulty Dan swallowed his laughter and said sorrowfully, though obviously without any real feeling, "Aw, Ruth, don't be angry. You can probably trade it in. How was I to know you had suddenly begun to act like a lady? Why, I bet you even speak with courtesy to young men now."

"Yeah, you ought to hear her on the telephone," Paul added before Rose broke in and told her husband to "give that baseball glove to Paul and stop teasing Ruth." At her words, Paul dove for the box, and exultantly shouted as he extracted the glove, "Man, I'll be the best pitcher around here next summer."

"I'll show you how to use the glove, Paul," Ruth said loftily. "Dan never could catch anything."

Dan threw up his hands and turned to his wife. "Do you hear that, Rose? Didn't I tell you she'd like the glove better than what you wanted to get her?"

"Give it to her anyhow, Dan."

Obedient to his wife's request, Dan slipped Ruth a long, thin box, which, when opened, displayed a pearl necklace—not real pearls, but not the ten-cent-store variety either. Roughly spinning Ruth about, he said, "Here, let me put them around your neck." That done, he teasingly tickled her under the chin.

Ruth pulled his hair in return. It was like being children again, when they were always battling about something. But now Ruth took refuge behind Rose instead of her mother. She stood laughing at Dan while his wife told him it served him right for the way he had acted. Ruth made a face at Dan, but Rose couldn't see that.

"A lone man can't win against a pair of women," Dan groaned, and eased himself into a chair. "Paul, get some music on the radio, will you?"

Ruth slipped her arms around Rose from behind and with her chin resting on her shoulder, and Rose's soft brown hair pressed against her cheek, she whispered in her sister-in-law's ear, "Rose, the necklace is beautiful. Thanks. And don't tell him I said so, but your husband's a pretty nice joe, too."

Waiting for her father to say grace before dinner, Ruth's eyes feasted on the golden turkey thrusting its legs up at her and inviting her to take hold of a succulent drumstick. She could almost taste the colorful orange carrots, green peas, the crisp white celery. A glacier of yellow butter was melting and running down the mountains of mashed potatoes. And the linen tablecloth, brightly polished silver, blue china, and centerpiece of flowers all set off by the joyous flicker of the candles at either end of the table, were as delightful to her eyes as the food would be to her tongue.

After dinner, which had proved to be exactly as good as it looked, Rose was the first one into the kitchen. With one hand she was trying to tie an apron about her; with the other she was trying to direct her mother-in-law from the kitchen. "Mom, you go into the living room with Dad. We'll take care of the dishes. You can have a holiday, too, Paul."

Paul cheered and ran off, but Mrs. Sterner objected. Overruled by her daughters and daughter-in-law, she went with misgivings to join her husband. Dan started along with her, but Rose seized him by the back of his coat collar. "Where are you going, dear?"

"To the kitchen," Dan replied, making an unwilling about-face.

"Congratulations, Rose," cheered Ruth. "You have him under control. He never used to help with the dishes before, except when you came, and then he was trying to make an impression on you."

"Oh, I've reformed, Ruth. You never have to do the dishes at home, do you, sweetheart?"

"Never alone, I assure you," Rose replied, drowning the first dishes in the suds; and her remark was emphatic. "Don't worry, Ruth, he's not going to sit around and get plump off my cooking without doing something in return."

The regular young crowd came in later that afternoon and danced and sang carols. Each recited the list of her or his gifts and listened to others do the same. It was nearly six o'clock by the time the last reluctant guest departed.

Supper on Christmas is a slight repast for most people. The Sterners had cold turkey sandwiches. Then, as on every Christmas night Ruth could remember, the family gathered in the living room for Mr. Sterner's reading of St. Luke's account of the birth of Our Lord. They sat in darkness save for a light for Mr. Sterner to read by—and that was behind the group—

and the faint glow of the crib in front of them. For the reading, Ruth sat on the floor, and during the conversation that followed she let her head fall back against Rose's knee. It was quiet, friendly talk that passed about the room; the whole atmosphere was like a warm embrace. Ruth shut her eyes and felt its happy assurance. She hardly remembered when they stopped to say a few prayers before the crib and went to bed.

The next thing Ruth knew it was the day after Christmas. Mom was waking the entire family early, because Dad always insisted that they attend the eight o'clock Mass on the two days following Christmas.

9

"SOME holidays! Girls, they were positively scrumptious," June Thompson was telling a group of her friends, when Ruth came into the cafeteria the day school began again. "Hi, ya, honey chile, I didn't see much of you during the holidays. Did you spend all your time at home?"

"I got around enough to satisfy me," Ruth replied.

"Well, dearie, I was just telling the girls that it was a scrumptious vacation—parties almost every night, dates and dances, and all the rest. Really, hon, I was out with so many different boys I can't remember all of them." June patted her blonde hair complacently. "I do remember seeing your friend Jim Stevens a couple of times. Surprised you weren't with him."

June waited for an explanation, so Ruth said nonchalantly, "Oh, I saw Jim myself." And that was the truth; she had seen him, even though she had had no date with him. Ken Carpenter had asked her to a party during the holidays, and Jim was there. Ruth had talked with him for a while, and danced with him once or twice, but everything was as formal as the conversations and dances she had at the party with boys whom she had never met before. She was not rude to him, but she was waiting for Jim to make the first friendly gesture. However, the nearest he came to righting the situation was in saying they would have to have a date some time. Otherwise he seemed quite satisfied with the companion he had that night. It was the new girl in town, Barbara Connell, and she looked like something straight from the society page of a Sunday newspaper. Her reddish brown hair had a lovely sheen; her hands, face, everything about her looked groomed to perfection. She had a glitter something like June Thompson's; it attracted boys to her. But, as Ruth told Pat Boyle, after she had been introduced to Barbara, she found her attractiveness more solid than June's. Barbara not only attracted, but her personality held you. Her voice was musical and mellow, the only voice Ruth had ever heard that was more pleasing than Pat Boyle's. And when she talked, Barbara said more than just words. Ken told Ruth that Jim had been taking Barbara out quite a bit lately. Almost unconsciously Ruth warned herself Jim wouldn't be calling her for many dates now, for, although it hurt her to admit it, she just didn't have Barbara's poise and cleverness. She could see why Mrs. Stevens liked her so. However, all of this was no business of June Thompson's.

"Really, I mean, hon," June chattered on, "Jim's a good kid. I might go for him myself if I didn't have Don Wright. Oh, I agree that Jim's a fair football player, but this is hockey season, and you have to admit, hon, that there just isn't another hockey player around like Don Wright."

"That's true, if you like hockey players," Ruth said tartly. Then to avoid an argument, she added, "I have to get something to eat. You'll excuse me, won't you?"

" 'Course, of course," June smiled knowingly. "I want to tell the girls about the New Year's party I attended. Girls, it was positively divine, so many nice boys. Let me describe . . ."

Ruth didn't hear the rest. She bought her lunch and found a place with Pat Boyle, Jane Arnold and some others—away from June.

By the end of the week Ruth was back in the regular swing of things. School, work on the paper and yearbook, study, school again. Mid-year examinations loomed threateningly. Tod had already asked her to go to the Catholic Students' Mission Crusade dance with him in February. And much to her surprise, Jim had phoned and asked her to a play at Ford's. However, disturbingly, her after-Communion talk with Our Lord on Christmas was on her mind. Since then she had been thinking about her vocation. She really didn't know what God wanted her to be. Sometimes she thought He wanted her to be a Sister, and she would try to picture herself as a nun. But the picture of herself in an evening gown was much more pleasing. When she thought of the apparent sameness of each day in a convent and the variety of a college girl's life, she felt that college was the place for her—she could think about the convent later. And at times she dreamed of how nice it would be to marry a good Catholic boy and be as happy as Dan and Rose. Nevertheless, since Christmas, the thought kept coming back, "Maybe God does want me to be a nun." It wasn't a new idea; she had considered it off and on for the past couple of years—ever since she had listened to that very practical talk during a retreat, about being very, very positive that you chose the right vocation—the one that would make you feel surest and happiest. Only it was more insistent now. She often prayed over it, but she couldn't make up her mind—it would be so nice to go to college.

"Come in," called Sister Elizabeth in response to Ruth's knock on her classroom door after lessons were over on Friday afternoon. Her voice was as vibrant as her actions always were. It seemed as spontaneous and natural as spring water, but years of effort made it Sister's servant. It could rise in anger, but only when she would allow it knowingly; and it could laugh effortlessly. Her voice was the image of Sister Elizabeth's character.

"Good afternoon, Sister. Busy?"

Sister Elizabeth's still youthful face broke into a welcoming smile as she looked up from the papers she was correcting. "Not particularly. What can I do for you?"

"Oh, I just thought I'd drop in to talk to you for a while," Ruth said, as she seated herself on one of the front desks.

Sister slid her papers into the drawer of her desk. "Did you have a good time during the holidays, Ruth?" Her blue eyes were fixed intently on the girl sitting in front of her.

"The best." Ruth's reply led to the next question about what she had done. Then she lost herself in telling everything that had happened during those free days. That's the way it was when a girl was with Sister Elizabeth. She'd sit and listen all day, manifesting true interest in whatever the girl had to say; she'd sit and enjoy it all as if it were her big interest and she had nothing better or more important to do. Occasionally she'd sit and talk with the staff of the school paper after classes until it was time for her to go to some duty in the convent. On those days there would be little actual work accomplished on the paper, but the girls went away feeling that they were liked and understood.

When Ruth had talked herself out about the holidays, she was prepared to ask about vocations. She laughed nervously, then said, "Look, Sister, after all I've just told you about dances and dates, you may think this is crazy. But do you think it's possible I have a vocation to be a Sister?"

"It's possible that *anyone* may have a religious vocation," Sister said pleasantly, almost teasingly.

"I know that," Ruth replied impatiently, "but I'm talking about me; you know, *me*, Ruth Sterner."

Sister refused to be serious. "You know we're mighty particular about the girls we take."

"I'm not asking about that, Sister, dear. I merely asked whether you think I might possibly have a religious vocation."

Sister's face showed unaccustomed lines as she rested her chin on her hand and asked, "You mean Ruth Sterner, the girl who loves to dance and go out with boys?" Ruth nodded. "I hardly think she'd have a vocation—at least not to be a Sister." Sister Elizabeth smiled warmly.

Picking up her books, Ruth said, "That's fine. Now I don't have to worry about that any more." She started toward the door.

"Ruth, you come back here!" And when Ruth was seated again, Sister asked, "Are you serious?"

"Y-yes." Ruth felt like a person on trial for her life. What if Sister told her she thought she had a vocation? What was she going to do then? She was hoping Sister would say she didn't have a vocation, so she could forget the whole idea.

"So you think you have a religious vocation?" Sister came and sat next to Ruth. "Let me catch my breath."

"Hey, wait a minute!" Ruth used an expression she had

picked up from Jim Stevens. "You don't get me that easily! I didn't say anything about *having* a vocation. I asked if you thought I *might possibly* have one. Now what do you say?"

"If you didn't think you had a vocation, why did you ask?"

"Because I thought I *might* or *may*, or whatever the word is, have one."

Sister Elizabeth's eyes sparkled mischievously. "Wait till I tell Sister Philothea her little friend Ruth is going to join us."

"Listen, Sister," Ruth said hastily. "I didn't say anything about joining anybody. And if you tell Sister Philothea, you can be sure I won't join. She'd be coming around trying to make me too pious, never wanting me to have any fun. If you tell her, or any of the other Sisters, I won't even mention vocation again."

"Why, Ruth, such impatience and petulance would never do in a nun."

"Well, I'm not a nun. And if you want to see a real display of anger, just you say something to Sister Philothea!"

"All right, Ruth, I'll be serious now. I shouldn't tease you about Sister Philothea when I know you don't get along with her. Don't worry, I won't say anything." Her eyes were intent, joyful, when they fixed themselves on the uncertain eyes of Ruth. "Now about that vocation. I think there is a good possibility God may be offering you a vocation. You have the necessary health, intelligence, and moral character."

"Yes, but there are lots of girls with better qualities in all those departments, and they don't have vocations. How do you know when you have one?"

"Do you expect the Holy Ghost to come down and tell you? If you do, you have a long wait coming. He usually doesn't hit people on the head with halos."

"I don't exactly want that. . . ."

"Well, do you know what you'd be giving up?"

"I think so, Sister."

"There won't be any more dates and dances, shows, fancy clothes or permanent waves. You won't know the thrill of falling in love with a young man, or the glory of having a baby of your own—a baby who is part of you and depends on you for all its needs."

"I know, Sister." Ruth was looking at the floor. She felt hollow inside, and it seemed as if the blood had stopped flowing through her veins. She wanted those things as much as any normal girl did.

"But that's not all, Ruth. A Sister's life is not easy—getting up early every morning, going to class day after day when it may be the last thing she wants to do, attending summer school year after year—that is, if she is with a teaching Order. She can't come and go as she pleases, or follow her own wishes and desires. She can't do any number of things other women can." Sister smiled, "But it's really not so tough, honestly it isn't."

"I wish I could be sure."

"Ruth, it isn't necessary to decide this afternoon. Suppose we both pray over it a while. I'll remember you every day at Mass. And you be sure to ask your confessor about this: after all, he knows better than anyone else how you stand with God. On your part, you ought to pray more and go to Mass more often, every day if possible."

"Yes, Sister."

"And study harder, Ruth. You ought to be over eighty-five in all your subjects—even the ones Sister Philothea teaches."

That matter was of little concern to Ruth. She didn't mind

studying a little harder. But she felt that no matter what she did, she'd never get over eighty-five in Sister Philothea's subjects! She was more concerned about something else. Timidly she asked, "What about dates?"

"What about them?"

"Is it all right to go out with boys, or must I stop?"

"Ruth, some Sisters would tell you that you would be endangering your vocation, or the seeds of your vocation, by going out on dates; and that's a real possibility. But personally I think it will do you more good than harm, if you go about it in the right way. God gave you your youth, and I think He wants you to enjoy it. It seems to me to be the best thing you can offer back to Him. When you go out, offer the evening to God, and always thank Him for your good times. Keep in mind that He may be calling you in a special way. Continue to ask His guidance, but go on leading the life of an ordinary young lady. It will be a means of testing yourself."

"Should I tell the boys?"

"Why?"

"It might not be fair to let them think that—that they may marry me some day, if they are never to have the chance."

For Ruth the problem was real, but Sister Elizabeth couldn't restrain her laughter. With some other girls she would have had to force herself not to laugh, but knowing Ruth as she did, she felt freer with her. "Most high-school boys aren't thinking about getting married for a long time. When they go out with a girl, it's because they enjoy her company, not because they're thinking of marrying her. That comes much later on. No, I wouldn't tell anyone if I were you. Should you make up your mind to become a Sister, you would have to tell them sooner or later. But don't say anything now."

"But what if one of them should be serious?"

"Do you think anyone is, Ruth?"

"Well, one boy asked me to go steady with him, and . . ."

"How do you feel about him, Ruth?"

Ruth was twisting her handkerchief about her little finger, not looking at Sister, talking in a near whisper. "I don't know. I felt awfully funny inside when he asked me. But I don't think I could be serious about him."

"Then just be careful; don't encourage him. When you go out with him, try to make it a double date. And of course you should tell this boy immediately if you decide to become a Sister." The sparkle came again into Sister Elizabeth's eyes; she put a hand under Ruth's chin and lifted her face. "By the way, it's not this Stevens boy I've been hearing so much about from some of your friends, is it?" Her voice was reassuring; it wasn't condescending or poking fun, but it was saying, "Come now, this isn't so serious as all that."

Ruth smiled back at the nun holding her face up to her own. "No, Sister, this one goes to Calvert Hall. We were in the same class through grammar school." She picked up her books. "Well, I feel better, even if we didn't decide anything."

"*We* are not going to decide anything," Sister said. "You're going to decide with the help of God."

"Thanks for everything, Sister. I'll be around to see you again."

Sister Elizabeth watched Ruth go out the door. After it was closed, she kept looking in that direction, seeing nothing, but thinking. The Lord works in strange ways, or at least His ways seem strange to people. There probably isn't a girl in Ruth's class who would pick her out for the convent, but God seems to want her. I hope I didn't give her too bleak a picture of the sacrifices it would cost her. Some other time I can give her the brighter side, but it's good for her to realize it isn't all easy. Even if the religious life is a life of companionship with God, we forget Him often; and sometimes He doesn't seem to want to associate with us.

"Dear God, look after Ruth." Sister Elizabeth prayed earnestly. "She'll make You a beautiful bride. And help me to do whatever I can."

10

WHEN the briskness of the air is no longer a fresh and fascinating thing, the football season is over. Clouds become leaden, then it turns colder and snows; or it remains in the thirties and boys begin to play roller-skate hockey in the streets. No snow came that January; so Paul and his crowd transferred their afternoon play from the lot in back of school to the levelest street in the neighborhood. Every afternoon the Baltimore Clippers faced some other hockey team in a tremendous struggle of noisy skates, still noisier boys, and tin-can pucks. Sticks flying, the boys scooted up and down the street in utter disorder. But the exhilaration of the game was theirs, and the thrill of competition. To them these games were as important as a big deal to a man in business; and they took them with as much seriousness.

As was the case every afternoon during the football season, Paul had to be called to come in for dinner. Ruth could hear his voice ringing above the others. It was thin and sharp, strained the way his bones seemed to be straining against his flesh, stretching it. Paul was growing rapidly; his skin was tight over his bones, barely enough to cover them. Ruth thought his vocal cords must be stretched in much the same way. When she came to the corner, she saw the boys madly swatting at the puck. It flew in one direction, then another, and the boys followed wherever it went. She called to Paul, but got no reply, the noise of skates and shouts drowning her out. Walking toward the group, she called again. Paul yelled back, asking what she wanted, the way he did every day, though he knew what the answer would be; it had been the same for years. Since she had no intention of chasing him, and since she knew he wouldn't come right away if she told him she wanted him for dinner, Ruth simply said, "Come here a minute."

"What do you want?"

"Come here and see."

Reluctantly Paul skated over to her. "What do you want?"

"It's time to come home for dinner."

"I'll be in soon."

"Now."

"No, I got to finish the game." The other boys were already calling to him to continue the play. Ruth expected her brother to skate away from her, so she stepped forward quickly and grabbed at him. Paul, who had foreseen the gesture, ducked under her arms and skated toward the pavement, between two parked cars and headed back into the street, keeping a slight distance between himself and his pursuing sister. His eyes were fixed on Ruth.

Suddenly she stopped and cried, "Paul, look out!" But it was too late. A car was coming down the opposite side of the street. The driver had his eyes fixed on the boys who were waiting for

Paul. He hadn't expected anyone to come from the other side; in fact, he didn't even see Paul. Not until the boy plowed into an end of the rear fender of his car and was knocked down did he become conscious of him. He slammed on the brakes and stopped.

Ruth had shut her eyes as she saw the car approaching; her cry of warning trailed off into a groan when she heard the sickening thud Paul's body made as it crashed into the car. For a moment she couldn't open her eyes. It was almost as if she thought she could wipe out the whole terrible scene by not looking at it. Her mind was confused; she felt weak and dizzy. Automatically she whispered a prayerful ejaculation and started toward Paul. His body lay on the street where it had fallen; all the boys had gathered around it. She pushed her way through them and stood next to the driver of the car, who was bending over Paul. Why had she chased him like that? It was all her fault. Paul didn't move. There was some blood on the side of his face. Maybe he was . . . maybe he . . . maybe . . . No, he couldn't be, he couldn't be dead. Ruth's heart stood still, but her lips quivered uncontrollably. "Is—is he all right?"

The driver of the car was a young man, about thirty. Though his face was tense and white, his hands moved calmly and carefully over Paul's body. "I don't know," he said. "I think this right arm is broken, but the other bones seem to be all right. I'm not absolutely sure, though. Don't know much about bones except the little I learned in the Army."

Ruth sobbed. The man, who had already begun to unfasten the skate on Paul's right foot, commanded, "Take off that other skate. I want to get him to the hospital." Although Ruth knew this was contrary to the rules of first aid, she dazedly did as she was told, sobbing all the while, wondering why

Paul didn't speak. "Relative?" asked the driver as he picked Paul up cautiously in his arms and started for the car. Ruth said she was his sister. Then the driver told her, "You'd better get in the back seat. You can hold his head on the way to the hospital."

Ruth gave the skates to the steadiest of Paul's frightened playmates and told him to go tell her mother and father what had happened.

"Yes," added the driver, "but be sure you say he'll be all right, and we'll call up as soon as we have any word. Got that?" The boy shook his head gravely.

"Take him to St. Joseph's Hospital, will you please?" Ruth requested. And the driver said he would. He told Ruth not to let Paul's arm move. "Maybe we should have put splints on it right away; but it's only a short distance to the hospital, and they can do the job right." Paul groaned and the driver said that was a good sign; probably he was just knocked unconscious by the impact. With her one free hand Ruth tried to wipe the blood from Paul's face. Now she could see that it came only from several scratches he had received when his face slid on the ground.

While Ruth was waiting for word from the doctor in the accident department, she telephoned home. Her mother answered, but she was too excited to talk or listen. Mr. Sterner was calmer, and told Ruth to make arrangements for a private room for Paul that night. He said that Mrs. Sterner and he were coming to the hospital immediately.

"Your brother has a broken right arm and his right side is pretty well bruised," the doctor reported to Ruth, "but it's nothing serious." The doctor who told Ruth these things was a young interne. Ruth asked him about a room for Paul, and he said he would make the necessary arrangements. His manner gave her confidence; it was so professional and sure.

When the young man who had driven the car was told there was nothing seriously wrong with Paul, he drew a deep breath of relief and said he was terribly glad. He slipped away soon after that and came back with some sandwiches and coffee. "Here, eat this, it'll do you good," he urged Ruth.

To please him, she managed to down part of a sandwich and drink some of the hot coffee, which did stop her trembling somewhat. She liked the man more when he said he was staying until her parents arrived.

After her mother and father had come, they were allowed to see Paul. He was sleeping soundly, his arm in a cast, his face bandaged. Since there was nothing they could do, Mr. and Mrs. Sterner decided to take Ruth home. In spite of her relief that Paul's injuries were not as serious as she had feared, she was still terribly white and shaken. She told her mother she was going to phone Jim to call off their theater date, but Mrs. Sterner urged her to keep her engagement. It would be good for her and help to take her mind off the accident.

Ruth finally agreed and, fascinated, she sat with Jim high up in the second balcony at Ford's, while, all about them, in the first balcony and in the orchestra people were filing into their seats. Everywhere there was a hushed murmur of conversation. As she watched the crowd, it was not difficult for Ruth to picture to herself the throngs that had filled this old theater in days gone by. Ford's is old, and Baltimore play-goers have been seeing shows there since the days of hoop skirts and bustles. Across the boards of that ancient stage have trod nearly all the great American actors and actresses. Ford's is a venerable place. And the atmosphere of the theater engulfs you while you are there. Waiting for a play to begin, your attention is so fixed on the stage with all its rich traditions that by the time the house lights are dimmed you have already absorbed automatically some of the tenor of the play.

Since the play that night was a modern mystery, Ruth wasn't familiar with it ahead of time. Neither was she quite sure what it was all about after it was over, though she didn't blame that on the show; some portions of it had her on the edge of her seat, but at other times she could not keep her mind from wandering back to Paul.

"Dandy show, wasn't it?" Jim asked as they were walking along Howard Street toward Lexington, where they intended to stop for some ice cream.

"Oh, yes, Jim!"

"Boy, when you see real people on the stage, the movies look like a lot of truck, just shadows, 'sound and fury, signifying nothing.'"

"Shakespeare again?" Ruth laughed.

"Yes. I wish we could have seen a Shakespeare play tonight."

"Remember a long time ago you were going to tell me how you came to know those lines?" Ruth was trying to recall the quotation Pat Boyle had given her from *Hamlet*, something about good night and flights of angels.

"Still want to hear?"

"Uh-huh."

"Well, Mr. Farrow, one of the scholastics at school, heard I was interested in becoming a lawyer. So one day he called me aside and asked me if it were true, and I said yes. Then he offered to work with me a couple of times a week if I wanted to do it."

"And he gives you all that stuff to memorize?"

"It isn't all memory. Some of it is exercise and some of it extempore speaking. But Mr. Farrow says men like Shakespeare and Demosthenes and Lincoln had something to say and they said it well. That's why he has me memorize some of their stuff."

"Didn't Ken say something about your wanting to be a politician—or shouldn't I say *statesman*—the night of the dance at school?"

"Yes."

"How come you want to be a politician?"

"Ideals, I guess," Jim said casually. "People are always saying politics are crooked, but I don't see why a man can't be honest, no matter what he does." Jim's brow was wrinkled. He looked so serious Ruth wanted to laugh. "Gosh, if the men who run the country aren't honest, how can the country be honest?"

"Lincoln was honest."

"Sure, so were a lot of others, but it wasn't easy. If political bosses had known they wouldn't be able to handle Lincoln the way they wanted to, he might never have been president."

"What do your folks say about your idea, Jim?"

"Dad thinks it's okay."

"What about your mother?"

Jim's jaw set, his lips pressed firmly together. Finally he burst out, "She doesn't understand. Since Dad's pretty well set now, Mother thinks Gil and I ought to forget about doing anything on our own and just ease along with him. Marry some society girl and get your picture in the paper that way, but don't do anything different or startling to get there. . . ."

Ruth was more certain than ever that she and Mrs. Stevens wouldn't get along. "Is Barbara Connell what your mother considers a 'society girl,' Jim? I think she's more than that."

"Yes," Jim replied. Ruth was not sure whether it was in answer to her question or in agreement with her statement. "But let's skip it," he suggested. "Let's stop somewhere and have a sundae. Do you want whipped cream, cherries, marshmallow *and* nuts on yours?"

Ruth responded quickly to his change of subject. "You left off the fudge sauce and candied ginger," she replied lightly as they turned into their favorite sweet shop.

After having their refreshments Ruth and Jim walked down Lexington Street toward Liberty to catch their bus. To one used to the broad boulevards of the newer American cities, Lexington Street in Baltimore looks like a pathway or an alley cut between the buildings. You feel as if you could stretch out your arms and touch the buildings on either side; and during the day you don't have to move them at all to touch the crowds that mill about, some on the sidewalks, some in the street mixed in with automobiles and streetcars, inching their way forward. Somewhere on the sidewalk you know there is someone selling old English lavender, and maybe a girl passing out samples in front of one of the nut shops, or a blind man playing an accordion.

When Jim complained that the street was too narrow for traffic, Ruth said that people didn't even suspect there might one day be such things as automobiles when they first planned such streets. "Anyway, I like them narrow, because they tell us the city is old."

"And what's so wonderful about being old? As far as I can see, these streets are the cause of a lot of traffic jams, that's all."

Ruth shrugged her shoulders. "Probably that's true, but there isn't anything you can do about it. You can't move the buildings to widen the streets, and the sidewalks are already pretty narrow. Anyway, they remind me of the past."

"The past—you can have it!"

"I don't want it, except to think about. You can't live without it; soon today will be past. Tomorrow it will be only a memory, but so much will have sprung from it, just as Baltimore today sprang from 'old town.' You can't know Baltimore until you know some of its traditions, its quirks, its lovableness. Change all the old things and you haven't got Baltimore; you have some other city in its place."

"You've got something there, Ruth—something I never thought about."

"Oh, I love to think about things like that. Just before Christmas I wrote an article for the school paper about all the things the Institute building has seen—old Baltimore, the big fire, the new Baltimore. It was fun. I get a real kick out of thinking of the days when Patterson Park was the Patterson estate and Jerome Bonaparte was courting Betsy Patterson against all the wishes of Napoleon; or picturing the battle of Fort McHenry with Francis Scott Key out there in the harbor writing *The Star-Spangled Banner*."

Caught up in Ruth's nostalgia, Jim said, "Bet you didn't know Robert E. Lee built Fort Carroll in the harbor before the War between the States."

"No, I didn't know that, but I've heard tales of the days the harbor froze so solidly that people could ice skate all the way from Light Street to Fort Carroll."

"That's all part of Baltimore, I suppose."

"Of course it is! Baltimore grew out of it, just as the great Johns Hopkins Hospital has grown out of a small building of the past century."

"But," Jim protested, "we can't live in the past."

"Who wants to? I like to watch things grow, too, and to think about the future. Take Johns Hopkins for example. Of course, I don't remember any of that growth—I'm not that old—but Dan watched them build the Welch Medical Library. And you must recall the Glenn L. Martin Company when it was 'the home of the Martin bomber' in one small administration building and a couple of hangars. Look at it now—it's gigantic!"

"Okay, okay . . ."

"I'm surprised at you, Jim Stevens! You want to be a politician and you don't want to remember the past. What kind of a platform are you going to run on?"

"The only platform I'm interested in right now is my proposal of more dates."

"Swell, I'll vote for you! Want to take me to my class dance?"

"Do I?"

"Fine!" Ruth stood up, "Come on, here's our stop."

As they walked along to her house, she told Jim about Paul's accident. He said he was sorry, told Ruth she could have called off their date, and asked what hospital Paul was in.

When they reached Ruth's door she started to say a brief good night, then smiled as Pat's quotation came back to her. "And just to show you I'm not completely ignorant of Shakespeare: 'Good night, sweet prince, and flights of angels sing thee to thy rest.'"

Jim bowed deeply with his hand on his heart, then said with a chuckle that someone had probably told her that pretty phrase.

Shortly afterward Ruth was in bed dreaming of flights of angels.

11

JIM STEVENS showed up at the hospital to see Paul the very next day. And if any action ever solidified a friendship, Jim's warmhearted gesture did just that. From the beginning Paul had liked him, but when he came to the hospital to see the younger boy, the football star became Paul's friend for life. Not only did Jim come to see him, but he also brought along a book of football photographs as a gift, and the two of them spent the afternoon poring over the pictures. That was the way Ruth found them when she came to see her brother. Paul was propped up in bed, Jim close beside him, turning the pages of the book.

Until Ruth was ready to leave, Jim said nothing about going, but as soon as she said she was starting for home, Jim said he had to go, too.

"Take you home, Ruth?" he asked. "I've got the car."

"But you have to get home, Jim. It's late."

"Not that soon. Come on."

Jim opened the car door for her and helped her in. It was his father's car, a shiny big black sedan, the only kind his mother approved of. After all, they had to keep up appearances, she had insisted; to which Mr. Stevens had replied with the threat that he would buy a smaller car for himself and save the "carriage" for state occasions. Much as Jim hoped his father would follow through on his threat, he knew he wouldn't because it would only bring down the wrath of his mother —and that wrath was much feared at home. Because it was so easy for her to be nice when everyone did what she wanted, the other members of the family had an unspoken agreement to let her have her way.

"Dad," Ruth asked her father on the way from confession that night, "do you think it's hard for Catholics to be politicians?"

"You don't mean *politicians*, Ruth. Call them public officers or something else. Most people think of politicians as crooks —and, unfortunately, some Catholics haven't found it any harder than pagans to be crooks." Mr. Sterner paused; he breathed almost as if he had had personal experience with the machinations of such politicians. "But to answer your question," he continued finally, "yes, I think it is difficult for Catholics to be good public officials."

"But there is a place for them, isn't there?"

"Indeed there is, Ruth. But the need is for intelligent men with courage and faith in their country. It takes a wise man to steer a steady course at a slow, sure rate of speed. The trouble with many Catholics who go in for politics is that they are in too big a rush to reform things or else they have a weakness in holding firmly to their course."

"Disinterest in public affairs on the part of the ordinary Catholics hurts too, doesn't it, Dad?"

"Disinterest on the part of too many good people in this country has done a lot of harm. Too many don't know the man they're voting for, what he's done, or what he intends to do. Too many don't vote at all. It will be a lot easier for a good man to get elected, and stay good, when Catholics—and others too—pay heed to the Pope's advice to Catholic women a few years ago. He told them it was the duty of women to take an interest in public affairs and to vote."

Ruth's eyes were fixed on her father. All this was most interesting to her. "What kind of policy do you think a Catholic should follow in politics, Dad?"

"It seems to me he should work with others as far as possible. He shouldn't attempt to change existing evils in one fell swoop, in which case he would probably end up out of office the next election. The man who'll be successful in public office is the one who supports everything that will be for the good of the people, and meanwhile gradually tries to do away with the wrongs that have come into existence through the years."

"I see."

Mr. Sterner wondered whether she did see, whether anyone understood the tribulations facing a good man in the much-abused field of politics. He wasn't sure he understood himself, except in a vague general way. He turned his eyes to meet those of his daughter, which were still fixed intently on him. "May I ask where you picked up this sudden interest in politics, Ruth? You aren't thinking about going in for a public career, are you?"

"No, of course not, silly!" she smiled. "It's just that Jim Stevens was telling me that he . . ."

"Jim Stevens? You seem to know all about him, young lady."

"Well, yes."

"Oh!" Mr. Sterner looked knowingly at his daughter, whose eyes suddenly lost interest in his face and found the cracks in the sidewalk more attractive. Giving her a reassuring pat on the shoulder, he said no more.

Neither did Ruth until they reached home. Then, as she started up to her room, she said she thought she would write her weekly composition on the duty of Catholic women to become interested in public life.

"What do you want to do that for?" asked her father, although his whole expression was one of knowing exactly why.

But Ruth only answered that she thought it was important, and that they might use it in the school paper if it were good.

"Oh, I see. And Jim has nothing to do with it?" Mr. Sterner headed for the living room. "Well, if you'd like to see what the Pope said on the subject, you'll find a copy of his talk in my desk. I show it to your mother every election time."

Paul was home from the hospital within a few days. He had to spend a couple of days longer in bed, and then he was allowed to sit up.

The night of her class dance, Ruth stopped in to see him before she left.

"You going out *again* tonight?" he asked.

"Class dance tonight, Paul. Big stuff. Like my dress?" She whirled around for him to get the full effect of the ruffled blue net.

"It's all right. Who you going with?"

"Jim."

"You like to go out with boys, Ruth?"

"Of course."

"Why? I don't like girls and I don't want to go out with them. They give me a pain."

"You like me, don't you?" Ruth questioned.

"That's different; you're my sister. But the girls in my class at school are always screaming and running to Sister, or telling tales, or something like that."

"And don't *any* of the boys like little girls?" Outwardly Ruth put the question seriously, but inside she was laughing at Paul, lost in a big bathrobe, with only his face and broken arm showing.

"No!"

"Paul," she said teasingly, "let me tell you a secret."

"What?"

"The girls don't like you, either."

"That's no secret! But if girls don't like boys, why do you like them? And why do boys like you?"

Ruth blushed at the guilelessness of Paul's compliment. "I didn't like boys either, when I was in the fifth grade, and they didn't like me. But things change after you get to high school."

"Why?"

"People have to love one another if they're going to get married, and you have to like a person before you can love him."

"Well, I'm not going to have time for girls. I'm going to play football."

"That's the way all little boys feel. Girls think they aren't going to have time for boys, either, because they have a lot of things they want to do."

"Like playing jacks and jumping rope!" Paul scoffed.

"But when they get older, God wants boys and girls to like one another. He wants them to go together and have good times. After high school is over, sometimes during college, God wants almost every boy to meet a girl he can like very much, a girl he can love, so that some day they will get married and have children, the way Mom and Dad did. Do you understand that?"

"Yeah," said Paul, "but I still don't think I'll ever like any girl."

"You will when you get older." A whimsical smiled played on Ruth's face. Just then she heard the doorbell ring. "That's Jim. Good night, Paul," she said and hurried from the room.

"So long." Paul listened to Ruth's heels clicking on the stairs. Then he heard voices below. If he yelled loud enough, Jim would hear him.

"Hi, Jim!" He waited a few seconds, then a masculine voice rang back, "Hi ya, Paul. Be downstairs soon?"

"Yeah."

"Be seeing you."

"So long."

Either of two things generally happens when a ballroom is overcrowded: if everyone knows nearly everyone else, there's a good chance the pleasure will be doubled; but if only a few are known to one another, the couples give up in disgust at the interminable collisions with strangers. It usually happens that Levering Hall, on the campus of Johns Hopkins University, is too small for the class dances of the Institute of Notre Dame, but tradition seems to keep them there. However, since only seniors and juniors are allowed to attend the dance, there is a great likelihood of each girl knowing a majority of the others present. So the fun is increased by the crowding—at least Ruth Sterner found it that way.

"I've really been happy tonight," she told Jim as the last measures of the final dance were being played.

"That's swell," Jim said with genuine warmth. "So have I."

More to attract attention than to be kind, Don Wright and June Thompson had invited a group to go with them to one of the road houses after the dance. Knowing she'd feel out of place where stronger drinks were served, and really preferring a Coke and ice cream anyway, Ruth wanted to stop at Murray's with some of her friends. She didn't want to be around when waiters questioned June or any of the others as to their age. Fortunately, Jim wasn't keen about the road house, either, so they refused the invitation.

Before taking Ruth home, Jim dropped off Jane Arnold and her escort, with whom he and Ruth had double-dated. Then he headed for Ruth's house.

"Going to the C.S.M.C. dance, Ruth?" he asked.

Taking the question more or less as an invitation, she replied hesitantly, "Why, yes, Jim, I'm going. Someone has already asked me."

"Wish I could have," he said, his hands gripping the steering wheel more tightly. "I wanted to, but . . ."

Ruth didn't know quite what to say when Jim stopped talking without finishing his sentence. Hoping he'd understand she wasn't boasting or anything like that, she said, "I had the invitation quite a while ago."

"Well, that's some consolation."

"What's the matter, Jim?"

"I'm going with Barbara Connell."

"I thought you liked her?"

"I do. Honestly, Ruth, I didn't mean it the way it sounded. Barbara's a swell girl, but I don't like *having* to take her out so much. Mother insists . . ."

"Oh, your mother!"

"Don't say it like that, Ruth. Mother's all right. She's got some wrong ideas, maybe, but she's really a wonderful person." Jim forced a laugh. "One of the wrong ideas she has is that she should pick out my dates for me. Barbara's society, all right, and Mother thinks I ought to like her more than I do."

"Your mother doesn't like me, does she, Jim?"

"She doesn't know you."

"I didn't ask you that, Jim," Ruth said quietly. She knew Mrs. Stevens didn't like her because of that night at Blakefield.

"Let's not talk about it." The tone of Jim's voice indicated an end to the conversation on that topic. "Anyway, I'm glad you're going to be at the dance. I'll see you. And Barbara and I will have a good time; she understands the situation. She just takes Mother's managing as a big joke."

When Jim left Ruth at her door, he said he wished the night weren't over. No Shakespeare this time, but she knew Jim meant what he said.

12

JUNE THOMPSON had a party on her seventeenth birthday. To Ruth her invitation came as a surprise—until June all but told her the invitation didn't hold unless she brought Jim as her escort. She and June had never been particularly good friends, but neither were Jane Arnold and June especially dear, and Jane also had an invitation. Ruth thought maybe June was hoping that Jane would recommend her for one of the big jobs on the school paper next year. But a party was a party, so Ruth asked Jim to be her escort and he accepted.

June lived in a big house on Joppa Road, at the north end of the city. She greeted her guests in a new ice-blue satin evening dress with one shoulder bare. Her hair was swept up on the top of her head in a hair-do more striking than becoming. Next to her were her father and mother. Her mother, who was dressed almost exactly like her daughter, only in sapphire blue satin, looked like June grown just a few years older and stouter and more sophisticated. She evidently doted over June, and gushily greeted her daughter's guests, while her husband, who looked completely bored, gave each of them a limp hand to shake.

Ruth got away from June and her parents as soon as possible. Even the room and its furnishings appeared to her to be soft and lush and somehow unwelcoming. A lot of fellows in expensive clothes were standing around some unfamiliar girls, most of whom were wearing pretty revealing kinds of gowns. Although some of these fellows were rather handsome, all seemed to be cut from the same pattern—tall and thin, sleek hair, clear skin, and languid eyes. Don Wright, hard and stocky, was a decided contrast to them. He came over to say hello to Ruth and Jim.

After a time, June's mother came in and drawled, "Children, the house is yours. You can dance here or down in the club cellar. Ping-pong down there, too. Have a good time."

As Mrs. Thompson left the room, Ruth could see her husband leaning lethargically against the front door, holding her wrap for her. Ruth thought he needed somebody to shake him into some kind of useful activity.

For a while everybody danced. Then couples began to sit around smoking. One fellow asked June if she had anything to drink. A maid brought in a tray loaded with Cokes, and the fellow began to open the bottles when June dismissed the maid.

"Got anything to spike this stuff with?" the same boy asked. While he was lifting the caps he talked without taking his cigarette out of his mouth. He poured some rum out of the bottle June gave him, mixing it with his Coke. Then he fixed another one for his date.

"Help yourself, everybody," June chirped. "There's plenty more where that came from."

"Turn out the lights," someone shouted. "Yeah," agreed another. "Lights hurt my eyes," shrilled a female voice. "Lights!" cried a few more.

Jim put a couple of glasses on top of Coke bottles, and said to Ruth, "Come on, let's see what the club cellar looks like."

There were already some guests playing ping-pong in the cellar, and two couples were dancing to the music of a band coming over the radio. It wasn't long before Ruth and Jim were involved in a doubles match with the fellow and girl who were playing when they came in. Since the other couple were very good, Ruth and the fellow, who said his name was Tom, paired off against Jim and the girl, Sue, after the first game. Then Tom suggested more Cokes. "Ought to be something to eat, too. I'll go scouting. Anybody want his Coke spiked?"

Ruth, who had never tasted anything stronger than wine, wanted only a plain Coke. She experienced a strange sensation when Jim casually told Tom to put a little rum in his.

"Phew!" Tom exclaimed when he returned. "It's so dark up there you can hardly find your way. Not many people dancing either. June's making all the boys kiss her a happy birthday."

More of the guests came to the club room as the night went on. June arrived, hanging on the arm of a dapper fellow Ruth had met earlier in the night. In her left hand she held a drink, and between the index and middle fingers of the same hand a cigarette burned.

"Ruth," June said, "Bill's just dying to dance with you." She shoved the youth toward Ruth, and turned to Jim. "Come on and dance with me, Jim."

"All right, June," Jim replied, putting his arm about her.

June stopped him. "I have to get rid of this cigarette and drink first."

"Set them on the table here," Jim said, pointing to a glass-covered table.

"I have to get rid of them upstairs."

"What's the matter with that table?"

"Nothing," June smiled demurely. "Only I want to put them upstairs. Come on, Jim, take me upstairs."

"Okay." Jim's word was cold and impersonal.

After June and Jim had gone, the boy dancing with Ruth asked, "Want to go upstairs, too? There's more fun there."

"I'd rather stay here, if you don't mind," Ruth answered.

Bill said okay, and kept on dancing indifferently. Tom, the nice fellow who played ping-pong so well, came over and asked if Bill would like to play ping-pong with his girl while he danced with Ruth.

Bill's face lit up. "Sure thing."

He played ping-pong halfheartedly, maybe one game, maybe less. Then he talked with Tom's date for a little while and they started for the stairs. Tom steered Ruth over that way.

"No you don't, Bill," he said. "It's ping-pong or nothing."

"Let's just sit and listen to the radio," suggested Tom's girl. Ruth knew she liked her forthright manner though she couldn't quite figure her out. The four of them drew chairs near the radio and listened to the music.

When June finally brought Jim back, Ruth could see that he was angry. To June's coquettish "thank you" he replied with a brusque "you're welcome." He glared at June when, smiling condescendingly at Ruth, she called to Bill, who tagged upstairs after her like a little puppy.

Turning to Ruth, Jim said abruptly, "Let's dance." With a minimum of courtesy, he said to Tom and his date, "Excuse us."

While dancing, Ruth could feel the tenseness that was in Jim.

He went through the motions without saying a word, his eyes looking out over her shoulder far, far away. When she asked him what was wrong, he answered, "Nothing." That's the way he was. When he didn't want to talk about a thing, he'd say to skip it, the way he had when they had been talking about his mother. His deep thoughts were for himself alone.

Before long, Jim suggested, "Let's get out of here. We can tell her we have to go to school tomorrow."

"All right, Jim," Ruth agreed quietly.

They went upstairs. It was nearly midnight. The darkened rooms there were heavily curtained with cigarette smoke. The only light in the front room came from the ornamental juke box supplying the music for the few couples still dancing. Here and there Ruth could see the red glow from the tips of the cigarettes of two people sitting close together. Not far from the juke box, so that some of its light fell on them, Ruth saw one of the girls from school and her date kissing. Jim called to June. They heard her telling Don Wright she'd be right back; then she came over to them. When Jim told her they were leaving, she said, "So soon?"

"Yes, we have to go to school tomorrow."

"Oh, school!" June laughed scornfully. "I wouldn't think of going myself." She walked toward the front door with them. No longer was she the piece of perfection she had been when they arrived; now her face was flushed and wisps of hair kept falling down and getting in her eyes.

After Jim had helped Ruth with her coat, he slipped into his, and expressed his thanks to June. She eyed him for some time before replying, enjoying his discomfort. Finally, she smiled wryly and said, "The pleasure was all *mine*."

"Hey, June." It was Don's voice.

"Coming," she called back. "G'night, Ruthie. Give my regards to the nuns tomorrow." Then she whirled around and left them.

Jim said little all the way home. Ruth knew he hadn't had a good time, and she felt that somehow or other it was all her fault. After all, she had asked him to go to June's party. She watched his big hands gently steering the car; it was like the night of the dance at Blakefield when she couldn't think of anything to say. Only then she had been embarrassed, while now she knew her feelings to be in agreement with Jim's. And when two people don't want to talk, the best thing for them to do is to keep quiet.

School the next day was more than tedious for Ruth. Her restlessness grew with each period until Sister Philothea caught her doodling during her class. Ruth couldn't decide whether Sister was unusually caustic, or whether it was her own feelings which were easily hurt today. Naturally she sided with herself, and threw the blame on the nun for reproving her "on the slightest provocation." It took no deep insight into character to discover in the eyes of the teacher a disdain for her distracting pupil. Willed or not, antagonisms make their appearances in the lives of even the holiest; and sometimes their unsightliness mars the beauty of grace. Nervous and high-strung, Sister Philothea was in constant conflict with herself because of her tendency to hasty, biting criticism, which was invariably followed by remorse. Yet she feared to appear a compromiser, so doggedly refused ever to apologize to a student. And she was always most careful that there was some ground for her criticism, however slight it might be.

While she was grumbling to herself over the injustices of life and the tyranny of teachers, Ruth said many things. One statement, however, stopped her short: "I wouldn't want to be like her for the world!"

It suddenly occurred to Ruth that she hadn't done much about trying to solve her problem of a vocation, of what she really did want to be like. She wasn't sure she had prayed over it very much—some nights, yes; but for the greater number she wasn't sure. She had gone to Mass specially only the morning after her talk with Sister Elizabeth, and for several mornings after that; but it became too much of a burden. Why the greatest action Man can do was a burden, she didn't know. She knew she was too tired or lazy to make *the* sacrifice. She had a vague recollection that she had intended to go to Mass the morning after her class dance; instead she had risen late and had had an argument with Marge which still hindered their relations. There hadn't been many serious thoughts about her vocation either, although she had talked to her confessor and received his approval. And now it didn't have the attraction it had held at Christmas. To be like Sister Philothea: the thought made her shudder! Some day she'd stop in and tell Sister Elizabeth it was all off.

On the way home from school Ruth complained to Pat Boyle about Sister Philothea. Today Pat, who took things philosophically, annoyed Ruth with her coolheaded facing of facts. "You can't have everything your own way all the time, Ruth. You get merit for doing difficult things; that's the way to get to heaven."

Ruth never could argue with Pat. Her disgust with school and life in general were still with her as she walked from the car stop. At home she found Paul, jubilant over his first day back at school. She thought how queer people are. The same thing can make some people sad and others happy. She wanted to laugh at herself—but couldn't.

13

"ARE you sure you brought Barbara only because your mother wanted you to, Jim?" Ruth's voice expressed the question which she couldn't put aside. All evening she had been wondering why Jim didn't go wild over Barbara, who, to Ruth's way of thinking, was exquisite. If she had asked herself the question once, she has asked it two dozen times.

"Not . . . exactly," Jim replied vaguely.

"I thought so!"

"Jealous?"

"No, I'm not jealous," Ruth said testily, surprised at the rapidity with which the words hopped from her lips before she could stop them and phrase them nicely. Words had a habit of doing that with her.

"Then what are you so anxious about? Afraid she's going to steal Tod?" Jim was using the ordinary chatter, not paying much attention to Ruth. "Why, she can do better than that any day."

"You don't know anything about Tod." Ruth's words were

clipped. She didn't know why she was taking up for Tod. She didn't know why her words were so without warmth.

"Enough to suit me. And if you don't mind my saying so, I think the guy's a lug."

Ruth pressed her lips together firmly and looked over Jim's shoulder while he prattled on. What in the world's the matter with me, she wondered. He's only teasing, and there's no reason for me to get upset; but I know that I am.

It was the night of the Catholic Students' Mission Crusade dance, and while Tod was reveling in Barbara's company, Ruth was dancing with Jim. It was strange the way things turned out. Usually it took a lifelong friend to get Tod to exchange dances, for on most occasions he was not interested in the dates his friends brought. To him new acquaintances were just so many names to be remembered for the night and forgotten the next day; they meant embarrassment and dull spots during a night's fun. But tonight he couldn't avoid meeting Barbara and exchanging dances, for Jim had brought her over and introduced Tod to her as soon as he saw Ruth and her escort enter the ballroom.

"I've heard a lot about you, Tod," Barbara had said buoyantly when he was presented. "Best back on Calvert Hall's team, weren't you?"

After that, Tod had been like a flower blooming in the sunny warmth of Barbara's smile. "I wouldn't exactly say that." He smiled back.

"Well, anyway, you'll have to tell me about football and Calvert Hall. I don't know much about either." Barbara beamed, warmth coming as naturally to her as the tint of her red hair. "And of course, I'd like to hear all about you."

"If you'll tell me about yourself in return," Tod agreed, surprised at his own forwardness—thrilled at it, too.

When Ruth caught herself feeling left out and thinking the conversation jejune, she became afraid to face her own thoughts. It's so easy for them to be kind and cheerful when you feel wanted, when you feel secure of yourself, but as soon as your position becomes the least bit unstable, thoughts about other people can be so ugly that you hate to recognize them as your own. They can belittle other people, color their actions, and rush blindly to your protection. Controlled, they make great-minded people; uncontrolled, they make small-souled individuals, the daydreamers who must stay wrapped up in themselves because reality is too real for them, when they have to face themselves and other people as they actually are.

After a time Jim noticed Ruth's silence. "What's the matter, Ruth? Have I won on the subject of Tod?" There was concern in his eyes, although he tried to joke. "You usually have the last word in these arguments."

"I'm not arguing tonight, thanks, Jim." Ruth, too, forced a smile.

"Want me to tell you what a swell dress you have on tonight?"

"No, thanks."

"Hey, wait a minute," he said seriously. "You knew I was only kidding, didn't you?"

"Yes, Jim, I know."

"Then, what's wrong?" He squeezed her hand gently.

They danced a while before Ruth said, "Jim."

"What?"

"Did you say your mother wants you to marry Barbara?"

"Whoa, wait a minute, not so fast!" Jim exclaimed. "Mother hasn't gone that far yet." He stopped suddenly and his smile faded. "But I suppose she will want it some day."

"You like her, don't you?"

"I told you, Barbara's a swell girl. I like her a lot because we always have a good time together, and she understands Mother. . . ."

"But I . . ." Ruth broke off. She was going to say, "But I don't understand her, so you like Barbara." But she didn't think that would be fair to anyone.

"She's a great friend to have, Ruth," Jim went on. "But I just know I couldn't feel about her the way I could about some others."

Knowing there was something wrong inside her tonight, Ruth knew she shouldn't ask any more questions. She had to fight with herself, and it was painful. But that something inside her made her ask, even though she knew with her feelings and with her thoughts what Jim would say. "Who, for instance?" came the question.

"You."

Both of them were embarrassed. Ruth stopped breathing, stopped everything except the motion of her feet and the word she couldn't put out of her mind. Like a bright neon sign the word YOU glowed there. Do what she would, the word wouldn't go out, and as long as it remained she was embarrassed. Forcing herself to look at Jim, she saw that he hadn't taken his eyes off her. Now that he had waited for her look at him, he didn't appear embarrassed at all. "Don't say that, Jim."

"Why not?"

Her mind was a cataract of confusion again. "I don't know, but just don't say it."

The return of Tod and Barbara separated them. Tod was bubbling over with enthusiasm for Barbara. Just as he couldn't hide his feelings when hurt or angry, so he had to show them when he was happy. "Ruth, she's going out with me next Friday."

Trying to share Tod's joy, Ruth said, "You'll have a wonderful time, I'm sure."

"I hope so. Gee, Ruth, I don't think I've met anyone easier to talk to than Barbara." Tod's choir-boy face beamed. "Did you notice how quickly we made friends? That usually takes a long time for me. But with Barbara everything seems different."

After the dance Tod and Ruth went to Murray's for ice cream and cokes. Jim and Barbara went with them, because as soon as Tod heard that Jim couldn't get his father's car that night, he had offered them a ride. When he had finished his ice cream, Tod asked Barbara to dance and left Ruth and Jim sitting at the table.

"Care to dance, Ruth?" Jim questioned.

"No, let's just decide which couple on the floor dances best." She didn't want to do much personal talking with Jim, and this would give them something else to talk about until Tod was ready to leave. She sensed that Jim felt much the same as she did.

After they had taken Barbara and Jim home, Tod hummed as he drove along. Ruth liked it because it made her forget herself and laugh at Tod. Not only could he not carry a tune, but it was also the first time she had heard him do a solo.

He stopped suddenly and for the tenth time that night asked, "Didn't you like her, Ruth?"

"Yes," Ruth answered once more.

"She's different, not like other high school kids. You don't hear her making a lot of silly remarks." Ruth recalled her own thoughts about Tod's first conversation with Barbara. "Barbara's grown-up," he enthused on. "When she doesn't have anything to say, she keeps quiet."

"You don't have to be quiet or sullen all the time to be grown-up. You can be a perfect clown and still be grown-up, as long as you know when to be what." Ruth's reply was more of a suggestion than a remark. "St. Philip Neri was a practical joker, but he was plenty grown-up."

"That's what I mean," Tod agreed. "Barbara's not quiet or sullen like . . ." He stopped. Looking questioningly at Ruth, he asked, "I was sociable tonight, wasn't I?"

"Yes, Paul should have seen you."

Tod was serious. "Paul and that gang of his don't like me. They think I'm big-headed, don't they?"

Ruth didn't say anything.

"I know they do," Tod said, "but I wish they didn't. I can't help it. When they come around and ask me to play with them, I feel like a fool. Suppose the fellows at school saw me, then what? I'd never live it down."

"You don't have to play with them, Tod, just be nice. Besides, I'll bet Barbara wouldn't laugh if she saw you playing with them. Neither would anyone else who is really *grown-up*."

"I never thought of that," Tod admitted. "No, Barbara wouldn't laugh. Ruth, I'm going to learn an awful lot from her; she's really grown-up."

Ruth lay in bed with her thoughts. She was trying to analyze her feelings impersonally while the night made its usual noises. Tonight the noises were neither pleasant nor unpleasant. A board in the floor near the radiator snapped its fingers to keep warm, and in the bed next to hers Marge breathed lightly, looking as if she were dreaming of flights of angels. Ruth was trying to decipher her feelings about Jim and Barbara and Tod, especially about Jim. Do I like Jim more than I should? Am I jealous of Barbara? What about Tod? When am I going to do some serious thinking and praying about that vocation? Outside a trailer truck lumbered down the street, and by the way it shook the house, Ruth knew it was as loaded as her brain was with thoughts—only she hoped in much better order. She tossed under the covers with the image of Jim before her. When Barbara appeared in the dream with Jim, she turned again, this time meeting Sister Elizabeth. Ruth tried to duck down a corridor, but she still heard Sister saying, "High school boys aren't thinking about getting married for a long time; they go with girls because they like them."

Today, as in Shakespeare's time, sleep still "knits up the raveled sleave of care." After wrestling with her thoughts, and tossing and turning in the struggle for more than an hour, Ruth was mentally and physically exhausted. Waiting only for a moment when she felt she was master of the situation, she fell asleep, sure of it.

14

THE priest who gave the retreat that year was tall and thin, like Abraham Lincoln, only he was more of a poet. He had fine, sharply chiseled features. His face would light up with the beauty of what he said with his organ-deep voice. When he moved his hands, which were long and expressive, they caught the eyes of his audience and swept them, like feathers suddenly captured in a draft, toward Heaven, or pressed them into their sockets with a scornful finger-thrust at evil. At such a thrust his eyes would glow and his lips would curl to reveal his teeth as he fairly spat out the words, "Shameful sin!"

The girls were impressed. After the first day, they were all agog. "I think he's darling," said June Thompson. "Looks like Gregory Peck, too."

Ruth said nothing the first day. But after the second day she was waiting for a streetcar at Monument and Aisquith Streets with a group of girls who were practically hero-worshiping the priest: "Did you see those eyes when he looked up to Heaven? . . . What a voice! . . . I could swoon every time he opens his mouth. . . . He's so manly."

At first Ruth tried to ignore them by looking at the monument to Wells and McComas, the Baltimore boys who gave their lives at the battle of North Point during the War of 1812 when they shot an English general. Since the monument is nothing to look at, her gaze followed Gay Street as it cut by the monument on its crazy jag across the town. But that didn't do anything to her ears, and finally she turned to Pat Boyle and exclaimed, "Oh, he's just an actor!"

Somewhat taken back, Pat replied, "You shouldn't say that, Ruth."

"Well, that's what he is," Ruth insisted. "All he does is stand up there and attract attention. What he says is all very pretty, but when's he going to say something definite? You get home and you ask yourself what he said, and all you can remember is something vague about good and bad."

"The success of the retreat depends more on you than on the retreat master."

"Sure, okay," Ruth sputtered. "But the retreat master is supposed to help. Has he helped you?"

"Not much," Pat had to admit.

"I had some important things I wanted to settle during these days, and about the only thing I've decided is that Father has beautiful hands." Ruth lowered her voice when they boarded the streetcar. "What I want to know is when I'm going to get something out of this retreat, something practical that I can use."

Pat, who wasn't as excitable as Ruth, said, "At least you'll get a good confession out of it."

"Don't tell me it's going to take him three days to get a

good confession out of me; he ought to be able to do that in one. When's he going to tell us something about how to be holy right now and later on? No, all he says is, 'You must pray, girls. And don't do or say bad things.' Then half the school falls off the pews and thinks he's adorable."

"Ruth, he may be vague, but not that vague," Pat admonished quietly. "You sound anti-clerical."

"If that means not liking this retreat, I am."

"Father has given us some positive things."

"What?" Ruth's retort was terse and rapid as rifle fire. "Pray: is that something positive? It's not negative; that's all. Did he tell us what prayer is, or how to pray, or what the best prayers are? Pray: they told me that in the first grade and every grade, but it's always vague, and about as effective as a tissue paper umbrella in a rainstorm."

"All right, Ruth, you win," Pat conceded with grace. "You're upset about something. Let's change the subject." It wasn't often that Pat was unable to argue with Ruth, but today Ruth wasn't interested in reason.

A retreat should be a time of refreshment and inspiration. It should be a time when you take stock of your struggle with Satan for your soul. Then it is that you should make repairs, bring up reinforcements, and plan attacks. From it you should come forth with vigor, confidence, a love of life and its purpose, which is to allow you to win a place in Heaven. But Ruth came out of hers bored. The priest had closed the retreat with a talk on vocations that was filled with a lot of stuff about the greatness of a religious vocation, walking with your head in the stars, and the army of God, without ever once descending to the practical realm of what to do about a vocation. "Pray, girls," he had ended, "that you may be worthy to walk with your heads in the stars."

Heads in the stars! All Ruth could think of was a character in a cartoon just after he got hit over the head with a club. She was so upset that when she ran into Sister Elizabeth after the last exercise, she could only mumble in reply to Sister's question as to how she had liked the retreat. And before Sister could suggest a talk, if she even had the idea in her mind, Ruth said hastily that she had to get right home—that she'd see Sister some other time.

"All right, Ruth." Sister Elizabeth was obviously disappointed and perplexed, but Ruth just couldn't talk to her today. She told herself this over and over again while she gathered her things from her locker and let them fall in a heap on the bench in front of her. Sister Elizabeth might bring up that vocation business. Golly, I'm sorry I mentioned it to her in the first place! After that talk today I don't feel attracted at all. Besides, the whole idea in general has lost most of its appeal. College looks pretty nice to me.

"Yes," she heard some girl say on the other side of the locker, "June says that Jim Stevens must have gotten tired of Ruth awful quick because he didn't bring her to the C.S.M.C. dance."

Ruth picked up her things and walked out.

"Hello, chicken." June Thompson turned on her best personality smile. "Where to?"

"Hi, June." The reply was unenthusiastic. Ruth didn't like people to say things about her when she wasn't around. "Home, I suppose. Nothing to do on the paper or yearbook today."

June fell into step with Ruth. "Good, I'll give you a lift."

"That's nice of you, June," Ruth replied, wondering where this sudden burst of generosity had come from. "But I'd take you way out of your way."

"Don't fret, honey chile! I don't have a thing to do." June unlocked the door of her car and slid in behind the steering wheel. "Besides, I want to talk to you."

"Well, it's your gas," Ruth said, knowing perfectly well that her statement could be taken in two senses.

The car was a shiny green coupe, June's birthday gift from her parents. It was one more reason for her popularity. While the engine warmed, June lit a cigarette, and in a puff of smoke asked, "Going to the Valentine dance at Loyola, gorgeous?"

"Hope so, but no invitation yet."

"Why, darlin', you must be slowing down." June was getting WITH on her radio, for she had to have music while she drove. "Don Wright asked me over a week ago."

Ruth refused to let June rankle her. "Guess I'm getting old and decrepit."

"Don't kid yourself, dearie!" June said. Looking at Ruth out of the corner of her eyes, she added, "But I'm surprised Jim Stevens hasn't asked you."

At first Ruth wanted to tell June to mind her own business. She saw the whole thing now: June telling the girls her suspicions, then waiting around and offering her a ride home just to ask her questions about Jim—to ask her questions about Jim to confirm her own rumor—not that June ever worried much about confirming rumors she started. To her they were just topics for conversation, and one simply had to have topics for conversation or there was no conversation. To have found herself in that situation ever would have been more than June's temperament could stand; so when things were running low, she always managed to start some new subject, generally one which attracted the attention of the girls to her.

But Ruth decided to be noncommittal. "Maybe he's taking Barbara Connell," she said. "You know he took her to the C.S.M.C. dance."

"Oh, I've seen them together before, and let me tell you that girl is *some* looker. Saw you with Tod Edwards, too. Wish I had had time to meet everybody, but there were so many of my friends there that I couldn't . . . You understand?"

"Certainly. Wasn't the dance a big success, June?"

"I rather liked it, but I'm looking forward to this Valentine dance with Don Wright. You know, not every girl can go with the best hockey player in the school."

"That's true," Ruth said. Of course, she told herself, not everyone would want to go with your hockey-playing friend.

"I know the girls will be jealous." June was half talking to herself. "I simply *must* get a new dress for the evening."

Not wanting to voice what she was really thinking, Ruth said, "Well, if I get there, we'll have to exchange partners for a dance." But she was sorry as soon as she said it, not only because she didn't want to dance with Don, but also because she didn't like the coy way June talked about Jim. Anyway, Ruth knew she wouldn't be going to the dance with Jim. He hadn't asked her yet, though she was pretty sure he would; but when he did, she had other plans. Now, however, she thought it would be delightful to throw a wrong scent toward June's snooping nose, so she murmured, "I don't think I'll be there with Jim."

"No?" There was a big "I told you so" hiding not very well behind June's eyes. "Anything wrong between you two?" she inquired.

"No, but I think he's going to ask somebody else."

"Aha!" June implied that she knew how it was—Ruth just

didn't care to talk about the fight she had had with Jim.

"But he's not the only Loyola boy I know."

June wasn't interested in other Loyola boys at the moment; for her Ruth's love-life was *the* thing. At every opportunity she tried to get Ruth to admit something had happened, and Ruth was enjoying June's being so completely fooled too much to set her right.

As Ruth was all but certain he would, Jim called her to invite her to the dance. When she answered the phone, his voice came across, "You going to the Valentine dance with anyone?" Behind the voice, by the way Jim had asked the question, Ruth could hear a plea of "Say no, say no." And when she did say no, she heard Jim breathe a sigh of relief at the other end of the wire.

"Boy!" he exclaimed. "I was scared Ken Carpenter would beat me to you. I told him I'd wham him over the head if he did, but he said he was going to anyhow. Will you go with me?"

Her heart kept telling her to say yes. She wanted to go with Jim, because she'd rather go anywhere with Jim than with anybody else. "Want to do me a favor, Jim?"

"I don't like the sound of this, but what is it?"

"Ask Pat Boyle to go with you."

"Hey, wait a minute! Ask Pat Boyle?" By the way Jim's voice trailed off, Ruth could imagine him sinking into a chair. But the voice came back strong. "Now look, Ruth, she's a nice girl and all that. But Pat Boyle . . ."

"Jim, really she's one of the nicest girls I know. If I didn't think you'd have a good time, I wouldn't ask you."

"Yes, I know, Ruth. But Pat Boyle . . ."

"Jim, you're being silly, really. You only met her once. You don't know what she's like."

"Yes," Jim cut in, "only once, but that was enough for me to see her."

"What's wrong with her?"

"Ah, Ruth, she's . . . Besides, I want to go with you."

"What's wrong with her, Jim?" Ruth was insistent. She wasn't going to let Jim get off the subject.

"Well, Ruth, she's . . ." Jim was trying to think of the right word to use; he didn't want to insult Ruth's friend. "Well, she's . . ." The same painful pause. "Look, Ruth, don't you think she's a little"—Ruth heard Jim swallow—"heavy?"

"She's not that heavy, Jim, and you know it."

"Maybe my eyes deceived me," he said meekly. "Honest, she looked pretty big to me."

"You certainly wouldn't call Pat fat, would you?"

"Well, maybe not." Jim wouldn't commit himself. "But, look, don't you want to go with me?"

"Yes, I do, Jim, but I want you to take Pat for a very special reason. I'll explain it all to you later."

"But, Ruth, I only met her once. I don't know her well."

"Please, Jim."

"But . . ."

"Please."

"Okay, okay, but you listen to me. We make sure to get some dances together or it's all off."

"Thanks, Jim." Ruth couldn't help laughing. "Of course we'll have some dances together. Romeo, you're wonderful!"

"Yes, I know." Jim was disheartened. One last possibility of getting out of this situation occurred to him. "Say, Ruth, maybe Pat won't accept. Then will you go with me?"

"Yes." A feeling bordering on hilarity tickled Ruth's sense of humor. It was such fun; Jim was so wonderful. Pat would be put in circulation, and June would be completely confused. "But don't worry, Jim," she prattled delightedly, "she'll accept."

"I was afraid of that. Look, when that chump Carpenter calls you, ask him if he's got a car. Mother is using ours that night, and I'd like to bum a ride with you."

"Jim, thanks." To have Jim do this for her tempered her joy with affection. "I really mean that."

"Okay." Jim's voice became softer now. "But remember I'm doing it for you."

She would remember, if for no other reason than that she couldn't forget it.

After the arrangements were made, Ruth was afraid her generosity had run away with her. After all, she wanted to go to the dance with Jim. And what would June Thompson say now? It didn't matter much what she thought, but she might say anything!

15

WHEN Ruth and Pat went to the Lyric together the following Sunday night, to listen to the Baltimore Symphony Orchestra, Ruth was surprised at her friend's conversation. Usually before the start of the program she'd explain exactly what to expect during each part of the performance, the various movements of the symphony, the additional selections of the orchestra, and what instruments to watch most closely. But tonight she was as excited as a little girl who has been invited to her first formal party and, caught up in the newly-experienced joy, has left her dolls to fend for themselves. So Pat had abandoned the music tonight; if it was going to win Ruth at all, it would have to do so without the help of her companion.

"Did you know," Pat asked excitedly, "that Jim Stevens asked me to go to Loyola's Valentine dance with him?"

"He did?" Ruth avoided answering Pat's question. "Pat, that's swell."

"Isn't it, though? And I think it's just about perfect that we're going along with you and Ken Carpenter. It'll give me a lot more confidence."

"Don't worry about confidence, Pat. Just be yourself and you can't help being a hit."

Smiling tremulously, Pat said, "Thanks." And the way she said it did things to Ruth. This girl felt things deeply—even a simple word of gratitude came from the heart. "Ruth," she requested, "tell me something."

"Yes, Pat, what is it?"

"How come Jim didn't ask you to the dance?"

"Pat, I'm surprised at you! You don't believe those rumors June started about Jim and myself being on the outs, do you?"

Pat sat still, pondering the attention-absorbing problem, the kind that makes you motionless and puts blank stares in your eyes—almost as if they were turned inside your mind, looking for the answer to the problem. She said she didn't believe much of what June said unless she were sure of it, but she couldn't help wondering why Jim hadn't asked Ruth.

Lost for an answer, Ruth resorted to a question: "What difference does it make?"

"None, I suppose. But it does seem strange, his asking me."

"I don't see what's so strange about it."

"Well, I do." Pat looked intently at her companion. "You're sure he didn't ask you?"

"I didn't say he didn't."

Pat didn't move, though she was evidently saddened and her voice dropped as she went on hesitantly, "And you—you told him to ask me?"

"Who said anything about that?" Ruth said hastily. "I only meant maybe he did ask me, and he did. But I have a date for the dance with Ken, so I couldn't go with Jim."

The orchestra was on the stage when Pat said, "But I don't know why Jim should suddenly decide to ask me."

Ruth had done enough hedging for one night. She was glad she could point to the orchestra and say, "They're ready, and you haven't told me anything about this symphony."

After a sprightly overture, the orchestra was ready for Mendelssohn's *Italian Symphony*. So richly relaxing was the music that Ruth couldn't help recalling the picture on Pat's album of an Italian lolling luxuriantly under a tree that shaded him from the sun. The whole thing bespoke warmth in the language of music, especially the second movement when the melodic measures of the violins predominated, imparting a spirit of security without strain such as exists when one is the friend of a strong man. To Ruth's mind it was beautiful, just as the magic of bows moving in unison and the enthralling gestures of the conductor's hands and baton were beautiful.

Pat didn't share Ruth's enthusiasm for Mendelssohn, Ruth discovered after the show, while they were waiting for the Charles Street bus. She was taken up with the last piece on the program.

"Well, I can't say I agree with you, Pat." Ruth reaffirmed her conviction, "I thought the *Italian Symphony* was wonderful, but that last thing . . ." She made a face.

"Oh, you just like pretty melodies, Ruth." Pat feigned impatience. "That last composition was technically more difficult to execute than any of the others."

"Well, they certainly executed it," Ruth agreed, unable to restrain the pun.

"Ruth, I'm afraid all you look for is a tune you can hum. A piece of music doesn't have to be that simple to be good."

"I still like a melody, but I guess they put in some of that other stuff for people like you. I hope you noticed, Miss Boyle, that the people agreed with me. If you paid any attention to the applause, you must have noticed that the *Italian Symphony* was the most popular thing on the program."

"Ruth, you're hopeless. That has nothing to do with our argument."

Before school the next morning, Ruth was trying to bone up some Latin for Sister Philothea's class when June Thompson sauntered up to her.

"G'mornin', gorgeous, Jim Stevens ask you to the Valentine dance yet?"

"I'm going with Ken Carpenter," Ruth said quietly. This'll slay her, she thought to herself, as she added, "Jim's taking Pat Boyle."

June reached dramatically for a chair. "He's taking Pat Boyle!" She gasped in utter amazement at the very thought of the idea; it made her legs weak; she had to sit down. If only Ruth weren't so serious, June would have laughed—the very idea of Jim Stevens taking Pat Boyle was a riot. It just couldn't be true.

"Look, honey," she said after gulping in a big breath of air, "you wouldn't kid little me, would you?"

"No, Jim asked Pat." Ruth placed a chip on the shoulder of her voice. "Anything wrong with that?"

June laughed sardonically. "No, gorgeous, not a thing. But your boy friend sure is slipping—from you and Barbara Connell to Pat Boyle. Now that *is* something to write about."

"Listen, June, Pat has a lot on the ball that you don't know about. She hasn't been around as much as some of us because she's a little too high class for . . ."

"You mean high *scaled,* don't you, dear?" June cut in.

Ruth's eyes burned through June without apparent effect. "To you that would make a big difference, wouldn't it—if class were measured by weight?"

"Put the damper on the fire, Ruthie, somebody's liable to get burned." June refused to get riled. "Sure, your *little* girl friend has a lot on the ball— Isn't Jim Stevens taking her to the Valentine dance? By the way, did it ever occur to you that Jim may be sailing that *tub* to make you sore?"

"No, it did not."

"Okay, sweetheart, but it still makes good news for my column when Jim Stevens ditches you and takes Pat Boyle to the Loyola Valentine dance."

"June," Ruth pleaded hopelessly—"she's got feelings—do me a favor and be careful what you say about Pat."

"Sure, honey, sure. I'll be careful what I say about her. Want to read the copy beforehand?"

"No," Ruth replied hotly.

"Or maybe you'd like to read what I'm going to say about you?"

"No, thanks, June."

Undaunted, June went on, "You know, dearie, I think I have the solution there. Jim's taking her to spite you, to make you jealous. It happens, you know. Boy and girl fight. Boy takes out wallflower. Girl jealous. Boy and girl make up."

"It's all so simple, isn't it?" Ruth said bitterly.

"For those who understand."

"Suppose you mind your own business."

"Sure, gorgeous, I didn't know you were so touchy about the subject." With a toss of her head, June turned to go. "I have to find somebody to give me a translation of our Latin homework.

I was so busy over the week end that I just didn't have time to do it."

Ruth was fuming. If only June had become angry, too. But, no, she was as cold and sharp as an icicle. Darn that June Thompson, Ruth said to herself, she makes me so mad—and nothing I say fazes her. She'll have everybody thinking Jim and I had a terrific row. Ruth picked up her books and started for class.

"Ruth," Jane Arnold fell in step with her, "what's this I hear about Pat going to the Valentine dance with Jim?"

"Now, don't you start, Jane Arnold, or I'll chew your head off. I just got rid of June Thompson."

"So it *is* true?"

"Of course it is."

"I just wanted to make sure. June told me, but I never know when she's telling the truth or when she's imagining things. I thought Jim would ask you."

"I'm going with Ken Carpenter."

"Good, we'll all see one another there."

During class Ruth didn't pay much attention to Sister Philothea, who spoke so knowingly, yet unconvincingly, about Latin. There was no doubt in Ruth's mind that she was one of the smartest teachers she had, but she always seemed to be saying, "This is beautiful, but you wouldn't understand, even if I told you. So why tell you?" or "This is an exquisite construction, but you wouldn't appreciate it. So why explain it?" or "Romans were great people, but all you're interested in is the movies." Well, Ruth thought, if that's the way she feels, she knows what she can do about it. Anyway, it was more interesting to survey the class and try to guess which girls had been out late the night before, or to note the ones who were paying as little attention as she was. She was looking at Caroline Hayes' new hair-do when she heard Sister Philothea call on her.

While the rest of the class squirmed uneasily, Ruth frantically tried to find a place to begin. Her eyes ran, unseeing, from the top of the page to the bottom. She wasn't even sure she had the right page. Blushing scarlet, she looked up at the waiting nun and said, "I'm sorry, Sister, I've lost my place."

"Why don't you say you never had the place?" Sister asked coldly. "That would be nearer the truth." She made, very deliberately, a mark in her notebook; round and round the point of the pencil spun, forming a black zero. "All right for you, young lady," she said, "we'll see about this. I want attention in my class. If you don't choose to give it, you may get out."

Ruth sat down shamefacedly. Bitterly she thought, she did that just to humiliate me. But why don't you pay attention? she chided herself. Must be awful tough to live with her, though.

Because some of the galley proofs had arrived from the printer, working on the yearbook that afternoon was exciting. To anyone with imagination, the finished product was easily visible. Already the girls were acclaiming it the best *Clarissian* the Institute of Notre Dame had ever seen.

Jane Arnold, who with Ruth was identifying the girls in some of the pictures, let out a howl. "Girls, look at this! Won't June just love this shot?"

Everyone gathered around Jane and had a good laugh at the picture of Class 3-C, June's class. Right in front where she could be seen sat June, but something had thrown a shadow on her chin so that her million-dollar smile looked like a rabbit's.

Marie Kenny said, "I can see her crying over it now. Then she'll come pleading, 'But, Jane, it's such a horrible picture, and I'm the only one who looks ghastly. *Please* have it taken over.'"

After their laughter had floated out the window, the girls settled down to work again until June arrived, late as usual. By that time the others had been through the galleys rapidly and were now proofreading very carefully.

"'Lo, everybody, sorry I'm late." She noticed the galleys. "Oh-ho, what have we here? The galleys? Let's have a look at them."

June was reading over Ruth's shoulder, unaware that all eyes were focused on her. "Oh, Jane, you didn't change those title heads as I suggested. The rest of the type is fine, but those heads just don't go with it. *McCall's* wouldn't run anything like that."

"This isn't *McCall's*, June. The change you suggested would have been expensive. Besides, we took a vote and the majority like it the way it is."

"That shows how wrong the majority can be," June said smugly. "Oh, well, you're responsible for the book. I only work here."

"Would you care to help me proofread these pages, June?" Pat asked.

"Sure thing, honey chile. I want to see what you have on the ball that has taken Jim Stevens away from Ruth."

Pat laughed self-consciously. "Nothing," she said.

"Oh, but you must have," June insisted. "Ruth says you have plenty on the ball."

Pat looked uneasily about the room. "That's nice of Ruth."

"Oh, come on, don't be bashful. Tell me what it is."

"June!" Ruth's voice rang out. Surprised at her own sharpness, she moderated her tone as she went on, "Leave Pat alone."

16

R UTH was still smoldering when she and Pat started home later that afternoon. Nothing much had come of her tiff with June, who had been just as surprised at the sharpness of her voice as she herself. With the air charged for an explosion, Ruth had waited, watching the color mount in June's cheeks. It was real this time, but just before things ignited Jane Arnold threw a bucket of cold water on the situation as she mustered enough courage to sound peeved herself and tell the girls to get to work on the yearbook and save their private feuds for later.

Out of the streetcar window, Ruth watched the people walking along or the water trickling from the dirty snow at the curb. She'd see a newsboy get on the car at one corner, walk through the car selling the *Sun* and *News-Post,* and get off at the next block. If it hadn't been for that, she might have thought they were continually passing the same houses all over again, so much were they alike, block after block of them. All of them red brick with white steps, red brick with white steps, red brick with white steps. She said no more than Pat, who sat next to her, doing nothing in particular. Probably reading the car ads, Ruth thought.

There was quite a crowd on the car, and Ruth had to wipe the haze off the window when she wanted to look out. That's what she was doing when Pat said, "Ruth."

"Yes?"

Pat kept her eyes on the books resting in her lap and without so much as turning to see whether Ruth was looking at her, she thanked her for standing up for her, as if Ruth had beaten a bully who was pulling her hair.

"Oh, forget all about that, Pat." Ruth felt so sorry for her friend that she found herself wishing she had done even more to put a stop to June's baiting of Pat. "Somebody ought to tell that goon to mind her own business once in a while—as if it would do any good."

For a time after that Pat sat silently, her eyes glued on her books, her fingers playing with one of them, opening and closing the cover nervously. Watching her without saying a word, Ruth could see a slight furrow cut in her usually smooth brow, and a watery glisten appeared every time light fell on her eyes. Sensitive feelings like Pat's weren't meant to cope with June's whip-like taunting, which stung deeply. Yet Ruth knew it wouldn't make much difference in Pat's attitude toward June. She'd treat her as she had always done, with greater fairness than any other girl in the school. But the pain wouldn't soon be forgotten.

"Ruth, I'm not going to the Valentine dance," Pat said in the same throaty voice she had used the few times she had spoken since boarding the car. She was swallowing her tears, and it seemed as if they were running down over her vocal cords, taking all the life out of them, the way dampness will take the life out of violin strings.

"Of course, you are," Ruth said as she turned and looked out the window. She wanted it to appear as if she had given an order and it was final. They passed a lone, bare tree that looked like a mistake which had never been corrected, and Ruth wondered if she hadn't been wrong in arranging this whole affair. But she wasn't going to change now, no matter what.

"No, I'm not," Pat replied without ever taking her eyes from her books. She was looking right through the covers and past the books, seeing nothing.

"Oh, yes, you are," Ruth said emphatically. "After Jim asked you and you said yes, you're going."

Pat bit her lip, and looking at Ruth through tear-filled eyes she asked, "Why did Jim ask me, Ruth?"

They weren't far from Ruth's stop now. "Come on," she said, "let's walk." It was still pretty cold out, and no one would think it strange to see tears in a girl's eyes the way the wind was blowing.

When Pat repeated her question, Ruth answered that Jim had asked her because he wanted to.

"You told him to ask me, didn't you?"

Ruth wasn't going to answer that question unless she had to. "You asked me that last night at the concert. Since when did I become Jim's boss?"

"Stop beating around the bush, Ruth." Pat almost choked. "Answer my question."

"That's got nothing to do with it. So what, if I did ask Jim to take you?" Ruth tried to brush off Pat's cares like crumbs from the table, but it wasn't so easy because Pat came right back with the same question.

"Did you ask him to take me?"

"All right," Ruth admitted, "I did ask Jim to take you. But that's no reason for your not going after you said you would. If you're going to let a little snip like June bother . . ."

"Here's your corner," Pat interrupted when they reached the point at which Ruth usually left her and went home.

"I'm not going home tonight until you tell me you're going to that dance, or give me a good reason why you're not going."

"I'm not going because I don't want to go." But there was another reason lurking in Pat's mind, that was evident; she *did* want to go.

"That hasn't anything to do with it, either, after you told Jim you would go. You don't have any reason for not going. If you were sick or something, that would be different, but you don't have any reason except June and she's no reason for doing or not doing anything."

"Well, I'm not going whether you think I have a reason or not. I do, and that's enough."

When they reached Pat's house, they entered and went straight to Pat's room where they continued to argue. Ruth thought she was winning her point until Pat turned on her suddenly and said, "Oh, hush, Ruth. I'm not going to the dance because I don't want all the girls at school to know Jim asked me because you wanted him to take me. When I want a date, I'll get my own."

Then she threw herself on the bed and began to cry with great big sobs that tied Ruth's heart in knots. What a horrible mess she had made of things!

"Pat, I'm sorry. I didn't mean to be a busybody. I didn't mean to hurt you. I only wanted you to go and meet a lot of nice people. Nobody knows why Jim asked you." She sat on the bed, touched Pat's hair gently, and repeated, "I'm sorry, Pat. Forgive me?"

"But June Thompson . . ." Pat choked and couldn't finish what she wanted to say.

Guessing what it was, Ruth replied, "Not even June Thompson knows. She thinks Jim did it to spite me, to make me jealous. She doesn't know, and no one is going to tell her. Anyway, nobody believes all the stuff she says."

"Well, I'm not going." Pat's crying was muffled in her pillow.

It might hurt Pat and ruin everything, but Ruth gambled on a new approach. "Well, that's fine, just fine," she said in exasperation. "It's wonderful. What about Jim? What's he going to do about a date?"

Pat didn't answer for a while—she was trying to sniff herself under control. "H-H-He c-can get another date."

"Of course, just like that." Ruth snapped her fingers. "He can always get a date any old time." She stood up. "I hope you're going to tell him the real reason you aren't going."

Pat started to cry again. "HH-H-He dd-d-doesn't w-want to go with a f-fat girl like me."

"Okay, Pat," Ruth said as if she were offended. "I'll call Jim tonight and tell him you don't want to go because I asked him to take you."

"That's not the r-reason, and y-you know it," Pat bawled.

Ruth set her jaw and said sternly, "All right, then, if that's not the reason, you're going."

"No, I'm not."

"Pat Boyle, I'm surprised at you. I thought you had some sense, but I guess I was wrong. I see you're just a big baby who is self-conscious because a drip with nothing in her brain pan sometimes calls you fat-stuff. You're worried about the opinion of a scatterbrained goof who doesn't remember what she says from one day to the next. She says you wouldn't know what to do on a date, and you say sure she's right, when you should be showing her she's nuts and that you can stand on your own, any place, any time. And she's the only one silly enough to laugh."

"No one asked you to get a date for me," Pat said in her own defense.

"And I said I was sorry, Pat." Ruth let her real feelings show before she made her last effort. "Call it off if you want, Pat. I'm going home. Of course, Jim'll think the world of both of us now, but that doesn't matter; we can patch it up. If you had any sense, though, you'd go."

"I'm not going," Pat said with emphasis and began to cry again.

Ruth picked up her things and started home, blaming herself for the whole mean mess. Now what was Jim going to say? Suppose he couldn't get another date, or had to take some girl he didn't like at all? Why couldn't June keep her big mouth shut? What a beautiful launching of Pat's social career! I suppose I shouldn't have tried to push it, she told herself. After all, Pat would have made her hit some day without any help from me, and I could have gone to this dance with Jim. Now maybe I won't even get to dance with him.

She was so absorbed in her own thoughts that she didn't know anyone was behind her until she heard her name called. It was Mike Hafey.

"Hi, stranger," she said, shoving her problems into another corner of her brain as Mike took her books. "Where are you headed?"

"Judy's."

"Spending all your time there now?"

"Not quite." Mike blushed. "But that's one of the reasons I haven't been around. Another is that I have a job on week ends."

"By the way," Ruth asked, "how was your prom?"

"I didn't know you could have so much fun." Mike's words fairly tumbled over one another, he was so eager to tell Ruth all about it. "Everything's been fun since I met Judy. I like everything I do when she's around ten times as much as I ever liked it before."

When they reached her house, Ruth took her books and thanked Mike. Then she stood on the steps and watched him walk into the glow of one of the street lights and past it. And all the while she was wondering why fellows like Mike go steady with the first girl they meet.

"It's about time," her mother said as Ruth dumped her books and hung up her coat. "Where have you been, Ruth?"

"I was down at Pat's," Ruth explained. "I'm sorry I'm late, Mom, but it was important that I talk to her."

"If it was so urgent," Mrs. Sterner smiled, "I suppose I can't object. There's something warm on the stove."

"Thanks, Mom. I'll clean up when I'm finished. Just leave all the dishes where they are."

When the dinner dishes were done, Ruth went to her room to study, but Marge was already at the desk, so she took her books and studied at the dining-room table. First she tackled her Latin because she knew Sister Philothea would be after her again tomorrow. She always was the day after she caught a pupil not paying attention or unable to translate. And today she had caught Ruth on both scores. But once she had finished the Latin, Ruth sat doodling, wondering what Jim was going to say when he heard Pat wasn't going with him. She pondered whether she should call him or let Pat do it. She finally decided to leave it up to Pat, hoping that she would change her mind. Her pencil traced a picture of a girl with a big mouth, and she labeled it June Thompson. Then she scribbled over it vigorously and resolutely went back to her studying.

17

"SORRY to keep you waiting, Ken," Ruth said above the rustle of her pink taffeta dress when she came into the living room where Ken was talking to Mr. Sterner and Paul.

"That's okay, Ruth." Ken got to his feet. "You look very nice." He stood almost a head taller than Ruth and seemed older than most high-school boys.

"Why don't you bawl her out, Ken?" Paul asked. "She always yells at me for being late."

"Yes, Ken," Ruth agreed, "you have a right to, you know. I'm ashamed of myself because I don't have any real reason for being late. Bawl me out if you feel like it."

Ken laughed and said it was all right but that they had better get started because Jim was sitting out in the car waiting. Ruth said good night to her father and sent Paul scampering by attempting to kiss him.

When they went outside, Ken pointed out his car, and Ruth could see the figure of a lone boy sitting in it. Golly, she hoped everything would go all right tonight! Pat had finally changed her mind but she had no enthusiasm for the date. If they didn't have a good time, she'd die.

"You should have brought Jim in with you, Ken, instead of leaving him out here alone."

"He said he wanted to wait outside."

When Jim saw them, he hopped out of the car and held the front door open for Ruth. Again she said she was sorry she was late and told Jim he should have come in with Ken. After that, somehow, Ruth could find very little to say until they reached Pat's home.

Pat looked quite attractive in her yellow gown and simple make-up. But she was uneasy and misty-eyed. Probably had a big cry, regretting her decision, Ruth thought. Well, she'd try to perk things up with some conversation as best she could.

"Jim," she asked, "what do you think of our foreign policy?"

"Needs to be strengthened," he remarked casually.

"If you ask me," Ruth went on, "what we need is some women running the show. Then we'd straighten out the world."

Jim and Ken laughed.

"Go ahead and laugh, but the Pope's on our side. He told the women to take an interest in public affairs."

"To take an interest doesn't mean to take charge, does it, Pat?" Jim asked, drawing his companion into the discussion.

"It might. He must have had a reason for telling women to take an interest."

"That's the girl, Pat," Ruth said enthusiastically. "The world needs women to run it. Look at the mess men have always made of it."

"Talking for yourself or the Pope this time, Ruth?" Ken inquired, taking one hand from the steering wheel and holding his arm up in front of his head in mock defense.

"Look at the silly boy, Pat. He thinks I'm going to hit him. Of course that's what men come to when they haven't got an answer, but I have an answer for you, Ken. I was speaking for myself and the Pope."

"When are you going to tell the Pope about it?" Jim broke in.

"Didn't you ever read what he had to say about women taking an interest in public life?"

"Now we're back where we started." Jim laughed. "All the Pope wanted was for the foolish females of the world to get out and vote. Secondly, he wanted them to know why they were voting, for what, and for whom, which is a big step forward, since most women usually vote for the handsomest man."

Both girls protested that statement, and Ruth added her last barb. "All right for you, Mister Politician. If you're right about that, you'd better stay out of public life because that face of yours wouldn't win you many votes."

"Descending to personalities, I see. That's a mark of a weak mind. When we reach that point," Jim said, "it's time to take the matter up in private."

"Gladly," Ruth replied, satisfied to end the whole discussion, as she saw Pat turn to Jim with some question. She had managed to get the two of them talking without undue strain.

It wasn't that she wasn't having a good time, Ruth knew that. But there was the knowledge that she could have been having a better time, as good a time as June Thompson seemed to be having, attracting attention in *another* new dress that made her look prettier than she was. At times Ruth repented her big-heartedness in asking Jim to bring Pat because, while Pat was obviously enjoying herself, it seemed evident that she wasn't being lifted off her feet, and that she'd probably enjoyed lots of concerts more than this dance.

When Ruth danced with Jim later in the evening, she asked him if he were having a good time, and he said he was because Pat was okay. "Of course, she's not you, but . . ."

Ruth's eyes met Jim's. "I appreciate this," she said softly.

"Ruth," he said, changing the subject abruptly, "Mother wants you to come out to the house for dinner next Sunday night. She suggested that I invite you."

Ruth was taken back. Mrs. Stevens wanted her to come to dinner! It sounded strange, too: Mother wants you to come. What about you, Jim? she thought. What's behind the invitation? Why should your mother suddenly want me for dinner, when she never seemed to want to even talk to me before?

"Should I come, Jim?" she asked candidly.

"I don't know." Jim halted. "I guess so. If I had suggested it, or Dad, I'd say sure, but I don't know. Mother's a strange one. Wanted to know how come I was taking Pat tonight. When I told her Pat was a friend of yours, she suddenly asked whether I wouldn't like to have you come to dinner Sunday night."

"Did she say anything about your taking Pat?"

"Not much. Forget about it."

"But should I come to dinner Sunday?"

"Yes, I suppose so. Mother'll be displeased if you don't."

"All right, then, I'll come."

At the close of the dance June Thompson came over to them, dragging Don Wright behind her by the hand.

"Oh, Ruthie, darlin', I've been trying to see you all night. Hello, Jim," she said with a flutter of eyelashes. "I wanted to exchange some dances, but Don has so many friends, and I had to save some dances with him for myself."

"That's all right, June."

"So nice of you, honey." June smiled her brightest at Jim. "I'd like to dance with you, too, handsome, but I guess that'll have to wait. Nice to see you two *together* again."

"Come on, Junie, the next number is starting," Don Wright said impatiently. "Excuse me, huh?"

"Somebody ought to blow the star dust out of that gal's eyes," Jim scowled as he and Ruth walked toward Ken and Pat. "What'd she mean by the way she tied her tongue around that *together?*"

"You'll be surprised, handsome." Ruth said it the way June had just done. "Keep your eyes open for the next issue of *Windows*. Unless I'm mistaken, you'll be mentioned in it."

"Sounds like it's going to be terrifically important." Jim frowned.

"Jim, before I forget it," Ruth said hastily, "if I come to your house for dinner Sunday, you'll have to promise to have dinner with us the following Sunday. I know Mother would love to have you."

"That would be a pleasure," Jim said.

After it was all over that night, Ruth thought how soon a night of dancing was forgotten. Not everyone of them, understand, she qualified the thought for herself, but an awful lot of them. She didn't expect to forget some of the dances with Jim; and she was sure Tod Edwards wouldn't forget the C.S.M.C. dance when he met Barbara Connell. Since then, she'd been out with Tod only once and all he'd talked about was Barbara. He did the same thing when he walked her home from church on Sunday. And Mike Hafey wasn't likely to forget the first time he danced with Judy Kemper. There were some things you kept stored in the memory within easy reach; others you locked up and forgot about. Some things you remembered because they were funny, and some because they were sad, and some because they were dear.

Ruth remembered a lot of things from grammar school, like the boys pulling girls' hair, or undoing their hair ribbons. There was the time when Sister was out of the room and Tod and one of the other boys had had a fight because the boy had said Tod was skinny. Then there were the valentines she received in the class mail box every year, and the Halloween parties, and the first time she thought boys were nice people. That was when a boy drew her picture during class one day, and it was very good. She still had the picture some place in her dresser.

There were also the memories of the Sisters who taught her: the young ones who were pretty and played games with the children; the ones who looked stern and had their students trembling most of the time because they feared extra lines to write; the older ones, like Sister Leo, who didn't play much but made all the girls and boys feel pretty smart because they knew how to ask the right questions and in such a way that the children could figure out the answers. In Sister Leo's class the pupils were always good because they were always happy, like Sister herself, whose eyes were forever laughing. It had been something like being in Heaven to be in Sister Leo's class. She was holy and she made you feel that God was in the room with you all the time; so you just had to be happy.

Ruth wondered why she was thinking of the past tonight. Was it because she was trying to recall the time she was happiest in her life? She didn't know; she only knew that when she thought of happy memories, especially early ones, Sister Leo's little bent figure and laughing eyes always came up. She would have done anything for Sister Leo, like cleaning blackboards or giving out papers, or anything she wanted.

But then Ruth thought of Jim and his mother. That dinner invitation! Jim hadn't seemed too happy about it. How was she going to act in front of Mrs. Stevens? She would be afraid of what she said, and how she said it. She knew she couldn't be natural in front of someone who would be constantly comparing her to Barbara Connell and girls like her. Oh, well, Jim would be there, and he'd know what she should do. She'd ask him to coach her beforehand so she would make a good impression on his mother. Of course, Jim would help her.

18

*J*HE damask tablecloth was creased so that it divided the table into perfectly even parts, and on it the plates were arranged with such precision that Ruth could picture the maid portioning out the distance between each place with a tape measure. Alined next to the plates was such an array of silver knives, spoons, and forks that she was sure she'd use the wrong one some time during the meal. And Mrs. Stevens was the type who would notice even the slightest slip. The table was beautiful, but somehow it scared Ruth. She had gone to fairly formal dinners and to hotels to eat but this was so frightfully elaborate. In front of her place there were three goblets of exquisite cut-glass: one tall and chesty, like some butlers she had seen in the movies; the others small replicas of the first. But Ruth didn't know what they were all for. She was sorry Jim was sitting next to her, because she would have had more confidence in watching him as he ate than she had in his brother Gil, who sat opposite her. Still, the array before him didn't seem to bother Gil. Ruth told herself she wasn't going to stare at Mrs. Stevens, who sat at the head of the table to her left.

"Dear," said Mrs. Stevens to Ruth as the maid began to fill the glasses while they ate their fruit-cup, "we have claret and sauterne. But if you prefer some other wine, just inform Helen and she'll bring it for you."

Ruth smiled at the maid standing beside her and said, "No, thank you, this will do."

So there is such a thing as white wine. Ruth had thought all wine was red; all the poets and storytellers spoke of wine-red lips and the like. She wondered what it would taste like, whether she would like it.

After the soup had been served, Mr. Stevens asked Ruth, "Still stealing husbands from their wives at dances, Ruth?"

"Not for more than one dance," she replied lightly without meaning to be pert, but Jim's mother evidently took it that way. The look on her face told Ruth she had made her first mistake of the evening. She should have prefaced her remark with "No, sir." And maybe that's all she should have said.

Gil said, "Hey, Ruth, are you . . ."

"Gilbert," his mother said with a look of thunder on her face.

"I beg your pardon, Mother," Gil said. Then he went on, "Do you like horses, Ruth? They're running in Florida now."

"Yes, Gil, I do," Ruth replied, although she wondered whether Mrs. Stevens would approve of her calling Gilbert Gil. "But I don't know much about them."

"They're wonderful, beautiful creatures. Nothing so slick and graceful as a race horse."

"I certainly like to see them in the movies," Ruth agreed enthusiastically.

"You mean you haven't seen them run in the flesh?" asked Jim's father.

"No, Mr. Stevens, I haven't."

"Well," he smiled graciously, "you'll have to get Jim to take you to the Maryland Hunt Cup this year."

Jim began to say he'd love to do it, when his mother broke in, "You know James plans to take Barbara to the Hunt Cup."

"Well, then," Mr. Stevens continued, "maybe we can take her to the Preakness with us."

The Preakness—something all Baltimoreans hear about, most of them talk about, but few of them actually see. Ruth would have given anything to go, to see the best of the thoroughbreds in the country matching stride for stride around Pimlico's old course. To Baltimoreans the Preakness is *the* race. There is a pretty famous race run a week or so earlier in Kentucky called the Derby, but they look on it only as a trial run for the Preakness. Oh, it would be so good to see it! Shivers ran up and down Ruth's spine.

"It's too soon to be deciding about that now," Mrs. Stevens said, looking sharply down her nose at her husband, as much as to say to him, "The idea of such a thing!" To Ruth she said, "You know Barbara, don't you, dear?"

"Yes, Mrs. Stevens, I do."

"A very nice girl, isn't she?" But the question was a rhetorical one, and Jim's mother went right on, "I tell James that Barbara is the type of girl I admire. She is lovely to look at, has all the social graces to perfection, and has a most charming personality."

"Yes," Ruth agreed, "Barbara is a wonderful person. She makes a hit wherever she goes."

"Precisely." Mrs. Stevens and Ruth had the same opinion

on one subject at least. "And what she can see in that boy she's going with is more than I can comprehend." Her jaw set firmly. "Of course, it may be one of those passing whims. It's very strange, the things that will fascinate a teen-age girl."

Knowing Mrs. Stevens meant Tod, Ruth said nothing—and felt awfully disloyal about it. She fastened her eyes on the juicy roast beef before her and ran her knife through it with the ease of slicing bread. Out of the corner of her eye she caught sight of Jim. His face was flushed, and suddenly it occurred to her that all Mrs. Stevens' talk about Barbara had bothered him.

The meat tasted good, but she didn't know whether to compliment Mrs. Stevens, since she hadn't prepared the food at all. She sipped the wine and wasn't sure she liked it.

When everyone had finished eating the main course and the maid had cleared away the dishes, Mrs. Stevens grew manifestly impatient because the dessert wasn't brought in immediately. Ruth felt sorry for Helen, who seemed to be so kind and courteous. She could hardly be expected to do things any faster, Ruth thought, since she had to bring in everything in individual servings.

It had grown quiet at the table, and Ruth felt that she should say something—anything—to break the tension, so she burst out, "I—I want to thank you for inviting me tonight, Mrs. Stevens."

"Not at all, dear." If Mr. Stevens had said it, it would have sounded real. But Ruth couldn't tell what was real and what wasn't when Jim's mother spoke, because it all came out in such an affected voice that she felt none of it could be real. Still, she knew that, no matter how artificially people talk, they have to say some things which are real and sincere.

"I want James to bring his friends to meet the family, and I'm sure we want to meet his friends. You see, dear, we knew all about Barbara Connell long before James ever took her out. She's from one of the finest families and such a nice girl. I like her more every time I see her. And I know that if I had had any daughters, I would want them to be like Barbara."

Again Jim flushed, and Ruth said nothing. Jim hadn't done much talking during the dinner, and Ruth wondered if he were as afraid of saying the wrong thing as she was. If it hadn't been for Mr. Stevens and his sense of humor, and Gil's enthusiasm for horses—both of which drew some forbidding looks from Mrs. Stevens—Ruth didn't know what she would have done.

After the ice cream, there were nuts and mints, and finally black coffee in the most exquisite little cups. Ruth thought they looked like Canterbury bells. She couldn't believe this was the ordinary dinner the Stevens ate every day, but they seemed so natural about it that she had to admit it probably was. After it was over, they went to the living room. There the maid came with cigarettes, placing them on small tables near the large easy chairs. Mrs. Stevens took one, along with her husband and sons.

"Have a cigarette, dear," she said to Ruth.

Many of Mrs. Sterner's friends smoked but Ruth's mother had asked her not to because she felt that she was too young, so she answered hesitantly, "No, thank you, I—I don't smoke." And for the first time in her life Ruth felt it was a fault, because Mrs. Stevens seemed so surprised.

"I thought all girls smoked these days," she said. And when the maid brought in some drinks and Ruth didn't take any, she urged, "Go ahead, dear, take a glass. It won't hurt you. Just sip it slowly."

Ruth took a thimble-sized glass from the tray. The taste wasn't like anything she had experienced before, but anything would have tasted badly by now. Mrs. Stevens was almost kind at times, but to Ruth it seemed that she was merely pitying her while saying to herself: "Poor, unsophisticated girl, she doesn't know any better!"

When Jim said he'd take her home, Ruth was greatly relieved, because then she could begin to feel like herself again without having to watch everything she did and said. Jim asked the maid to bring Ruth's coat, and ran up the stairs, followed by his mother's disapproving eyes. He reappeared again in a few seconds with something in his hand that looked like an onionskin bag. He placed it on one of the tables and went to get his own coat.

"James, is that your monogram?" asked his mother.

"Yes, Mother."

"Are you going to give it to Barbara as I suggested?" And the question was a suggestion all over again, maybe even a warning that he had better give it to Barbara.

"No, Mother," Jim replied as he slipped one arm into his overcoat and picked up the package again. He wasn't offering any hints as to what he was going to do with it. "Ready, Ruth?"

Jim's mother said good-bye to Ruth sitting stiffly in her chair, but his father walked to the door with them. "It was nice having you, Ruth. Come again some time."

"Thank you, Mr. Stevens." Then Ruth was out in the car with Jim, driving toward her house. For a time they didn't say anything, but finally Jim pointed to the package between them on the seat of the car. "That's for you, if you want it."

"But, Jim, it's your letter for playing football."

"I know what it is. And I know I'd like you to wear it."
He didn't look at her at all, as she slipped the monogram from
the bag and fingered the knotty chenille as gently as if it were
silk. Of course, she wanted it; she'd be proud to wear it. She
held the letter against her cheek.

"But your—your mother wants you to give it to Barbara,"
Ruth said hesitantly.

Jim's face flushed. "Who earned the letter, anyhow? Mother
hasn't anything to do with it. And I don't want to give it to
Barbara. If you don't want it, it'll stay in my room. But Barbara's not getting it, that's for sure."

"Really, Jim," she said softly, "I'd like to have it, but . . ."

"But what?"

"I don't want to cause any trouble between you and your
mother."

"Listen, Ruth," Jim said hotly, "if you want the letter, take
it and forget about Mother. There are some stickers with the
school seal on them in the bag for Paul, too."

Overcome with emotion, Ruth whispered, "Thanks, Jim,"
and became silent.

"Ruth, did Mother embarrass you tonight?" Jim began again.

If she had said no, Jim would have known she was not telling
the truth. So she said, "A little."

"I'm sorry."

"Oh, she didn't mean it, Jim."

"I'm afraid she did," he replied in dead earnest. "I think
Mother invited you just to show me that Barbara can handle
herself better in any company."

"Well, I guess she showed you, all right," Ruth said sadly.
A tear formed in the corner of her eye. "I wish she had asked,
though. I would have admitted it without the experiment."

"Who gives a hang about that? You didn't do anything wrong. To tell you the truth—well—you had better 'social graces' than Mother!" Jim exploded. He made Ruth feel that all the hardships of the night were nothing; it didn't make any difference to him.

When they pulled up in front of Ruth's house, Jim didn't move to get out of the car, so neither did Ruth. She sat looking straight in front of her down the street, feeling that he had his head turned toward hers with his eyes searching into her mind. She wished he'd say something, but she was afraid to turn and say anything herself.

"Ruth," he finally said. And as she looked around, Jim's face leaned toward hers and she felt his lips softly on her cheek, just at the corner of her mouth. Then he moved quickly, saying as he sprang out, "You were swell tonight." He circled the car and held the door open for her. She got out without saying a word, unable to say anything, just feeling the swift softness of his kiss. She didn't look at Jim, and he didn't look at her as they walked to the front door.

Here she held out her hand. "Good night, Jim."

He took it in his and held it warmly, not shaking it, just holding it. And he looked into her eyes for the first time since the kiss. "You didn't mind, did you?"

She swallowed and said, "No, Jim. Good night." Then she pulled her hand from his and ran into the house. She stood just inside the door with a heart that raced, skipped a beat; raced, skipped a beat, and danced.

19

"HEY, Ruth!" Paul met his sister at the front door as she came in from school the next day. "Look what I won in the spelling contest today." He held up a holy picture which his teacher had cut from *The Messenger of the Sacred Heart*, pasted on wallpaper and decorated with ribbons. Ruth remembered the stack of them she used to have at one time, but she couldn't recall what had happened to them. Once they had meant so much; now they were just memories.

"Swell, Paul," she said. "Come up to my room and I'll show you what Jim gave *me* last night."

"What'd he give you?" Paul inquired as they started up the stairs.

"You wait and see." She beamed. "You'll be surprised. It's something special." On reaching her room, Ruth went straight to the dresser, opened the top drawer, and handed Paul the stickers Jim had sent him. "These are yours."

"Oh, boy!" Paul exclaimed. He was going to say more, when Ruth interrupted him.

"And *this* is for me." Pride stood out all over Ruth as she held Jim's varsity "L" in her hand, her fingers gliding over the blue and gold chenille, her eyes fixed on her brother, who stared at the letter in awed admiration.

"Gosh!" Paul's eyes opened their widest. "Did Jim *give* that to you?"

"Of course." It sounded as if it were the most natural thing in the world, as if she herself had expected it all along, and had received it with the greatest calm,—which she obviously had not!

"Let me see it." Paul held it before his chest—it reached to his waist. "Boy, just wait till I play for Loyola; I'm going to win a whole lot of letters. And *no* girl is going to get *any* of them!"

"Stingy."

"I'm not stingy. What're you going to do with it?"

"Wear it on the back of my trench coat. I've already got Tod's 'C' on my jacket."

"That thing—I wouldn't be seen with it. Hey, what's happened to Tod, anyway? He hasn't been around much lately."

"Thought you didn't like him?"

"Don't worry, I don't."

"Well, just don't forget to thank Jim for those stickers when he comes to dinner Sunday night."

"Is he going to eat with us?"

"That's what you usually do at dinner, isn't it?" Ruth laughed at Paul when he exclaimed indignantly, "You know what I meant!"

Windows appeared that week, as scheduled, and the first thing Ruth did was to turn to June Thompson's column. She smiled as she read what were subtle hints about Jim and herself. They were so veiled that she thought no one would know what June was talking about. But she couldn't help wondering what June would have written if she had been free to say what she pleased, if the Sisters allowed a real gossip column in the school paper.

Not one to be restrained by what she termed "dictatorship to the press," June amplified and clarified what she had written until the girls began to ask unendingly, "Oh, Ruth, did you have a fight with Jim Stevens?" "What'd he do to you?" "What did *you* do to him?" Someone giggled. "Is it true, or just June sounding off?" "Pat steal your boy friend?" Some of the girls sympathized with her; some were just plain curious; but most of them just asked teasingly, "What happened to your one-and-only?"

Though Ruth had meant only to return the quips, she found herself feeling strangely out of tune with her words as she said as casually as she could, "When did *he* become my one-and-only? You don't see me sitting home crying, do you? Maybe I found something better." That at least would pique June's curiosity, she thought, all the while telling herself she'd explain her seeming disloyalty to Jim when she saw him. It would be a real shock for June the next time she saw them together.

So completely did Ruth shatter the effect of June's gossip that by the end of the week no one asked her about it any more. Most of the girls took it for granted that, whatever the reason, Ruth wasn't the least bit worried about what June said. Only Pat Boyle, who realized she had been the cause of the whole thing, had the real explanation. Then Ruth started the corridors buzzing again the next Friday by wearing her trench coat to school with Jim's letter very conspicuously displayed on the back.

On Saturday Ruth did the shopping for the next day's meal with particular care. She often did this to help her mother. But today's marketing was extra-special because Jim was coming for Sunday dinner. Along the route through the old Baltimore market, which took her from this stall to that to purchase the many different items of food, she met Judy Kemper.

"Hi, Judy, how's your basketball coming?"

"We're having a good year," the regular forward on Catholic High's team answered with enthusiasm. "Beat Southern yesterday. How come you're not playing for the Institute?"

"Not good enough. I went out for the team, but the coach decided she had enough players who are much better than I am."

After glancing around to make sure no one was within hearing distance of them, Judy said seriously, "Ruth, I was talking to Mike last night. . . ."

"Dating you steadily now, isn't he?"

"Yes, that's what I wanted to say. He told me you were the one who told him to ask me to his prom."

"I only told him he ought to ask someone."

"Well, anyway, I want to thank you. We had a wonderful time. Mike's a . . . well, he's . . . You know what I mean. He's not shy at all after you get to know him. He's so different then. Thanks again," Judy said through moistening eyes, and hurried away.

When Ruth had picked up quite a few of the things on her mother's list, she headed for Decker's store, just across from the market. The handle of the now loaded basket cut into her arm, and she let it slip down into her hand where it hurt less but seemed to increase in weight.

Pete got over to wait on her as soon as he could.

"Hi, ya, beautiful! What can I do for you today?" Pete took Ruth's list and began stacking things on the counter. "You should have been over to the C.Y.O. last night. We had a great time."

"I'll be there next week," Ruth said as she tried to find room in her basket for the various articles Pete was piling up. "Right now I've got to hurry home and help tidy up for tomorrow. We're having a guest to dinner."

"But, Ruth, you can't carry that heavy load. Here, leave it with me and I'll deliver it the first chance I get." Pete came around from behind the counter and picked up the basket. "You won't need any of this stuff before this afternoon, will you?"

"No, thanks, Pete. See you this afternoon. Say hello to Betty for me."

"Gladly. I take every opportunity to say hello to Betty."

When she reached home, Ruth found that her mother was out and that Paul had skipped off without doing the tasks assigned to him. Deciding she could easily add his chores to her own, she shrugged her shoulders and went to get the vacuum cleaner.

After Marge had finished the cleaning upstairs, Ruth joined her in the kitchen, and as the girls were preparing lunch, she said, "Pete Decker's going to deliver our groceries this afternoon. Wouldn't be surprised if he hung around for a while. Pick out some records he likes, if you go down to the cellar."

"All right, I could go for a bit of dancing," Marge agreed as she took up some of the things Ruth had removed from the refrigerator and began putting them back. "We're not going to have dinner," she explained. "Mom is meeting Dad downtown. We don't even have to use the dining room; we can eat here in the kitchen."

Paul didn't show up for lunch, so when the girls had finished, they washed their dishes and put things in order. Then Marge went to the cellar to listen to some music, while her older sister completed her cleaning.

The last thing Ruth got to was the clothes closet, and when she had hung the coats in order, she closed the door with a sigh of relief. Momentarily she leaned against the closet, surveying herself in the mirror on the wall opposite. She smiled at herself and fluffed her longish black hair. As she did so, she suddenly wondered what she would look like in a veil. Fascinated, she reached into the closet and pulled out an old black scarf which she put on her head and gathered under her chin. "Horrible!" she said, making a face. She slid the scarf farther back on her head, allowing her rich hair to show. "That's it. Jim would like me better that way, I'm sure. Yes, I think I'll go to college before I decide about becoming a nun."

"Hey, Ruth." She heard Paul call as he closed the back door. She slipped the scarf into the closet just before her brother reached her.

"Hi, did Mom leave money for me to go to the movies?" he asked, out of breath from running up the stairs.

"She usually does," Ruth said coldly.

"Can I have it?"

"I suppose so." And she handed him some of her own money, since she didn't really know whether her mother had left him the price of a movie. When Ruth made no other comment, Paul wanted to know what was the matter.

"You ought to know."

"I don't know anything. What's wrong?"

"Why didn't you come in for lunch?"

"I'm going to bring a sandwich to the movies with me."
Paul started toward the kitchen, sending a boyish whistle echoing through the house. Then Ruth suddenly remembered that
it was Lent and called her brother back. Paul didn't come all
the way; he stood by the dining room table and demanded to
know what Ruth wanted now.

"You're not going to movies during Lent, are you?"

Why did she have to remember that, when he had forgotten
all about it? No, he wasn't going to movies during Lent, but he
could have gone and enjoyed himself, and everything would
have been all right because he had forgotten that it was Lent.
Now he'd have to do something else.

"But some of the gang are going and I don't want to miss the
show," he was saying as Ruth advanced toward him. "I'll give
up candy instead."

"I thought you said you were giving up *movies* for Lent."
Ruth held out her hand for the money.

"Aw, but, Ruth . . ."

"No buts about it. Give me my money."

"Well, I guess I can use the money, if Mom left it for me,"
Paul said, holding the change tightly in his hand.

"But Mom didn't leave that money. It's mine. And you can't
have it to go to movies after you resolved not to go during
Lent. You know Mom wouldn't give you any money for that."

"Suppose I don't go to the movies," Paul said hopefully as
a new idea came into his mind, "can I have the money?"

"You little robber, you!" Ruth gave in with a laugh and tried
to throw her arms around her young brother. He slipped away

agilely and said, "Thanks, Ruth. I didn't really want to go to the movies anyway. We'd rather tape up some hockey sticks with the tar tape we can buy with this money."

"Hey, you, come back here with that," Ruth called after Paul who was already out the door, oblivious of the fact that he hadn't had anything to eat—or had he? Ruth smiled to herself. "The little monkey!"

20

THE next morning Ruth was up in time for early Mass, from which she hurried home to help her mother with the dinner, because everything had to be perfect for Jim. If the distances between places at the Stevens' table had been exact, Ruth was determined that they would be just so at the Sterner table to-day, and she got out the tape measure to make sure of it. Insisting that they use the best silver, she arranged it until she was satisfied that it looked as perfect as the silver had at Jim's house the week before. Between making a cake batter and putting it in the oven, and fixing a salad, Ruth put the china and glasses on the table, and added a graceful flower centerpiece she had arranged as the finishing touch.

When Jim arrived, Ruth met him at the door and took his hat and coat. "Make yourself at home," she said, "while I put your things away."

Jim was looking at the latest issue of *Windows* when Ruth came into the living room and sat down next to him. "You write anything for this one?" he asked casually.

"Nothing that would interest you," Ruth replied, trying to be just as offhand as he had been. Of all things, why did he have to pick up that paper? She had intended to put it away when she cleaned yesterday.

As he was about to fold the paper and put it down, Jim's eye was attracted by the mention of Ruth's name in June Thompson's column. "Wouldn't be talking about us, would she?" he questioned. Looking at Ruth, he chuckled, "Serious business, eh?"

"June thinks so." Ruth sighed as she let her head rest on the back of the sofa. "And she certainly has the girls talking. And of course I wouldn't tell them it wasn't true. What I said was that you're just another boy, and all that sort of thing."

"Oh!"

"And when they asked questions about it, I said they wouldn't see me missing any dances because of you."

Subdued, Jim said, "I guess you had a lot of fun."

Sensing suddenly that Jim would have preferred to have her deny what June wrote in the paper, her previous feeling of disloyalty came back to her, disturbing as a dash of cold water thrown on a person basking in the sun. With some embarrassment she said, "Of course, all my friends know it isn't true. They know I'd rather go out with you than with anyone else, Jim."

He smiled self-consciously as Paul re-entered the parlor to announce, "Dad's home, so we can eat now."

After grace, Jim helped Ruth with her chair. Warmed by her smile, he began to look after all her needs until Mr. Sterner said, "She's big enough to ask for what she wants, Jim. Eat your dinner and enjoy it; she won't starve."

Without any of the strain, Jim fell into conversation with her father about the old and new Loyola, and with Paul about sports. And he didn't overlook praise for Mrs. Sterner's cooking. That put him in good standing with Ruth's mother. But Paul corrected him when he congratulated her on the cake.

"Mom didn't make it," he managed through a too-full mouth oozing chocolate at its corners. "Ruth did."

"Well, your mother probably taught her how, so I'll congratulate them both. How's that, Paul?"

"Okay with me. I don't care much who makes it as long as it's good." And he filled his mouth again. "*Mmmmmm*, I like chocolate cake."

"It's really that good, too, Ruth," Jim agreed.

"Thanks, Jim." That made the dinner a complete success— he liked her cake!

Although Mrs. Sterner wanted to do the dishes herself and let the girls off for a change, they insisted on doing them. Jim argued, "You worked hard enough preparing the meal. We can at least do the dishes for you, Mrs. Sterner." The novelty of doing dishes held for him a strange homey delight, unknown to those who have to wash dishes often.

"Thank you, Jim, but I'd better do them. I don't like to trust boys with dishes. After watching my own, I know from experience what terrible dish washers they make. Besides, you might get splashed."

"We can give him an apron," Marge volunteered. "That'd make him look cute."

"And," Jim added, "Ruth and Marge can inspect my work."

"No, thank you, Jim."

But with even Paul anxious to do the work, and with all of them repeating that she was *not* going to do it, Mrs. Sterner finally gave in. Then Ruth handed Jim a frilly apron which he threw over his head. She tied a big bow behind his back. Paul draped his arm with dish towels and took delight in showing him where to put the various plates and saucers after they were dried.

"We ought to have you to help with the dishes more often, Jim," Marge said. "This is going much more smoothly than usual. Most of the time we have to chase Paul all over the house before we can get him to do any work."

"I do as much work as you do," Paul retorted.

"I'll bet he does," Jim agreed.

"See, what did I tell you?" Paul shot at Marge.

Almost as if in answer to Mrs. Sterner's dictum about not trusting boys to do dishes, Jim let a glass slip from his hand and crash to the floor. Looking at it stupidly, as if wishing it would come back together again, he said, "Gosh, Ruth, I'm sorry!"

At the obvious consternation in his voice, Marge giggled, but Ruth laughed out loud. "Well, don't stand there looking silly," she said mercilessly. "Pick up the pieces."

"Don't worry, Jim. I break plenty of them. We've got more," Paul consoled him. "I'll pick up the pieces for you."

"Be careful, Paul. Don't cut yourself," Ruth warned. And as Jim stooped to help her brother, she added, "Get on with your drying, Jim. I can't spare both of you. Mother won't say anything about the glass, but *I'll* be cross if we don't finish soon."

When the work was completed, Ruth began to push Jim, apron and all, toward the door. "You lead the way, Paul. Marge, stay with me in case he tries to escape."

In the living room Ruth announced, "Mrs. Sterner, this *wretch* broke one of your best glasses."

"Shame, shame, SHAME!" chanted the Sterners before they burst out laughing. "Oh, Jim," cried Mrs. Sterner in mock distress, "I don't know how I'll ever replace that glass!"

When he could stop laughing with them, Jim said, "Really, I'm sorry, Mrs. Sterner, and I'll get you a new glass. Thanks for being so nice about it."

"That's all right, Jim." And the way Mrs. Sterner smiled and looked at him told him she meant it. His mother would have said the same thing, but Jim knew that with her it would not have been all right. "Now you see why I don't like boys to do dishes," she said as she relaxed in her armchair again. "But don't you even think about replacing that glass unless you don't want to remain a friend of mine."

"What do you have planned for the rest of the afternoon, Jim?" Mr. Sterner asked.

"I've made arrangements to meet Charlie Kelly and Edith Welch at the zoo in Druid Hill park. After that, Edith has invited us to her house for a buffet supper followed by whatever she has planned—probably dancing and listening to the radio."

"Then Ruth won't be home for supper?"

"No, sir," Jim replied, "but I'll have her in before ten tonight."

"I've finished my homework," Ruth chimed in, just in case her father needed a little persuasion.

Before leaving the house that afternoon, Ruth insisted that Jim come to the cellar because she wanted to show Paul something. "He thinks you're a sissy, you know."

"I don't!" Paul almost shouted as he followed them down the cellar stairs.

"You said dancing was for sissies, didn't you?" Ruth questioned gleefully.

"I never said Jim was a sissy."

"Girls have a conspiracy against boys, Paul, always picking on us," Jim said in a way that cemented his friendship with Ruth's little brother. "I know you didn't say anything against me."

Ruth put Paul in a chair and said, "Now you watch this." She put on a lilting record. Probably this whole business is a ruse to get a few extra dances with Jim, she told herself, but I like it anyway.

Later, when she and Jim reached the zoo, it was nearly four o'clock, and since it was a warm day the people were out in droves. Little children running in and out of the milling throng made happy noises. Still younger ones were too thrilled with big red balloons and the strange animals to say anything— they just threw up their feet in sheer joy and brought them down on thudding heels. It was only the hold of parents on their hands that kept them from tumbling to the ground in their gladness.

"Jim, look at that!" Ruth was smiling and pointing to a tiny girl in her mother's arms in front of the lion's cage. The lion had roared, and the baby was trying to hide herself in her mother's shoulder. About all that could be seen of her was the gold of her hair and the red bow tied on to it.

Jim wanted to stay and watch this small girl, but they had to look for their friends. "I told Charlie we'd meet them near the elephant house."

Passing the concession stand, Ruth laughed at the tiny tots who were eating ice cream and getting as much of it outside their mouths as inside, and the ones who were drinking soft drinks with mouths which looked as if they would suck in the entire bottle. "Jim," she pleaded, "buy me some peanuts."

After meeting Charlie and Edith, Ruth wanted to throw peanuts at the monkeys. "Watch me hit the one in the corner on the head with this nut," she boasted.

The others jeered when she missed. "I'll do it *this* time," she kept repeating, as time and again she threw and missed. When she did hit him, she had just about emptied the bag of nuts, and contentedly she decided to eat the remaining ones herself. The almost-spring-weather made her feel as frisky as some of the monkeys swinging about in their cages, and she challenged the others to a race to the drinking fountain. Jim let her cover half the distance before he started, but he still beat her to the goal.

"Meanie," she gasped above panting laughter.

"Better be careful," Jim threatened, pointing to the near-by alligator pit, "or I'll throw you in with them."

"I dare you."

Seizing her arms, Jim began to lift her off her feet. Her face came very near to his and she said in his ear, "Jim, put me down; people are watching us."

He looked at her, stopped laughing for a few seconds—Ruth thought he was going to kiss her again—then he only laughed some more and let her go. "Be good now," he warned, "and don't go daring people to do things."

After romping about the park for another half-hour, the four young people set out for Edith's house. And soon—it seemed about as long as it took a sky rocket to fade on the Fourth of July to Ruth—they were on their way home. Then Jim kissed her good night; and for the second time Ruth couldn't say anything and had to hurry into the house.

21

It WAS raining. Big drops of an early spring shower splattered against the window beside which Ruth was sitting as she rode the streetcar to school. Teeming with people—office workers, laborers, students, maids—the car smelled of stale air, wet hair, and damp leather seats. When people shuffled toward the back of the car at the urging of the conductor, Ruth heard dirt grinding under their feet; and the girl in the seat in front of her was tracing a face on the steamed-up window and getting a kick out of it. Outside, she saw through the haze on the window an occasional woman struggling with an umbrella threatening to turn inside out at the behest of the wind that ran and whistled, and scattered rain like a boy in summer with a hose.

On such days school is dull, and Ruth found herself nodding sleepily during nearly every class. Everyone's spirit seemed dampened and only simulating activity, while the lights in the room tried desperately to take the place of the sun, but their glow was only a ray, a sunbeam not the sun, and they gave no warmth. Not until the Principal came to distribute reports during the last period was Ruth able to arouse herself to anything more than passivity. That the Principal said nothing when handing over her report surprised Ruth, for she nearly always had some comment to make, either of encouragement or warning. But today she said a cold nothing, and as soon as Ruth had glanced at the marks on her report card, she knew why. It had been a rebuke, an un-needed one, for Ruth's heart sank to her toes and she almost trod on it as she walked back to her seat. She managed to put a blank look on her face in an effort not to register any sign of her inner feelings to the eyes of the whole class which she felt to be on her. Upon reaching her seat, she looked once more at the marks on her card, slumped in her chair, and slid the card into its envelope in one mechanical motion.

After the final period was over, Ruth hurried to Sister Elizabeth's classroom, praying all the while that none of her girls would be there and that she might have a good long talk with her. Although there were still a few girls with Sister, Ruth went in anyhow and asked if she might have a talk with her. Sister said of course, the way she always did, and told the other girls she'd see them the next day after school.

When they had gone, she turned to Ruth and asked, "Well, Ruth, did the rain wash your smile away today?"

"Look at this," Ruth muttered and handed the report to Sister Elizabeth.

The nun studied the marks carefully, her eyes moving from the card to Ruth's face, which was turned from her, and then back to the report. "Well," she said after her examination, "there must be some reason for this, Ruth. What's the matter? Haven't you been studying? Too many dates?"

Though she felt the genuine solicitude in Sister's words, Ruth was upset and, immediately on the defensive when dates were mentioned, she blurted out, "Not studying and dates don't have anything to do with it. It's Sister Philothea, that's all. She doesn't like me; she tries in every way to find something she can lower my marks for, and if she finds anything, she takes off as much as she possibly can for it."

Knowing that when a girl is perturbed and near to tears it's almost impossible to reason with her, Sister Elizabeth nevertheless attempted this with Ruth, making use of all the tact she possessed and coupling it with her sympathy. "Ruth," she said in a voice soft enough to slip by the girl's defiant stare, "you don't like Sister Philothea, and possibly she hasn't any great affection for you. But you don't honestly think, do you, that Sister would mark you unfairly?"

Disarming as the nun's words were, Ruth was moved only to state her accusation in an indirect way. "Look at the other marks then. How are you going to account for the difference?" She blinked her eyes and squeezed a tear out of the corner of one of them.

In an attempt to steer away from any mention of Sister Philothea, Sister Elizabeth tried to encourage Ruth. "But, really, Latin's the only poor mark you have, Ruth. Your English mark is above eighty and only a little below your other grades."

"Yes, but it should have been above the others. And I'll bet you I know more Latin than a lot of girls who got much higher marks than that seventy of mine."

"I'm sure there must be some reason for the marks, Ruth. Perhaps the reason is a misunderstanding of your ability. Whatever it is, I'm sure Sister Philothea didn't give you low grades for no reason at all." When Ruth opened her mouth to reply, Sister went on, "You don't think that's right, I know. Maybe Sister was mistaken, but I'm sure she wouldn't do it purposely. And if you think the marks are the wrong ones, the best advice I can give you is to forget about them and prove the mistake with the grades you get on your next report."

"Forget about them?" Ruth choked. "But what are my mother and father going to say? They'll want an explanation. And what do you expect me to tell them?"

"What can you tell them except that you think you didn't deserve them? It will be difficult to explain, Ruth. But your parents are reasonable people and if you tell them in a rational, quiet way that you think Sister Philothea made some mistake, they'll certainly be willing to wait for the next report to see that you can do better, especially since your other marks are all above average." Sister smiled at Ruth and went on. "It's one of the many hard things that will happen in your life. Though you may feel you're willing to face all of them, except the ones that aren't your own fault, you will find that you will have to bear even those things that come to you through no fault of your own as well. In fact, those are often the hardest to face, because everyone wants justice done her by others. But no matter where you go or what you do, you won't escape entirely from injustices of some sort." Sister went from where she had been standing near to Ruth and sat at her desk. "But suppose we both try to forget about this one mistake, even if it looks like a tremendous one to you right now. It won't be so bad in a few days, I assure you. That's the way it is with most of our troubles. They look big only while we actually have them. Afterward they sometimes seem very funny."

Twisting her class ring around and around on her finger, Ruth looked up at Sister Elizabeth and gave a halting smile that was a lame attempt to show her gratitude and to laugh at herself. She wouldn't worry about the marks as long as she was with Sister, she knew, but the thought of them would be like a bully waiting around the corner of her mind for her as soon as she left the room.

"You haven't been around here for a long time, Ruth," remarked Sister Elizabeth in an effort to open another conversation on whatever subject pleased Ruth. "What have you been doing with yourself, besides disagreeing with June Thompson?"

"Oh, lots of things." Ruth smiled and felt warmness run all through her suddenly, the rush of memories racing with her blood. And then she began to talk with a new flow of words, telling the nun all that had happened since the last time she had been in to see her, forgetting completely why she had come to her that day.

While Ruth talked, Sister wondered; she watched the glow in the girl's eyes. Had Ruth lost something, or found it? She felt as if she herself were losing something in the joy that accompanied Ruth's words. Though she continued to smile outwardly, she began to feel empty inside. And after the girl had run on through all the joys that had been hers, Sister felt constrained to ask the question she had been tempted a thousand times to call her in and ask her. "Ruth, have you given up thinking about a religious vocation?"

The question took the laughter from Ruth's lips. She looked at her friend and thought she could see in her eyes all the hopes she had had, the prayers she had said. And she felt for a moment as if she had failed the nun. But when she thought of her own uncertainty, she answered, "No, I haven't given up thinking about it, but I think I'll go to college first."

Sister Elizabeth folded her hands. "Why do you want to do that?"

"I just can't make up my mind now," Ruth said simply. "I'll be more mature when I've finished college, and then I'll know my own mind better."

"Have you done much praying and thinking about it, Ruth?"

"Sometimes."

"And you feel you don't have a vocation?" The question came straight and clear, just a question with no hint of the answer expected.

"Sometimes," was Ruth's uneasy answer.

"But sometimes you think you have one still."

"I never thought I *had* one; I thought I *might* have one. And sometimes I think I still might have, but it's all so uncertain that I've decided to go to college first." But down inside her Ruth felt she was hedging; she didn't want to face the issue. And Jim Stevens had something to do with the whole thing. "I've been meaning to come in and tell you."

"Oh," Sister said and sat without further comment for a few seconds that seemed eternity to Ruth. Looking at her hands and thinking about something, posing a question for herself and weighing possible distinctions before placing it, the nun sat, not seeing the girl before her. Finally she looked up and asked boldly, "Ruth, do you know what you're doing?"

Ruth looked out the window at the wet street still being washed by the rain. "I think so."

Very calmly Sister said, "I doubt it, because I think you're running away from a vocation. You aren't giving God a chance."

"I'm not running away from anything," Ruth replied with a

deal of fiery warmth. "If I were sure I had a vocation, I'd say so right now, but I'm not sure at all, nowhere near it. And I'm sure I like the way I'm living now. I like dates, and dances, and friends. It seems to be a choice between an uncertainty and a certainty. I don't want to give up the things I like so much now unless I'm sure I have a vocation."

"All right, Ruth." Sister Elizabeth's tone of voice was very quiet as she proceeded. "When did you first begin to feel you didn't have a vocation?"

"I'm not sure." Ruth was confused. She tried to remember when it was, what had happened, why. She wasn't certain about anything—everything was such a mess. It was probably after one of those dates with Jim that she had first thought about not having a vocation—after one of those dances. But which one? Was there one at which she had had a better time than all the others? She couldn't remember.

As if reading her mind, Sister Elizabeth broke the silence. "Has that boy anything to do with it?"

"I think so, Sister."

"But I thought you told me you couldn't get serious about him?"

Then it dawned on Ruth that Sister Elizabeth was thinking about Tod Edwards. "Oh, no, Sister." She couldn't help the laugh which escaped her—to compare Tod with Jim! "It's not the one I mentioned the last time I was talking with you." She became very serious again. "No, this is another one."

"Then it must be that Jim Stevens the girls mention," Sister guessed, but her statement was really a question, and Ruth answered it as such—in the affirmative.

"I see. Do you like him, Ruth?"

"Very much."

After another pause during which the nun studied the girl, Sister began, "Well, Ruth, I don't want to seem to be pushing you into a vocation. You probably wouldn't stop going with this Stevens boy if I suggested it anyhow. And then, maybe you don't have a vocation." Ruth smiled hopefully before Sister continued, "But since you haven't completely lost the idea, I'll ask you to do only one thing."

"What's that?"

"Give it a chance. You'll never decide as long as you keep shoving the idea into some pigeonhole in your mind every time it comes up. It's something like people who come to visit you; if you keep telling them to come back later, the time will come when they will stay away for good. And if you'll only try to work this thing out during these last days of Lent, I'm sure you'll be able to make up your mind one way or the other. Then if you decide you like boys and that sort of thing better, I won't say anything because I'll know you at least gave Our Lord His chance. Everyone isn't called to the religious life, and marriage and motherhood are perfectly beautiful vocations, too. Don't forget that, Ruth."

When she left Sister Elizabeth that afternoon, Ruth had forgotten all about the report card. She had bigger things to think about, vital things. She didn't even notice the rain that was still falling.

22

"RUTH, can I take you out tonight?" Jim asked. There was a ring of urgency to his voice even before he added, "I've got to talk to you."

Hesitantly Ruth said she'd ask her mother, though she knew what the reply would be before she posed the question. Since that report card she wasn't allowed out more than once a week end, and here was Jim on the phone asking her to go out on a week-day night. The expected no came without hesitation on the part of Ruth's mother.

"But, Mom," she pleaded, "Jim says it's important. He has something to tell me."

"Does he have to see you to tell you?" her mother asked drily. "Can't he tell you over the phone?"

That was Ruth's chance to score. "You know what you'll say if we spend a long time on the phone."

"For heaven's sake, Ruth, it's not going to take him all night, is it?"

"But he doesn't want to tell me over the phone—and it's important."

"I don't care how important it is," Mrs. Sterner repeated. "You're not going out tonight because you have school tomorrow, and I'm not going to have you get another report like that last one if I can help it."

"But, Mom, I told you that report was all a mistake. There won't be any more like it."

"You're keeping Jim waiting on the phone," replied Mrs. Sterner, indicating she had said all she intended to.

"Please, Mom." Ruth tried her last and most heart-wringing plea, but it had no effect. She went to the phone and told Jim she couldn't go out because her mother wouldn't let her.

"Well, I'm coming over anyhow," Jim said with determination, and hung up before Ruth could say anything else.

She went and told her mother, "Jim says he's coming over anyhow. Now I've got to see him. You know he wouldn't do that unless he had something really important to say."

"He shouldn't do it for any reason." Mrs. Sterner put down her sewing and looked at her daughter. "And you're not going out with him. I'm surprised at Jim. I had a higher opinion of him."

"But I've got to see him, Mom. You don't understand."

"I understand that he's going against my wishes and trying to force my hand."

"He's not doing anything like that, Mom," Ruth insisted, "at least, not purposely. Jim's got something important to see me about and"—her voice became high-pitched and as determined as Jim's had been over the phone—"I'm going to see him."

"If you expect me to shout back at you, Ruth, you'll have a long wait." Mrs. Sterner began to sew again. "If you were younger, you'd get a spanking. But you're old enough to realize you will be deliberately disobedient if you go out with Jim tonight. When he comes, I'll not say anything to him; it will be entirely up to you. If you go out with him, remember you are disobeying me."

"All right," Ruth said, as she swallowed a lump in her throat. She went upstairs to change her dress before going out with Jim. She hurried to be ready when he arrived, because she knew his reception would be a cold one. She was waiting at the door for him when he came. She called to her mother, "I'll be back as soon as I can, Mom," and she went out.

Since Jim had come on a bus and had no place in particular to go, they decided to walk—no place in particular.

"What'd your mother say when you told her I was coming anyhow?"

"She still wouldn't give her consent; she said I was being disobedient." And her actions bothered Ruth more than anything she had ever done. It was the first time she had been coldly, deliberately disobedient.

"I'm sorry if I've caused you any trouble, Ruth," Jim said. "But I had to talk with you. Mother insists that I take Barbara Connell to the Mothers' Club dance Easter Monday."

"But, Jim, you asked me to go."

"I know, but it seems Mother made these arrangements with Barbara's mother quite some time ago, and she insists that since she made her engagement first, I should tell you it's all off." Jim stopped and looked at Ruth. "I couldn't tell you that over the phone. I had to be here to explain."

Ruth nodded her head and murmured, "I understand."

"You don't understand at all, Ruth, if you think I'm going to take Barbara after I asked you. I did that before, but not this time. When Mother told me about it, I said I wasn't taking Barbara and I didn't stay to argue with her about it. I said I was going out. I called you from a drugstore."

"Well, Jim, I don't know what to say."

"Look, Ruth, if you'll still go to the dance with me, I won't pay any attention to Mother at all. That's what I wanted to tell you tonight."

Ruth heard her heels clicking on the ground, striking mournful notes, beating a dirge. She looked at Jim and said, "But she's your mother, Jim."

"I know," he answered, knitting his brow. "But she hasn't any right to make dates for me without telling me about it. Some day we've got to face the fact that Mother isn't running my life for me as she used to when I was a kid and it was her place to do it. If you'll go with me, I'll take you."

"But she'll be angry, Jim." Ruth thought of her own mother. "And hurt." She didn't want to hurt anybody anymore.

"But it's got to happen some day," Jim said, "and it may as well be now. Dad will understand, I'm sure, when I explain it all to him. It's all right, isn't it? After all, I did ask you. Let Mother worry about Barbara now."

They had walked quite some distance by the time Ruth said, "Jim, you'd better take Barbara. I won't mind not going, and everything will be better that way."

"But it's not fair to you. I'm not going to take her, and that's all there is to it."

"Yes, you are, Jim." It pained Ruth deep down inside to say it, the way it did when she had turned away from her mother and come out tonight; she wasn't going to be the cause of Jim's mother being hurt too. "I'm not going with you."

"Don't you want to, Ruth?"

"Of course, but it would only cause a lot of trouble," Ruth replied. She turned around. "Let's start back."

"Want a Coke or some ice cream first?"

"No, thanks."

Jim took up the subject again. "But look, Ruth, if you want to go, let's go."

"No, Jim."

"But, Ruth, I want you to. I don't want to take Barbara or anyone else. I just want to take you."

"I'm sorry."

"Well, then," he insisted, "come with me just because I want you to."

"No, Jim." The words came slowly to lips that quivered as they formed the words that were so contrary to the way Ruth actually felt. "I'm not going, and that's all there is to it." After trying a smile that didn't come through with anything like reality, she gave up the attempt and said, "Let's not talk about it any more."

When Jim didn't reply, Ruth knew he was angry and hurt. And because she knew he wanted her to say she'd go to the dance with him, she felt she was betraying their friendship. Friends are supposed to want the same things, supposed to be united in will, and here she was doing the opposite of what Jim wanted her to do, the opposite of what she wanted to do. She was right and she knew it, but all her feelings were against her, just as Jim's were; only she wondered if he knew underneath it all that she was doing what she thought was right, the best thing. If she acted otherwise, she wouldn't have been happy, whether she went to the dance or not. This was the only way.

After that, Jim answered her questions in monosyllables, and when Ruth wasn't plying him with questions he said nothing. By the time they reached her house Ruth was finding it as difficult to talk to him as it was for her to try to carry on a conversation with Sister Philothea, who generally answered her with finality and in as few words as possible. At the door Jim said good night briefly and hurried away.

Inside, Ruth hung up her coat and went to her mother, who was still sewing. Mrs. Sterner didn't look up at her daughter. She kept her eyes fixed on her fingers working the needle and thread through the cloth in her hands. As she worked, she rocked slowly back and forth, the old-fashioned rocker creaking with each backward motion like an old lady stiff in the joints. The light fell on her mother's face and Ruth thought she looked sad, tired—almost old. Sorrow pulled at Ruth's heart. She hesitated in the doorway as she said in a voice barely above a whisper, "I'm sorry, Mom."

There was no reply save the steady *creak . . . creak . . . creak*. Perhaps the fingers moved a little more rapidly, Ruth wasn't sure, but the head hadn't altered a bit. It was still at the same angle, bending over the work. Whether it was or not, it could only appear to Ruth a weary head, bent with sadness, and she couldn't leave it that way. "Mom," she began again, but she couldn't go on. The tears choked her.

"Yes, Ruth?" came the response. The head was still bent over the needlework. But a mother couldn't ignore a daughter's contrition.

"Mom, I'm sorry." Ruth rushed across the room and fell on her knees beside the rocker, letting her head fall into her mother's lap. "I'm sorry."

Mrs. Sterner carefully got her sewing out of the way of her daughter, as she said very calmly, "All right, Ruth, don't cry."

But Ruth couldn't help it—too many things had been kept back too long. Now they poured out with her tears. She told her mother how she just had to see Jim that night, how she couldn't help not liking his mother. Her sobs became bigger, longer, as she told of her confusion over the report card, the struggle over what to do in life. "It's all so—so hard," she said as she dropped her head into her mother's lap again and let the tears run freely.

To cry with her daughter would have been an easy thing for Mrs. Sterner to do. Her eyes glistened like broken glass in the sunlight. She sat looking at the head in her lap, gently twisting a strand of the soft black hair about her finger. Now she was sure childhood had gone from her daughter's life; she was grown-up, feeling the growing pains of adulthood. How often Ruth, the child, had cried at her knee over broken dolls, or skinned knees, or stomach aches. But now it was Ruth on the threshold of womanhood, crying over life's problems.

"Ruth," she whispered kindly, "you're nearly a woman now and you can begin to see that you have to face your own problems; when you were a child, there was always someone to take care of them for you. Then others could always soothe away the pain. But now you begin to see that life's a conflict, a conflict fraught with happiness, perhaps, but nevertheless a struggle. It's the fight to win Heaven, the carrying of the cross Our Lord spoke about.

"There are various ways of fighting the battle; call them vocations. Every vocation is a finding of something and a giving-up. When you mentioned the sisterhood just now, it brought to mind the prayers I've offered that one of my children would enter religion. What you find there is God. In marriage you find a husband who gives you his love, children, companionship. But in every vocation you should find the help that's going to enable you to win the prize of Heaven."

It wasn't often that Ruth's mother had spoken to her like this. Almost without her mother noticing it, she sat on the floor and rested back against her mother's knees. Her sobs had subsided and she was drying her eyes when her mother said, "I don't know much about the religious life, but I do know that the vocation I chose has been all I could ask for here on earth. I wouldn't trade your father and you children for all the money in the world. But that doesn't mean it has all been easy; marriage means responsibility. To make any kind of success of it you have to be willing to give and take, especially give. That's why love is so important. When you love enough, the giving doesn't count; it's what you want to do. Caring for a husband and children, keeping house, washing, and the like leave you little time for doing lots of things you enjoy. If you think that's easy, ask anyone who's been through it. But ask the ones who knew what to expect and still wanted it, and you'll find that none of them wants to change it—ever."

Mrs. Sterner finished speaking, and for a while both she and Ruth sat quietly, pondering their own thoughts. It was Ruth who broke the silence when she said, "Mom, tell me about you and Dad. How did you meet? Where? When did he ask you to marry him? How long did you know him before he kissed you the first time?"

"That's a long story, Ruth," Mrs. Sterner replied with a serenely happy little laugh. "It brings back such a mass of memories. I'd hate to skip any of them, and to tell them all would take such a long time. Besides, I could never do justice to the way I feel about your father. And since the whole is colored by my feelings, he probably didn't impress me half so much then as I think he did."

But Ruth kept plying her mother with questions, and since Mrs. Sterner was not reluctant to talk, she and Ruth sat up until they heard Mr. Sterner come in from a meeting he had attended that night.

"You'd better get to bed, Ruth," her mother suggested. "Remember what I told you about vocations, any kind. You give up things because you've found something better. In marriage you give up other men because you've found the best man, then you give up other things because of your children who become your pleasure and your treasure. If you become a nun, you'll be giving up marriage, not because it isn't a glorious thing, but because you have found something much better, infinitely better. You'll be giving them up because God calls you."

Mrs. Sterner kissed Ruth and hugged her tightly. "Good night, dear." She didn't look old or tired now—she was smiling a young smile. Ruth kissed her father and ran up the stairs. She didn't go to sleep. She knew her mother and father were talking, perhaps about her. She loved them; they were so wonderful. She loved God for giving them to her. She loved God. Yes, she loved God more than anyone or anything. She wanted to do things for Him to show her gratitude. Her heart swelled with life and love.

23

ON EASTER SUNDAY the entire Sterner family went to the Solemn High Mass at their parish church, to join in celebrating the Resurrection of the Lord. In a manner befitting the wonderful occasion, the altar was ablaze with dozens of candles which set off the glory of the pure white lilies against their background of green. And not to be outdone by the decorations, the music for the feast carried the joyous spirit of conquest, victory, happiness. Ruth thought that if anyone made half an effort, he could hear angels singing alleluia, while the sunlight streaming through the windows told her all nature was joining in the commemoration of Christ's victory over death and sin and the devil. And on such an occasion it was only right that the birds outside should accompany the ringing of the bells at the Consecration. Without a doubt it was God's day, and Ruth felt near Him.

A call from Jim after Mass and before the Sterner family Easter dinner made everything seem just about perfect to Ruth.

If Jim wasn't angry any more, and everything else made you want to sing, what further could you ask? It was one of those days that made you smile at everyone and everything, such as the little boys dressed up in new Easter outfits, afraid to play or run because they might scar their shiny shoes; or little girls with grown-up hats and gay pocketbooks swinging from their hands or shoulders; or Yardley's cartoon in the *Sun*, showing George Washington looking down from his monument on Charles Street and smiling at all the pretty girls passing by in the Easter parade.

Ruth smiled back up at old George Washington that afternoon as she walked past the monument with Tod Edwards, Pete Decker and Betty Cranwell, and Mike Hafey and Judy Kemper. Continuing northward on Charles Street, the group met fewer and fewer paraders, but when they approached Twenty-fifth Street the crowds began to increase again. It all reminded Ruth of the pictures she had seen of the Easter Sunday promenaders of the '90's, when the men in blazers and straws showed off their ladies, who wore Gibson girl outfits with bicycle-sleeves and bird-hats with lace that tied under their chins. As she thought of it, Ruth could almost hear the hoofs of Baltimore's best carriage horses and the rattle of the carriages after them. Then there would be the jingle of a bicycle bell or the sound of a policeman's whistle, and the policeman would have one of those old helmets and sideburns. Although times had changed, Ruth thought that the spirit of the people must have remained pretty much the same, for they could hardly have been happier than the Easter paraders of today.

Tod especially was happy today. Evidently forgetting he had to act grown-up, he laughed and talked like any other high-school boy his age. Ruth thought maybe he had learned that you don't always have to be grave and serious to be grown-up. Today he'd talk on any subject, but there was one on which he was eloquent. To get him to give a full-length speech—something Tod never did before—all Ruth had to do was mention something about Barbara Connell. Tod would launch into a full biography of the girl.

"You know, Ruth," he said as he closed one episode of Barbara's life, "I think she's about the swellest girl I've ever met." A far-away look came into his eyes and he remarked with feeling, "Gosh, she's pretty, and always so nice to me. . . ." Tod hesitated when it struck him for the first time that he'd been concentrating almost exclusively on Barbara all afternoon. "You don't mind my talking about her, do you, Ruth?"

"Not at all, Tod." It was interesting to observe this new Tod, who had so much life and enthusiasm—confidence, too—in contrast to the old one who was always trying self-consciously to impress people that he was grown-up. Before now he hadn't made much of an impression on Ruth, but here was a boy with some drive. "I'm glad to hear all about you and Barbara."

"Thanks, Ruth, but I guess I have been boring you." With a shrug of his shoulders, he reiterated his one reason for talking so much on one topic, "But you don't run into somebody like Barbara every day. In fact, I've never met anybody like her, and since I can't find many people to talk to about her, when the chance does come I guess I forget about everything else. I didn't think you'd mind so much, because you're different, too, but I've known you so long that you're more like a sister."

When they reached Seton, it seemed that the whole group suddenly came upon people they knew. Betty Cranwell greeted a lot of girls from school, and most of the others also saw friends among them or among the groups congregating in front of Sts. Philip and James' Church, on the other side of the street. Milling in and out between these groups was a steady trickle of young people stopping in to pay a visit to the Lord. And into this thin line Ruth and her companions made their way before continuing on out Charles Street, past Johns Hopkins University, across University Parkway, and on to Bedford Square where St. Paul Street runs into Charles. Here the footparaders thinned out again, leaving only the line of polished cars, as varied in color and design as the girls' powder blues and greens and the boys' gabardines, to go on past Loyola College and Notre Dame of Maryland and some beautiful suburban homes.

From the bus, which they boarded at Bedford Square, Ruth reviewed the paraders once more. She reached home just in time to help her mother and Marge with the preparations for the evening meal.

Without noticeably withdrawing from the conversation during the evening, Ruth thought about herself and her life. What were dancing and the pleasures she held dear? Wonderful things, but when you compared them with the service of God in religion, they were of no eternal value. What was one home and one family? A nun adopts the whole human race. What was Jim? A friend she'd always remember and pray for, but even Jim was nothing when Christ was calling her to know, love, and serve God. Ruth was certain now that Our Lord was calling her; she felt some tinge of the joy that would be hers in her quest for sanctity. She could change her generous love for people into a desire to lead them to God through her prayer, work, and example. There was no confusion now; everything was clear. Christ was offering her a vocation. With a humble "Thank you, Lord" Ruth accepted. She was going to be a nun.

"Hello, there, Sister Mary Elizabeth, S.S.N.D.," Ruth called out as she entered Sister Elizabeth's room after class the day they returned from the Easter holidays.

"Hello, Ruth, why so formal?"

"I was wondering how I'd like to be called Sister Mary Elizabeth, S.S.N.D. Any objections?" Ruth carelessly flung her books down on a desk and stood with feigned impudence before the nun.

"Don't be so smart, young lady," Sister replied playfully. "Vocations are nothing to joke about."

"Oh, I don't know. They strike me as being rather ordinary things. Everybody has one of some sort. What's so special about yours?"

"It's the very best there is," Sister said proudly.

"So I've heard," Ruth replied with a toss of her head. "But I expected a greater thrill than the one I've got. In fact, I get more of a thrill out of riding the roller-coaster."

"Stop your nonsense, Ruth."

"But I'm perfectly serious, my dear Sister." Ruth felt like throwing things in the air today, just to watch them float to the ground like streamers at a parade. It was a day for marching and singing. She felt lighter than air. "I'm trying to tell you I've decided. I've made up my mind."

"Well, it's about time you stopped playing hard to. get," Sister feigned severity, "and settled down to something serious."

"Oh, is that so?" Ruth pulled up a chair for herself. "Well, I've always heard about the happiness of a vocation. When does it begin? I still don't like the idea of giving up every-thing."

"You are in a hurry, aren't you?" Sister Elizabeth laughed. Then she turned serious. "Ruth, I think you'll make a lovely Sister, and as for that idea of sacrifice—I stressed those things because I didn't want you to overlook the fact that you will be giving up much. But a vocation is something positive."

Sister Elizabeth went on to explain all that a religious voca-tion gives. It makes all God's children the object of your love. The world is open to a nun. As a missionary, nurse, teacher, social worker, she goes looking for souls. Disheartening at times, it is nevertheless a thrilling expedition because you are doing God's work and you know that He is beside you, offering encouragement and eternal happiness.

"As a School Sister of Notre Dame you will probably spend your life in a school and you will have the opportunity of teach-ing the hundreds of youngsters who pass through your class to walk in the way of the Lord. Those you teach are influenced by you, then they influence others, who in turn influence still others, until it's impossible to estimate the tremendous amount of good wrought by a single nun in a classroom."

But Ruth, who was willing to wait to find out those things, was interested in one special thing just now, and she broke in on Sister's narrative to ask her, "When did you decide you had a vocation?"

"I thought I told you all that before."

"Well, all right, but how did you feel about it?"

"Pretty much the way you seem to feel right now."

"I must say, you're not much of a help. But, anyhow, they're only lead questions to asking all about this life. I really don't know much about it. What will be expected of me?"

The room sang with laughter as Sister Elizabeth gave expression to the joy given her by Ruth's question. "Just good will, Ruth," she replied. "You'll find out about other things as they come along. You'll have a regular schedule of prayer, reading, instruction, work, and recreation. With God's help, the burden becomes light. And you are doing these things together with the most wonderful people in the world, people just as determined to love and serve God as you are. Basketball, a little party, work change into thrilling events under the circumstances. I'm sure you have heard laughter coming from the Candidates' building here at school. And I'm just as certain that you are the type of girl who will like the life. Only remember this—you won't change completely overnight, so don't expect everything to be easy. But, for heaven's sake, don't go in with the idea you're a martyr and that everything is going to be difficult. Everyone, no matter what she does in life, has trials. Some things in the convent will not be easy, but for the most part you should be very happy." Then, in a businesslike manner, Sister continued, "We'll have to arrange for you to make your application. Some Saturday soon you'll be able to see the Sisters who are to interview you. Then you'll have to have a physical examination by your doctor. By the way," Sister changed again suddenly, "have you mentioned this to your parents yet?"

"I've talked with my mother, but I haven't told my parents of my decision yet."

"You had better do it then. You must have their permission, you know."

"I'm sure they won't object."

"No, I don't think they will," Sister agreed. "Now where was I? Oh, yes, last of all we'll have to get your clothes—you'll enjoy that, I'm sure."

"You won't tell any of the Sisters or the girls about this, will you?" Ruth asked with some solicitude.

"Not unless you want me to."

"I'd rather not tell anyone for a while yet."

Sister looked at Ruth and queried, "What about the boy you said you liked so much the last time? Don't you think you ought to tell him?"

"That's a strange thing. Before I was concerned about Jim, but now I don't think he'll mind when I tell him." Ruth pictured Jim's feelings as being pretty much the same as hers, and now that she had decided she had a religious vocation, it wasn't a part of her mental make-up to consider any reaction but joy. So much was this the case that all obstacles and difficulties seemed to fade into nothingness. Today she wasn't to be bothered; it had been that way since she had made up her mind. And even when she mentioned not wanting to give up things, those things were more fictitious than real. It wasn't until she entered the front door of her home that she began to wonder what her mother and father would say when she told them that she wanted to become a Sister. That they would give their consent, she was sure, but she hoped they'd make no show about it, because she wouldn't know what to do if her mother cried, or if everyone asked a lot of questions. Then what would Paul say, she wondered. And Marge?

After dinner, while Mrs. Sterner was helping Paul with his lessons, Ruth, instead of going to her books, sat in the living room with her father, talking about anything that bobbed up as a topic for conversation, sometimes not talking at all, just watching the ashes glow in her father's pipe. Postponing the question which came time and again to her mind, Ruth thought how handsome her father was, though she knew it was only to herself he appeared so because she saw and loved the man himself, not merely his appearance.

"Dad," she asked during one of those periods of silence, "what would you say if I told you I wanted to become a nun?"

Setting his pipe down and looking intently at his daughter, Mr. Sterner asked, "Do you want to be one?"

Ruth nodded, and he took up the pipe again, sucking on it for what seemed to Ruth a long time—too long in fact, for she broke in, "Well, aren't you going to say anything?"

"Yes, Ruth." Mr. Sterner blew out the smoke slowly, meditatively. "I'm glad, and I'm proud, and I'm grateful. It'll be hard to lose you, Ruth, but we couldn't lose you to anyone better than God." He sat forward in his chair. "Have you told your mother yet?"

"No, sir. You don't think she'll cry, do you, Dad?"

"Of course not," he replied as he rose and walked across to the door. "She may cry a little the day you leave us, but not tonight." He called his wife and when she came into the room, said, "Ruth wants to tell you something."

"Mom, do you recall the talk we had the night I went out with Jim a while ago? You remember the night, don't you? The time you said I couldn't go?"

"Yes, Ruth," Mrs. Sterner said with a note of expectancy in her voice.

"I want to go away to become a Sister."

Taking her daughter in her arms and holding her tightly to herself, Mrs. Sterner said in a voice full of emotion, "Ruth, you don't know how happy that makes me. It's the answer to the prayers Dad and I have said that one of you might have a religious vocation. When did you decide, dear?"

As plainly and briefly as possible, Ruth told her story, including all she thought necessary to obviate questions from her parents, who surely would want to know everything. Her one hope was that they wouldn't ask her question after question, not that she didn't want to answer them. But talking about one's vocation seemed like bragging about winning a gold medal at school. And as if sensing their daughter's feelings, Mr. and Mrs. Sterner contented themselves with asking but a few points beyond those Ruth gave them.

Ruth was receiving a congratulatory kiss from her father when Paul called, "Hey, Mom, when are you coming back to help me?"

By the time his voice had died down, Paul himself had followed it into the room where he looked at his parents and sister standing so close together there. "What's going on, anyhow?"

"Paul, Ruth is going to become a Sister," said Mrs. Sterner.

Without waiting for more information, Paul was out of the room, running toward the stairs, shouting, "Hey, Marge, Marge, Ruth's going to become a Sister."

And Marge came bounding down the stairs, asking if it were true. While Paul, back in the living room again, was saying, "I hope you'll be a good-looking Sister, like Sister Gerald in the sixth grade. Gee, wait till I tell the gang you're going to be a Sister. Bet it will put me in good with the Sisters at school, too. Then I won't have to study any more."

"Paul," Ruth cut short his effusions, "I don't want anyone to know yet, not even the Sisters. Understand?"

Quizzically looking at Ruth, like a boy in class who has been told his "correct" answer is wrong, Paul asked, "What do you want to be a Sister for, if you don't want people to know?"

"I'll tell them in due time. I haven't been accepted yet, but when I have been, you can tell everyone you please." Ruth smiled, but emphasized again, "Remember, I don't want them to know now." Then turning to her parents and Marge, she said, "You won't tell anyone, will you?"

After all had promised to tell no one, Ruth threatened Paul, "And if you tell, I won't even let you come to see me in the convent."

"Aw, I won't tell anybody," Paul agreed, though still somewhat puzzled over his sister's attitude. He wanted to be a football star years from now, and though he wasn't one yet, he wanted the whole world to know about his plans. But girls are funny.

"Then, if everything is all right," Ruth once more addressed her parents, "I'm going up to study. Oh, yes, I'll have to see Dr. Bowman for a physical examination, but I guess he can keep a professional secret."

After Ruth left the room, Mr. and Mrs. Sterner sent Marge and Paul back to their lessons. That left them to talk over the blessing that was theirs, but they soon ran out of conversation and each sat dreaming of the past, dreading the departure, and wondering about the future. Already they were able to enjoy the first visit with the young nun in her new habit, and years later, thrill to her success with her first class, and love her more as she became holier and always happier. Each knowing what the other was thinking, they smiled at one another; and Mr. Sterner filled the room with the aroma of his pipe, puffing away steadily the way he always did when he was meditating.

24

By THE end of the week spring had burst forth in all its glory. Anointed with the chrism of sunshine, plants and animals took on a new vigor, a new life; and even men felt a new strength coursing through their bodies. Almost as if in proof of the point, Ruth and Jim, Marge and Joe Milo, Tod and Barbara Connell, and Mike Hafey and Judy Kemper pedaled with vim as their bikes rolled out York road, passing along the way lawn after lawn in which the green blades of grass had cut their way through the brown sod. The farther they got from town, the deeper they penetrated into the bewitching sounds and smells and sights of springtime.

Once out of the city by way of Towson and the Delaney Valley Road, they headed into beautiful open country, broken now and then by a neat farm, its patches of land evidencing fresh plowing or the first green slips that would turn into various vegetables. When they passed a plowed area, the air would be heavy with the moist smell of new-turned earth; then hardly more than a minute later the sweetness of some wild-flowers growing along the side of the road permeated every-thing. And all the while the tires of their bikes joined in a cheerful *hmmmm* that changed to a *humph* when they crossed the bump of tar between each section of concrete.

It's fascinating, a bike ride in the springtime, with the steady push-push of the pedals over level stretches of road, the strained uphill struggles, the free exhilarating downgrade rush when the wind fans your face and brings tears to your eyes. Then the long drift followed by lazy pedaling.

After reaching the top of one of the hills, Ruth halted and pointed to the waters which were blocked up behind Lock Raven Dam. They were visible between the trees like crooked mirrors.

"We'll be there soon," she said to the others.

"We'd be there now," Jim boasted, "if you girls weren't so slow."

"Is that so?" Marge asked. "Who wanted to stop for the sundaes?"

"I didn't hear any of you object."

The unspoken challenge was all Ruth needed; she made it explicit. "I'll race you to the top of the next hill, smarty."

"Okay," Jim agreed, "and the loser pays for the ice cream at Murray's on the way home."

"If there's going to be a race, count me in," said Judy, "though I don't know why anyone should be in a hurry to get anywhere today, it's so beautiful."

"Anybody else want to get in the race of the century?" Jim called out. "We'll give the ladies a handicap."

When everyone agreed to take part, Jim added, "All right, you girls start. When we think you have a big enough lead, we'll follow. Okay, go!"

Barbara shot out in front of the others at first, but Judy and Ruth were soon up with her. Marge was only half-heartedly in the race.

"Look at Judy and Ruth go," Mike cried excitedly. And pride forced him to emphasize the Judy.

"We'd better start, too, if we're supposed to catch them," Tod suggested. "That hill isn't very far away."

"Okay, let's go." And the boys shoved off in pursuit of the girls.

Barbara had dropped behind, and Ruth was tiring rapidly as the girls started up the incline, but Judy, whose basketball experience kept her in trim, pedaled steadily forward, widening the distance between herself and the others. And by the time the boys passed Ruth, she was losing ground but cheering for Judy to beat them.

As Jim sped by her, he called, "Throw me a rope and I'll tow you."

When Ruth reached the top of the hill just behind Joe and Mike, Judy was boasting, "Well, you boys pay for the ice cream. That'll teach you to be careful about challenging people to races in the future."

Ruth held up Judy's hand and proclaimed her the winner and new world champion. But Jim tried to turn Ruth's victory upon her by telling her she had the wrong sport.

"So have you, brother," she retorted, "if you think bike racing is yours."

"I notice you were still puffing and groaning up the hill while we waited for you, and you suggested the race."

"That's all right, the girls won," Ruth defended herself. "It wouldn't have looked good for two of us to come in before you boys."

After a rest, the hikers moved on toward Loch Raven at a more leisurely pace. Crossing over the first bridge and zigzagging with the road along the water's edge, they breathed in the scent of pine, the perfume of thousands of trees greener than usual against the blue and white sky. Over the second bridge and up the road that clung to the side of a hill above the broadening water, they pushed to where they stopped for a moment to look back at the array of pines lined up like soldiers guarding the water. They shoved off again, down an incline, past a ravine full of dead leaves from years and years ago. Then the dam and their destination.

Parking their bikes, they walked over to the dam to watch the immense carp that swam near the top of the water and sprinted toward any spot where something touched the surface and caused a stir. The fish would swim right up to the spillway but never follow the water that slid over the restraining concrete to continue on to the second and older dam which was visible in the distance.

It wasn't long before Marge was suggesting that they find some place to build a fire. "I'm starved!" she exclaimed.

It took no speech-making to have the motion pass. After their ride, all of them were hungry and ready to do justice to a campfire dinner.

"One of you Boy Scouts prepare the fire," Ruth commanded.

Even cold sandwiches were savory today, and the odor of the gurgling brown coffee, pungent and fresh, brought a delicious *mmmmm* from all of them as they spread out on the ground around the fire, eating their lunch with avidity. As the fire disappeared, they continued to sit about, or to sprawl on the ground looking up at the sky without saying much, for satisfaction and security are eloquent testimony of comradeship. And though the fire became a lone crackling ember that sputtered out in death, there was a warm breeze blowing capriciously about.

"It's wonderful like this," Jim commented to no one in particular. "Too bad life can't be this way all the time."

"Yes," agreed Tod, who was next to Barbara and happy.

When Ruth was away from the raucous city, listening to the quiet country, which spoke only in the pleasantest of modulated tones through the music of the birds or the whispering of the wind in the trees, her mind was drawn automatically to God. And she wondered if that wasn't the way God had intended it to be when He fashioned the world with its beauty of sound and color and smell. For isn't it His beauty that dwells in the peacefulness of sky and earth and water? And so different is it from the sounds that clatter through the streets of the city, with its smoke-encircled, mathematical buildings.

A stop at Murray's for some ice cream and dancing interrupted their homeward journey by way of Loch Raven Boulevard, and it was late afternoon by the time they reached home, after covering well over twenty miles.

"Thanks for the invitation, Ruth. It was a swell trip and a great idea," Jim said. "We'll have to do it again some time."

"Thanks for us, too," called Mike, who hadn't even gotten off his bike. "Judy and I'll be running along."

"Glad you liked the trip," Ruth replied, noticing for the first time that Judy was wearing Mike's class ring.

"And I'll be moving on too, Ruth," said Tod. "I told Barbara I'd ride home with her."

After Joe Milo had said good-bye and Marge had gone in, Jim remarked to Ruth, "Tod seems to have fallen for Barbara in a big way. I'd have volunteered to go along with them, since they have to go my way, but I don't think Tod would have liked that."

"I don't think so, either." Ruth smiled and sat on the steps. "So I guess poor Romeo will have to ride home alone."

"It certainly looks that way. Wouldn't want to come along, would you?"

"I've had enough bike riding for one day, thanks," Ruth shook her head vigorously. Then suddenly she said with seriousness that didn't lack surety, for her decision still gave her a feeling of security, "Jim, put your bike down and sit here with me for a while; I want to tell you something."

When Jim sat next to her, Ruth knew she liked him more than the rest, and when he was clearly apprehensive, she knew it wasn't going to be as easy as she had thought it would be to tell him. She couldn't begin what she wanted to say.

"Well?" he asked without taking his eyes off her face, which he was endeavoring to read.

She tried to be matter-of-fact. "Jim, I won't be seeing you much more."

"Huh?" If she had slapped him, she couldn't have made him appear so hurt. Jim searched for her eyes, but they turned from his. "Hey, wait a minute, did I misunderstand you?"

"No, Jim, you heard me." Everything outside her stood still; it was motionless, dead. Ruth turned her face to Jim as she explained, "I said I won't be seeing you much more because . . . because . . . well, (and the words rushed out as the blood mounted in her cheeks) I'm going to the convent in August."

"Oh." Jim sat in silence for a few seconds, then he put his hands on the step to shift his position, and his right hand touched Ruth's. He patted it, then took the fingers in his hand, his thumb moving over the knuckle of her middle finger. "Gosh, Ruth, that's swell, swe-l-l." He almost swallowed the repetition. He drew his hand away, adding, "You'll make a swell nun."

While Jim's fingers mechanically tied and untied his shoestrings, his eyes were fixed on them, but Ruth was sure they didn't see what they were looking at. For Jim's mind was on other things, and she would have given anything to know what he was thinking. But no matter what his thoughts were, she knew he would have wanted her to tell him the way she had. "Jim," she said, "I wanted you to know before anyone else outside the family."

"Thanks, Ruth." He looked up momentarily from his shoes. Then suddenly tying the strings again, he said, "Look, this doesn't mean I can't take you out any more, does it?"

"No, Jim." Ruth brightened up immediately. When she had made her decision to become a nun, she had thrown all the tremendous trifles of life out the window of her mind. Tremendous and good and wonderful as they were, they seemed petty and selfish when looked at through the eyes of a person in love with God. She could never be completely satisfied with them when there was God, when there was an entire world for which she could work and pray. In the convent she would give her all to winning souls to Christ, not just herself or the family that might be hers, but the whole world of men. The trifles weren't for her. On the day of her entry into religious life, they would be put aside forever. But until that time she would use them. She would act like a normal high-school girl —with the one exception, that she had chosen God. After trying to explain this to Jim, she concluded, "So I thought maybe you wouldn't want to take me out, once you knew."

"Hey, wait a minute! What do you think I am?" Jim objected. "I'd be a heck of a Catholic if I interfered with a girl who's going to the convent. Ruth, you know I admire you more than any girl. But I would never try to get you to change your mind. Even so, if you were going to Europe in August, I'd want to see you between now and then. Do you see the parallel? August is a long way off." His face glowed, partly from joy, partly from the sun which had shone on it all day. "We can have a lot of fun before then. I'm asking you right now to come to my prom."

"And I'll accept your invitation, if you'll come to my prom with me."

"It's a bargain."

"Jim, we will have a lot of fun between now and August, won't we?"

"You bet we will!" Jim was lighthearted again. "Hey, I was so surprised I forgot to say congratulations."

"Thanks, Jim."

"Ruth," Jim looked at her, hopefully expecting the right answer, "do you suppose people will think it strange if you go on dates after they find out you intend to enter the convent?"

"Some of them will but they shouldn't," she answered almost defiantly. "What do they expect me to do, act like a nun before I am one? That's why I'm not going to tell most people till later. How can a girl be a nun outside the convent? If she could, there wouldn't be any use of ever entering one."

Jim glanced at his watch and said, "I'd better be on my way home. The folks'll be wondering what happened to their little boy Jim. But I appreciate your telling me about your vocation. Is that why you'd never tell me what you planned to be?"

"I really didn't know, Jim. But that's why I wouldn't say

what I was thinking about. Honestly, I just made up my mind myself."

"Okay," Jim laughed, "I believe you. It wasn't any of my business anyhow."

"But it was."

"No, it wasn't."

"It was."

"Okay, it was. But I have to go now. Well, I'll see you soon—Sister."

Ruth held onto the handlebar of Jim's bike and said, "You will pray for me, won't you, Jim?"

Jim was flustered, stunned. Imagine anyone asking him to pray for her, especially a girl going to the convent. It wasn't like any of the other times when people asked him to pray for them, when it was just a formula as meaningless as good-bye. But now it was something real, a girl asking him for his prayers, and he hardly knew what to say, since he always considered his prayers pretty powerless in comparison with other people's. His prayers were important—the idea jolted him pleasantly. "Of course, Ruth," he murmured as he touched her hand once more before starting off down the street.

25

The Faculty and the Graduating Class
of
The Institute of Notre Dame
Baltimore, Maryland
announce their
Commencement Exercises
Thursday afternoon, June twelfth
at three o'clock

R UTH addressed the last of her invitations while she hummed a tune she had heard the circus band play when Pete Decker took her to see "the greatest show on earth," which had come to town shortly after the excitement over the Preakness had subsided. Mr. Stevens didn't remember to invite Ruth to the race, but she didn't care. The tune she was humming now was *The Entrance of the Gladiators,* and as she hummed it

Ruth could picture again the elephants lumbering into the rings. Or, better still, she could see them leaving to the same tune, because they were followed immediately by a parade of clowns who made the children howl with delight over their crazy antics. One little boy in front of Ruth had laughed so hard he lost his ice cream, but he didn't care—clowns were better than ice cream, until the clowns were gone.

Because the circus is a delightful thing to remember, and because this was the last one she would see, Ruth had tried to take a mental picture of it. She had fixed in her mind everything about it, from the dust that rose in the air when it was trampled by thousands of feet to the staccato jamming of the circus band and back to the barker's, "Hear ye, here ye, step right up this way." Clearly printed on her mind were the lights, the colored tent, the red hot dogs and yellow lemonade and pink candy-floss, all mixed in with visions of animal acts and men and women of utmost skill, who swung so gracefully in the trapeze act.

And not to let the other senses have the advantage, Ruth had tasted just about everything she had ever had to eat or drink at a circus from the time she attended her first when she was in the fifth grade. Ice cream and peanuts and candy-floss were so mixed with Cokes and lemonade and hot dogs that Ruth was amazed she hadn't become sick, while Pete had enjoyed it all, thinking she was acting just like a kid. And she was, only Pete didn't know why.

But the circus was gone and Ruth was licking stamps, thinking how the time had flown since Easter. Here we are, she thought, with the exams over, the prom tomorrow night, and graduation next Thursday. Word had also come that she had been accepted by the School Sisters of Notre Dame and was to enter the candidature on the feast of St. Augustine, August 28. So she had made up her mind to begin telling the people she intended to tell.

Saturday Ruth did her usual share of the housework, listened to the radio, had her hair fixed, and was more than excited the whole day. For it was her prom day, the day she had waited for even more than she had graduation. After a light supper, she went upstairs to dress.

Later, when Paul came up to tell her Jim had arrived, he said, "Gee! You look pretty tonight, Ruth."

Since it came from Paul, it meant his remark was an exclamation and not just a compliment, for boys, especially little brothers, are not in the habit of passing out compliments. Yet he could have said nothing that would have made his sister happier, because if there was one thing Ruth wanted to be tonight, it was pretty, the way every girl wants to be on the night of her prom.

When she entered the living room, Jim stood up and confirmed Paul's statement. "Ruth, you never looked better than tonight."

"You look handsome yourself in that summer tux of yours."

Ruth's gown (she had a new one, even if she were going away—Marge could use it after she was gone) was of yellow organdy, with a full skirt, ruffled from top to bottom, and a green sash about the waist. It made her feel as cool and fresh as she looked. To her mind it was the perfect summer formal, which was enhanced by the corsage of yellow roses Jim had brought.

Only a few minutes after they had entered the ball room of the Sheraton-Belvedere Ruth and Jim had their program of dances completely filled out. And since Ruth had helped select the numbers the orchestra was going to play, she made certain there would be a few waltzes; and now she made sure that she would have all of them with Jim.

While they danced Ruth, who was feeling exuberant, teased Jim about the number of times he had gotten his picture in the Loyola yearbook. He parried her thrusts until he noticed Ruth's parents and directed her gaze toward them.

"Yes, I know," she said. "Didn't I tell you they were going to be chaperones? We're having the next dance with them."

Jim said swell, and after the dance they walked over to Ruth's mother and father. Jim asked Mrs. Sterner if she would dance with him, and they left Ruth with her father.

When Ruth had glided out to the center of the floor with her father, she commented, "You don't seem to have lost any of your skill over the years, Mr. Sterner."

"No, you children and your mother have kept me in trim."

"Sir, I do not relish being called a child. You must realize," she said haughtily, "that I'm to graduate from high school next week."

"Oh, I beg your pardon, young lady," her father said the way she knew he would say it, because it was the way he had been making mock excuses ever since she could remember. "It was a slip of the tongue."

"Your apology is accepted." Ruth smiled. She loved dancing with her father who had been her first real dancing partner. When she was very small her mother used to pick her up and dance around with her in her arms to the tune of old-time songs on the radio. But as soon as she learned to dance, Ruth liked nothing better than proving it to her father, who never failed to make a fuss over her and tell her she was the best dancer in the whole wide world. And even when she had some notion that her father's statement might not be true, she loved to have him repeat it to her.

After the dance, Ruth and Jim went to the two-thirty Mass at St. Vincent's. Both received Holy Communion and were impressed by the number of others from the dance who did the same thing.

Following the Mass, they drove to Child's restaurant for a breakfast of bacon and eggs. Then they drove home slowly as the sky was beginning to lighten toward the east.

"That's the last one, Jim."

"Last what?"

"The last Institute dance for me."

"Yes, August is getting pretty close." Jim paused, then said quietly, "The folks want to go to Ocean City in a couple of weeks, but I'm trying to talk them into waiting until the last part of August."

"Do you think they will?" Ruth hoped they would.

"No," Jim said like a little boy who knew it was the right answer but still wished it weren't. "Mother'll go when she plans to go, and there won't be any stopping her."

"Oh," Ruth murmured.

There was determination in Jim's voice when he added, "Don't worry, I'll fix it up some way to stay in the city myself. Dad won't be going to Ocean City."

"You'll miss a lot of fun at the beach," Ruth warned.

"I guess," he agreed casually. "But I think I'll find the city more interesting until about the twenty-eighth of August."

"Thanks, Jim," she said. "I appreciate it. You know, I'm going to miss nights like tonight."

"You'll get over it."

"I hope I won't be homesick."

Such conversations never run in any logical sequence, Jim found, for there was only one thing in his mind and it had nothing to do with Ruth's homesickness. "Ruth, you will let me have the last date with you, won't you?"

"Certainly, Jim." The answer came as something long decided on. Then Ruth burst out laughing. "Gracious, aren't we the serious ones? I wish you could meet Sister Leo at the parish convent—she's been there for fifteen years. And since she taught me in the third grade, she's just about the happiest person in the world, now that I'm joining her. She says she can retire and to a life of leisure as soon as I'm ready to take over the third grade. She's wonderful, Jim; you'd like her, always full of fun. She teases me all the time. And I tell her I'm going to get my last permanent wave three days before I enter."

"What name are you going to have as a Sister?" Jim made a face. "Whatever you do, don't let them tag you with one of those crazy things nobody can pronounce or spell."

"I don't know what name they'll give me, because the Sisters tell me you're never certain until you get it what name you'll have, though they do allow you to suggest a name you'd like."

"Do you know which one you're going to suggest?"

"Yes, I do."

"What, Ruth?"

"It'd be nice if I could be called Sister Mary James, wouldn't it, Jim?" Ruth felt herself blushing as Jim stopped the car in front of her house and looked at her.

"Are you serious?"

"Yes," she answered, knowing that the simple statement conveyed more meaning than a whole book of explanations. Then, still embarrassed, she laughed again. "But it will be quite a while before I get a new name. Thanks for tonight, Jim."

Jim watched the door close; he hadn't even said good night; at least he couldn't be sure whether he had or not. The happily astounded boy drove home with his thoughts, repeating over and over to himself, "She wants to be called Sister James."

26

WHAT'S the matter with you tonight, Ruth?" Mrs. Sterner asked of her daughter who was sitting in her room listening to the radio. "You've been moping around the house all day, and now you're up here alone."

"There's really nothing the matter, Mom." Ruth knew it didn't sound convincing. And Mrs. Sterner, who had gained a certain amount of intuition in raising her children, was quick to take her up. "I'll guess you wanted Tod to take you to his prom tonight. Is that the trouble?"

"I suppose so." Ruth turned off the radio.

"Well, don't you think you've been out enough recently?"

Ruth squirmed in the chair, pulling her feet up under her. "Oh, I have, Mom, more than enough. But this is his prom."

"But you told me yourself Tod has been taking this other girl out regularly."

"I know," Ruth replied, forgetting for the moment that Tod didn't know she was going to enter the convent, "but he can take Barbara out all he wants after I'm gone. And August is getting awfully close . . . and . . . well, I just wanted to go to as many proms as possible. I guess I was a little disappointed that Tod didn't ask me since we've been friends so long."

"Suppose we just sit up and talk," Ruth's mother suggested. "Will that make you feel any better? You know we won't be able to do that much longer either."

To Ruth it was evident that her mother wanted her to say yes, and suddenly she wanted it, she wanted it more than anything else, the way she used to love to sit up and tell her mother all the things she would like for Christmas when she was a little girl who searched for big stockings to hang by the fireplace. "Swell," she said, hopping up, "you sit in the chair and I'll stretch out on the bed." She lay with her face propped in her hands. "You know what we missed this year, Mom?"

"What, Ruth?"

"June week at the Naval Academy. I forgot about it completely until I saw the pictures of the presentation of colors in the paper. You know, that color girl looked just the way I always thought I'd look when I became the color girl and wore a beautiful white dress with a blue sash." Ruth winked at her mother. "I never told you I was going to be color girl, did I?"

"No, Ruth, you didn't." They both laughed, and Mrs. Sterner added, "But you wouldn't have surprised me if you had, the dreams that come into that head of yours!"

"Well, did I tell you Tod is taking me to Gwynn Oak next week? I'll bring you a brass ring from the merry-go-round if you want."

Mother and daughter talked long that night, and by the time Mrs. Sterner left the room Ruth had almost completely forgotten about the dance. But it came back with a rush just before she climbed into bed after saying her night prayers. "Darn it all, I wanted to go to that dance."

If anyone had told Ruth when she was a freshman that graduation would be a sad affair, she would have laughed at the person, because there was nothing she so much looked forward to as a day of joy and accomplishment. But as she sat on the stage that Thursday afternoon, her high school completed, her diploma waiting for her, it wasn't all joy. She was happy, but there was also sadness at the thought of leaving the Institute and the friends who had meant so much to her during the past four years. Now, she thought, it's our turn to see what we can make of this weary world; and she wondered what the old building was thinking about the girls who were leaving today.

Before the exercises had begun, Ruth had told some of the girls she was going to enter the convent. Now she could feel the eyes of some of them resting on her. What were they thinking? Their congratulations had bordered on envy, causing Ruth to wonder why she rather than many of the others had been chosen. But the girls didn't leave her time to think; they began teasing her about the events she would miss and the broken hearts she would leave behind when she went away. Some said it would be a shame to have her hair cut and hidden beneath a veil. And Ruth was surest of their esteem of her vocation, when nearly all of them promised to send their children to Sister Ruth to be taught.

When all the speech-making and other functions proper to graduation were over, Ruth was glad to get down off the stage to greet her family and introduce them to some of the Sisters and a few of her classmates. After that, Mr. Sterner, as was his custom on special occasions, took the family to the Candle Light Inn, just outside the city limits, for dinner.

It was the old Tod who took Ruth to Gwynn Oak park the next week, and he seemed ridiculously out of the spirit set by the roar of the roller coaster speeding up and down and around, with girls screaming at each loop and dip. He was just as much a contrast to the joyous music of the carousel. He was reserved, quiet, mechanical. When Ruth teased him, he didn't laugh; and when she mentioned Barbara Connell, he talked just long enough to change the subject. It was so evident he wasn't having a good time, though he did whatever Ruth asked him to, that after a while neither was she. When Pete Decker and Betty Cranwell wanted to go boating, Ruth and Tod went only to follow the wishes of their friends. But Tod paddled their canoe listlessly and spoke only when spoken to.

Ruth had decided to tell him tonight that she was going to enter the convent, and now that they were alone, she thought it as good a time as any to do so.

"Tod," she said, "I won't be seeing much of you any more."

Without looking at her, Tod replied, "If you're sore about Barbara Connell or something like that, forget it." Tod kept dipping the paddle into the water mechanically. "We had a fight the other night. I'm finished with her for good."

"You know me well enough, Tod, to understand that I wouldn't say so, even if I were jealous of Barbara." Ruth decided to wait until Tod was feeling better to tell him about her vocation. But now that she had started the conversation, Tod wouldn't let her drop the subject.

"Then what's this stuff about not going out with me any more?"

"I said not *much* more. But forget it."

"No," Tod said insistently, "I want to know. What were you going to say?"

"I was going to tell you, Tod, I'm going into the convent in August."

Tod stopped paddling. "Ruth, you can't do that," he pleaded. "There are lots of girls who can be nuns, but you—you." His voice trailed off. Then it bounded right back with firmness. "No, you just can't do that."

The lights of the park were reflected on the water, and they moved like mocking fingers pointing at Ruth with each ripple of the water's surface. They were like the fingers of those people who couldn't or wouldn't understand what she was doing and would ridicule her for wasting her life in a convent. If only Tod weren't one of them, she could snap her fingers and ignore them. "Tod, I'm sorry I told you tonight," she whispered. "I wouldn't have if I had known about Barbara."

"That's got nothing to do with it, Ruth. I've always liked you better than any other girl." Tod took up the paddle again.

"I don't think you would have said that a little over a week ago," she said kindly, hoping he'd listen. Oh, why did he have to have a fight with Barbara at a time like this? Why couldn't it have happened after she was gone? Still, Ruth was sorry for him.

Tod was almost crying when he protested, "I would have."

"I'm sorry, Tod." Ruth couldn't bear to look at him because she felt cruel. To her, every laughing light on the lake, the shrieks coming from the roller coaster, all the happy sounds, seemed sneers.

"Ruth, you don't have to go to the convent. You can do a lot of good in the world. You don't have to go . . . you don't."

"Yes, I do, Tod," she answered quietly, though it hurt her to see Tod in such pain. And almost as if to soothe her own discomfort, she trailed her hand in the cool water.

"But you don't, you don't," he insisted. "Ruth, I don't want you to go. Please stay."

"I have to go, Tod."

"No, you don't. No one does. Why do you have to go?"

"Because God wants me to." With tears in her eyes, Ruth urged, "Tod, please try to understand. Dates and dances have been fun. But after they're over, what are they? What good have they done for the world? I want something bigger than that. I want to love God with all my heart and to make the world love Him. Do you understand?"

"No!" he raised his voice. "It's not fair. I need you. Barbara doesn't mean a thing to me."

"Oh, you'll forget all about me as soon as you make up with Barbara," Ruth tried to smile, thankful that they were away from Pete and Betty. "Come on, congratulate me before I tell the others."

"No, I mean it, Ruth. I don't want you to go away."

"But I can't refuse the greatest gift God can give a girl, just because you're selfish." Ruth hated to put it so bluntly, but this tremendous trifle was beginning to ruffle the peaceful calm of her soul. "Honestly, you act as if I'm doing this to hurt you." When she received no reply from Tod, she suggested that they go back to the shore, since their time on the lake was about up anyhow.

Pete and Betty reacted pretty much the same way the girls in her class had done when she told them, but it didn't make Ruth very happy because Tod's accusing eyes were on her all the time. Why can't he understand? Make him understand,

Dear Lord.

It wasn't much fun to sit under a tree and listen to the music coming from the open-air ballroom with a boy who was pouting. Happy couples passed by, chattering away, and now and then breaking out into a laugh which blended with the music. It was lost on Ruth, though, for all the time Tod sat at her side, saying nothing, his very silence objecting to her vocation. Never had she longed so much for a night to end. She prayed someone would suggest going home. She wanted to get away, away from Tod and his silence, his brooding eyes.

When Tod left her at the front door, Ruth thanked him, but he turned to walk away without a word. "Tod," she called.

He came back still without saying a word, and without looking at her.

"Tod, can't we be friends?"

Continuing to stare at the ground, he mumbled, "Yes, if you'll say you're not going away."

Fearfully she put her hand under his chin and lifted his face. "Tod, please try to understand."

"I don't want to understand," he snapped, pushing her hand away. "We can still be friends if you don't go away."

"Is that the only way?"

"Yes."

"Then," she said, "I'm afraid we can't be friends."

"Okay." Tod turned and walked away.

"Good night, Tod," Ruth said softly, and ran into the house.

As she undressed for bed, tears ran down her cheeks. Why does it have to be like this? I wanted everyone to be so happy about my vocation. Why can't Tod understand?

Ruth said some pretty quick night prayers and crawled into bed. Tears slid down her cheeks. She turned over, buried her face in her pillow and let the tears flow freely.

"I-I w-w-wanted to be s-so happy t-tonight," she sobbed softly. "Darn that old vocation!" But that only made her cry the more. "Of course I don't mean that. Well, darn Tod, then. . . . No, I don't mean that either. I'm sorry for him—poor, selfish Tod. Oh, I don't know what. . . . I want to please everybody. Make him understand, Dear Lord. Make him understand. Make him . . ." She cried herself to sleep.

27

ONE night Ruth went to sleep in June and woke up in August; time was taking a rollicking run through the pages of the calendar, and still Ruth found herself wishing that it would go faster. For she was anxious to enter her new life, despite the fact that she loved her trips down the bay with her family; the swims, tennis, and dances. Of course, any night Ruth was home some of the neighborhood crowd would stop in to talk, dance, and have a coke. And there were the treasurable occasions when the family had their "last time" for many things.

If Ruth wanted to remember how much time was passing by, she had only to think of Tod who had not been around since the night at Gwynn Oak. And the further she got into August, the more Ruth wanted him to come to see her, because she wished to part friends with everybody. She attempted to catch him after Mass on Sundays, but he was always hurrying away when she caught a glimpse of him. All through July and August, she had kept hoping he'd come around, but he didn't. Ruth was thinking about Tod as she prepared for her last date with Jim, when Paul came into the room.

"Are you going out *again?*" he asked.

"*Yes*," Ruth said impishly, "I'm going out *again*."

"Gee, will you have to change when you become a Sister! Sisters don't go out all the time."

"That's right, Paul. They have other, very important things to do—and delightful things, too." She tried to kiss him, but he slid under her bed. "But I'm not a Sister yet."

"I know it. And you're not going to kiss me either."

"Will you miss me, Paul?" Ruth asked as she put on her hat.

"I don't know." He came up on the other side of the bed. "I guess so."

"Well, I'm going to miss you, but I want you to grow up to be a great man."

"I'm going to be a great football player."

"Great men are better than great football players."

"That's what *you* think."

"Well, maybe you can be both," Ruth suggested.

"Yeah, that's a good idea; I'll be both."

Marge came in to say Jim was downstairs. Paul beat Ruth to the living room, and by the time she got there he was already sparring with Jim, showing him a new hook he had learned.

Jim had gone to Ocean City with his mother and brother in June, but he had driven to Baltimore several times to see Ruth. Today he had returned with his father and was going to spend the week with him. As he and Ruth drove toward Gwynn Oak, Jim told her about it and asked, "Are you sure we can't have one more date, Ruth?" And Ruth thought how white his teeth looked in contrast to his tanned skin. When she didn't answer him, but only kept smiling at him, Jim added, "You aren't going away until Wednesday, you know."

"I know, Jim, but I've told you before that I'm spending to-morrow with Pat Boyle and Tuesday I do whatever the family wants to do. No more dates."

Jim dropped the point. "All right, we'll talk about that later. Let's enjoy this night of dancing anyway."

"Good idea."

The whole atmosphere of the open-air ballroom was delicious. Ruth could almost drink the coolness which was mixed with the distant echoes.

June Thompson and Don Wright were there that night, and when June caught sight of Ruth, she hurried over to her, asking, "Hi, gorgeous, *what's* this I've been hearing about you?"

Ruth smiled to herself, very happy that June hadn't been the first to know about *this*. "What, June?"

"This business about the convent. You're not serious, are you?" June made a face, as if the very idea of a convent were repugnant to her. "You're not the kind of girl who's supposed to become a nun, honey chile."

"Of course I'm serious, June."

"Well, that beats me!" June threw up her hands. "I'm sorry for you, gorgeous. I think nuns are great, but you couldn't get me into a convent for anything in the world. Imagine! It makes me shudder to think of it."

Ruth laughed. "I hope it won't be as bad as all that."

"Bet you don't last six months, sweetheart. You're not made for that life." June raised her very thin brows and opened her eyes wide. "And what's Jim going to do now?"

Ruth wanted to kick her in the shins for embarrassing Jim. Instead, everyone became silent until Don Wright spoke up.

"What do you say you dance with me?" he said to Ruth with a

silly grin. "I never did dance with a girl who's going to the convent."

Don was no rescue at all, and Ruth wanted to get away from him and his remarks, which were less subtle than June's, if such a thing were possible. "Say," he remarked, "a gal who can dance like you shouldn't be in a convent. Just like June said, you aren't made for that. Neither's Junie. What'd guys like me do if the pretty gals all went to the convent and the uglies stayed home?"

"Jimmie boy, you'll have to take me out when Ruth goes away," June said coyly at the end of the dance. "Well, gorgeous, Don and I have to run." Then she snickered.

"Sure, I'll take her out after you're gone," Jim grumbled. "I wouldn't waste a nickel to call her up, much less take her out. How do you like that? Practically asking for dates with another fellow when she's out with Don?"

"Let's forget them, Jim."

"Forget them? Doggone it, she made me mad with that talk about you not lasting six months and your not being the kind to be a Sister, and what am I going to do when you're gone . . . I . . ."

Ruth put a finger on Jim's lips. "She didn't realize what she was saying, Jim." She smiled at him. "Come on, smile now."

"I think you're the perfect type for anything, Ruth." Jim smiled back at her. "I'm glad you don't let June's chatter bother you."

On the way home that night, neither Ruth nor Jim talked much. Although Ruth had planned everything she was going to say, as she remembered so well doing once before, the words wouldn't come. But when they reached home, she felt she just had to say something, whether she wanted to or not. "Well, Romeo," she began, "it's been wonderful knowing you. . . ."

"Ruth," Jim interrupted, "can't we have just one more date?"

"I wish we could, Jim. But really I should spend some time with my family—I want to. They haven't seen so much of me lately."

"I guess you're right," he said sadly. He looked at her. "Let's save the good-bye until Tuesday night. I'll drop over for a little while then, and I promise not to keep you from your family. Okay?"

"Okay!" Ruth smiled. "I appreciate tonight, Jim."

"Not as much as I do."

The farewells meant only the end of tonight.

On Monday the Sterners ate out again, all together for the last time, in Ruth's honor. Tuesday afternoon the young people from the neighborhood came to say good-bye and Tod was with them.

"Tod," Ruth beamed, "I'm so glad to see you!"

"I had a mighty tough time dragging him over," Pete Decker spoke up. "But I told him he wasn't going to let you go away without saying good-bye."

"Won't you all come in for a while?" Ruth invited.

"No," Pete replied in his capacity as official spokesman for the group, "this is our last, final, and official good-bye. Ruth, we hope you'll love it, and think of us once in a while. We'd like to give you something to remember us by, if you'll only tell us what you can use."

Ruth swallowed a lump in her throat. "Thanks, all of you. I have everything I need, but you don't have to worry about my forgetting you. I couldn't do that if I tried. You've been too swell for that."

The others went, leaving Mike Hafey and Tod behind. Mike

told Tod he only wanted to see Ruth for a minute, so Tod moved away to let him say what he wanted to.

It was the same bashful boy Ruth remembered from the parish C.Y.O. who addressed her, "Ruth, I wanted to ask you to pray for Judy and me. I've got an office job at Bethlehem Steel, and I want to give her a ring for Christmas." He blushed redder than Ruth had ever seen any girl blush. "Then we can get married next summer."

"Mike, that's grand! I hope you and Judy will be very happy."

"Thanks, Ruth," Mike replied as he started to back away. "Don't forget to pray for us. And good luck to you." He was walking down the street, very rapidly.

Tod came over and sat on the steps next to Ruth.

"Thanks for coming over, Tod," she said. "I wanted you to."

"I wouldn't have if Pete hadn't come around."

"Good old Pete, he knew I wanted to say good-bye to you. . . ." Ruth broke off what she was saying. "Tod, you don't think I sent him over, do you?"

"I thought that at first," he admitted, "but nothing could have made me come if I didn't want to. Pete couldn't have done it with the help of the whole gang."

"Then you're not angry with me any more?"

"Yes, I am," Tod said frankly, as he fumbled with a key ring he took from his pocket. "I still wish you weren't going. But you think you're doing right, so I'm sorry for the way I treated you."

"Tod, you're wonderful!" Ruth rumpled his hair, and he smiled for the first time since he'd come. "Have you made up with Barbara yet?"

His smile disappeared. "No!"

"Why don't you?"

"If she would only call me up . . ."

"She's probably saying the same thing. You still like her, don't you, Tod?"

"Ye-es, I think so."

"Then why don't you make up?"

"Because I didn't start the trouble in the first place. It was her fault."

"But, Tod," Ruth tried to strike one of his strong points, "don't you think it would be more manly for you to apologize?"

"What for? Because she got sore? No, thanks." Tod stood up. "So long, Ruth."

"Well, wish me luck, Tod."

"No."

"But why, Tod?"

"Because I hope you don't stay."

"Tod!" she exclaimed. The cry was forced from her like any cry that comes after a sharp, sudden pain, but Tod didn't notice it. He was walking down the street, hands in pockets, shoulders stooped. Ruth could have cried for him, but she shook her head and went into the house. Poor, selfish Tod, she thought again.

28

THE Sterners had their last dinner together that night. It was a merry affair, with everyone recalling all the funny things that had happened while the children were growing up. And even Paul, who now considered himself pretty old, related some of the funny things he remembered from his childhood. But most of the stories were about Ruth and the things she had done, how she had pulled the ornaments off the Christmas tree one year, and how she cried when the head of her favorite doll was crushed, and how after that she didn't want any more dolls—she wanted to play with Dan and his gang, she wanted a baseball glove, she wanted anything but what a girl should want.

It was a long, leisurely meal, since no one was in a hurry to get it over with. During one lull in the conversation, Ruth turned to Paul and asked, "Well, Paul, are you going to kiss me good-bye, or is it still for sissies?"

"Wait till the time comes," Paul said unenthusiastically.

"But I guess I'll do it."

"And, Ruth," Dan warned, "you'll have to be careful not to kick people in the shins the way you did me, or you won't last long."

"Is that so?" she replied laughingly, trying to reach her brother's ankles under the table. "Well, anyway," she said, "I want all of you to be on your best behavior tomorrow. We have to make a good first impression, you know."

They all laughed, and were still laughing when the doorbell rang. "That's Jim," Ruth said as she ran for the hall, leaving everyone else still seated at the table. She opened the door and asked Jim to come in.

"Thanks, Ruth. But I won't be staying long. I know your folks want you for themselves tonight."

"They can spare me for a few minutes. Come in and sit down for a while," Ruth urged.

"All right." Jim stepped rather stiffly into the living room and sat down.

"Remember the first time you sat in that chair, Jim?"

"No."

"Well, it was the first night you took me out."

"Do you remember the first time I took you out?" Jim smiled.

"Do I? I can tell you everything we did from the beginning to the end." Ruth experienced the joy of it all over again. "First of all, you were sitting there looking like a scared rabbit, but after . . ."

"I believe you, Ruth, but we haven't time for a step-by-step account." He leaned back in the big chair. "I remember when you first impressed me; it was before the St. Paul football game. You were with Jane Arnold and made quite a hit with me. After that I used to look for Jane at the other games to see if you were with her, and then I forgot all about looking for Jane and looked only for you."

Much as she wanted to reminisce, Ruth had some things she wanted especially to say, and they'd never get said if she and Jim got to reviewing the past. Somewhat uneasily, and trying to make it sound natural, she said, "Now, Jim, you listen to me. I've planned everything I want to say to you, and I want to be sure I say it all and don't forget anything. You just listen, and don't interrupt me; otherwise I might not get through it all."

It wasn't much different from what she had planned to say to him the Saturday before. And though it still seemed a little strange to Ruth—words do such a poor job of saying what we really mean—she knew it was say them now or never. So she went on, "First of all, I want to say thanks for all the wonderful times we've had—that means every single time I've been out with you, no matter where. And I appreciate the things you told me about yourself and your plans for the future . . . and . . ."

"Hey, wait a minute," Jim leaned forward in the chair. "I was going to say those things to you."

"Don't interrupt," Ruth commanded. "In the convent I'll do a lot of praying. So you may be sure I'll be praying for you, Jim, that you may be a successful lawyer and politician; but even more, that you may be an outstanding Catholic and do great work for the Church. You will pray for me, too, won't you, Jim?"

"Sure, Ruth, certainly." Jim was again struck by the incongruity of this girl asking him to pray for her, as if she were the one who needed it and not the other way around.

"And finally," she said, "I want to say I won't ever forget the things we did together, the places we went, the fun we had. In the future I expect it to be easy to think back on them and then say a prayer for you and the others who shared them with us." She let her head rest against the back of the chair. "That about completes my little speech. Now if you have anything to say, it's your turn."

Jim folded and unfolded his hands, pressed his arms on the chair, brought his hands together again as he spoke. "Ruth, I can say thanks to you for all the things you thanked me for. I've told you this before, but I want to repeat how I felt about you: I think you're the nicest girl I've ever met. I'm sure you'll make a wonderful Sister and that the kids you teach will be crazy about you. But I do hope you won't forget the times we've had together, and that they will always be pleasant memories for both of us in the future. And if I ever amount to anything, I hope I'll remember it's probably due to your prayers."

"We did have fun, didn't we?" Ruth added, no more anxious than Jim to end it all with a good-bye. "And all these things we did will be memories, tomorrow's memories. I hope they'll be as much fun."

"So do I." Jim looked straight at her, remembering the time her eyes had flashed blue fire. "I don't want to forget them ever."

"That's kind of you, Jim," Ruth said softly. She loved his eyes, his unruly hair. She wished within herself that there was some easy way to say good-bye, some pleasant way rather than this, though it wasn't anything she would have missed. To say good-bye to Jim was hard, but not to see him before she went would have been agony.

"I didn't mean it to be kind, Ruth." Jim spoke slowly, as if thinking of each word before he formed it. "I meant it to say how I felt."

Although Ruth had wanted this to be as free and easy as a date, everything was stiff and formal. She hadn't wanted it to be that way at all, but she knew they were both anxious about the end. For this was the end, and they couldn't shove it back again as they had done before. Now they both knew that they had to say it.

"Well, Ruth, I'd better be on my way." Jim rose from his chair. And handing her a black Eversharp pen and pencil set, he said, "Here's something I thought you might be able to use."

"Jim, it's beautiful!" Ruth's hand shook a bit as she took the gift from him. "But you shouldn't have done it. A set like this is expensive."

"I know it." He smiled, pride and affection in his eyes. "And I paid every cent of it with my own money. But you deserve it."

"I-I appreciate it, Jim." Two big tears welled up in the corner of her eyes, and Ruth bit her lower lip to keep them back.

"I know you do," Jim said warmly. "Didn't I say you deserved it?"

"Yes, but . . ." Ruth couldn't go on—the tears wouldn't let her.

"No buts about it. If you like it, I'm satisfied." Jim laughed a little. He gave her his handkerchief. "You'd better wipe your eyes, or Paul will think you've been crying."

Ruth thought of her family for the first time since Jim arrived. In the beginning she had heard them clearing away the dishes and things; but they were surely finished with that by now. Weren't they wonderful to let her have her time with Jim without bothering her? But wouldn't Paul tease her if he saw tears in her eyes? She smiled. "That would be disastrous, wouldn't it?" She dried her eyes and handed the handkerchief back to Jim. "Thanks."

They walked to the door together. Jim turned and held out his hand. "Well, Ruth, I don't like to say good-bye, but I guess this is it."

In a quick second Ruth had pushed Jim's hand aside and kissed him. Then she took his hand in both of hers, and in the warmth and firmness of the grip were all the feelings she wanted to convey, especially gratitude and affection. "Good-bye, Jim. Thanks for everything."—And he was gone.

She watched him get into the car and drive off, and she made a feeble waving motion which she knew he didn't see. A tear slipped down her cheek before she could catch it. Now Paul would know, but she didn't care. Jim was gone—his smile, his hands, his laughter—he was gone.

"Hey, Ruth," Paul called, "can we come in now?"

"Yes." And tomorrow even Paul would be gone. It was sad; it hurt. But there was something deeper that took away most of the pain; it was the sense of doing what she knew all of them really wanted her to do. It was more than that, it was the sense of accomplishment of God's will. When Ruth turned to smile at her family as they entered the parlor, she knew a joy, a real joy of love for them and a goal. They were all that was dear to her. She loved them, she loved them tonight with a womanly love that penetrated to her soul. Now she knew what they had been to her, what they were to her now. She couldn't embrace them all at once, so she threw herself into her mother's arms and hugged her tighter than she had ever done before. Her tears wet the side of her mother's face, but she kept saying over and over, "I'm so happy, I'm so happy." Fire lit in the blue pools of her eyes and she saw visions of the big things that were hers to do . . . TOMORROW.

4114